PISHTACO

Lord of the Lost Inca Gold

Mark Patton

EDGE SCIENCE FICTION AND FANTASY PUBLISHING
An Imprint of HADES PUBLICATIONS, INC.
CALGARY

Pishtaco
Lord of the Lost Inca Gold

Copyright © 2023 by Mark Patton

EDGE SCIENCE FICTION AND FANTASY PUBLISHING
An Imprint of HADES PUBLICATIONS, INC.
P.O. Box 1414, Calgary, Alberta, T2P 2L6, Canada

The EDGE Team:
Producer: Brian Hades
Cover Design: Brian Hades
Cover Art: David Willicome
Book Design: Mark Steele

HARDCOVER ISBN: 978-1-77053-230-4

EDGE Science Fiction and Fantasy Publishing and Hades Publications, Inc. acknowledges the ongoing support of the Alberta Foundation for the Arts and the Canada Council for the Arts for our publishing programme.

Library and Archives Canada Cataloguing in Publication

Title: Pishtaco : lord of the lost Inca gold / Mark Patton.
Names: Patton, Mark (Author of Pishtaco), author.
Identifiers: Canadiana (print) 20230448194 | Canadiana (ebook) 20230448445 | ISBN 9781770532250 (softcover) | ISBN 9781770532304 (hardcover) | ISBN 9781770532243 (EPUB)
Classification: LCC PS3616.A88 P57 2023 | DDC 813/.6—dc23

FIRST EDITION
(20230516)
Printed in USA
www.edgewebsite.com

Publisher's Note:

Thank you for purchasing this book. It began as an idea, was shaped by the creativity of its talented author, and was subsequently molded into the book you have before you by a team of editors and designers.

Like all EDGE books, this book is the result of the creative talents of a dedicated team of individuals who all believe that books (whether in print or pixels) have the magical ability to take you on an adventure to new and wondrous places powered by the author's imagination.

As EDGE's publisher, I hope that you enjoy this book. It is a part of our ongoing quest to discover talented authors and to make their creative writing available to you.

We also hope that you will share your discovery and enjoyment of this novel on social media through Facebook, Twitter, Goodreads, Pinterest, etc., and by posting your opinions and/or reviews on Amazon and other review sites and blogs. By doing so, others will be able to share your discovery and passion for this book.

Brian Hades, publisher

CHAPTER ONE

The Spider

Sunlight poured through the dormer windows of her bedroom. As Miss Penelope Farquhar's pupils adjusted, she saw a small speck hovering just above her bed, as though it was floating in the light. The sight of it provoked enough curiosity in her so that she gave up any further attempt at getting more sleep. Throwing her sheets aside, she got up to investigate.

The bed was a four-poster. What Miss Farquhar discovered was a newly woven web anchored upon two posts at the foot of the bed with a spider contentedly seated in the middle of its orb. Though it was a smallish spider it had managed to produce an enormous web.

There were often lots of conversations going on in Penelope's head. However, on this occasion it was only her own voice that she could hear as she thought, *Its relaxing now but what an undertaking for this little fellow. It must have spent all night working on the construction, traveling great distances, spider-wise, to accomplish this task. Perhaps its ambition is greater than I suspect? Perhaps it has no desire to snare a housefly or an errant moth that had been lured into the bedroom last night from the glow of my reading lamp? Perhaps it had been staring down at me for quite a while and just couldn't muster enough gumption to give it a go and try its luck at catching me?*

The idea of being the spider's prey amused Penelope so much that she got back into her bed and raised her hands and feet into the air as though she was a dead fly.

But the spider didn't move.

Penelope was laughing at her own antics and was wishing the spider could too, when her attention was directed to her fingernails and toenails, which she was still dangling above her. They were fabulously done. She had had them painted black at Carmen's Get Nailed, Spa and Beauty Salon. Carmen had adhered special decals to them — the ones with skull and crossbones.

Penelope was a stickler about her nails and her appearance in general. Once she was out of her bed not a yellow hair on her head would be allowed to independently seek its own direction. It was her body, and it was all going to be under her control. Her weight was permitted to range between one hundred and twenty-five pounds to no more than one hundred and fifty pounds. She would have ordered her body to grow a bit in stature but realized that there were just some elements of her existence that she couldn't control. Short she would always be, she couldn't change that — but in her dreams...well that could be quite a different story. That's why the skull and crossbones. They were her signals.

"Had a talk with my brain last night." Penelope had decided to continue with her joke and engage her new spider acquaintance in conversation. She loved animals, insects, reptiles, plants; around these creatures, she felt at home. Around people...not so much. She could never get away from them.

The presence of this spider did give her a little cover. And in the scheme of things talking to a spider was saner than the conversations she normally had with herself.

"Yes, I had a talk with my brain just before I fell asleep. Way overdue, if you ask me. I mean, my brain is mine and it's supposed to represent me. After all, I'm the one who goes about using it... well, most of the time. And no, I don't care to hear your opinion on that topic. I assure you that I'm doing my best with it. Guess I could have gotten a better one, but this one is okay as far as brains go... a little eccentric...still, it is a very smart model. But that's only during the daylight hours. One of the problems with this brain of mine, and I'll grant you that there are some doozies, is its singular lack of imagination when it goes to sleep.

"Do you think that is because of some sort of union regulation that governs brains? I mean an official time when they're not required to think?" Penelope paused, allowing the spider some time to venture a guess, and, when it didn't, she giggled and took up where she had left off. "I bet that it is a union thing. Must be where that required eight hours rest comes from. Mine goes on strike if I don't get enough of the stuff. I suppose it is all about some kind of contractual agreement with the rest of my body — official time off for brains so that they can go out and play with all of those thoughts and emotions that they have had to put up with during the course of their workday.

"But it's not like I ever place great demands upon my brain. You know, I don't force my brain to conjugate Latin verbs. Okay, I do make it apply itself to an occasional differential equation, but I've never forced it to devise a theorem for supersymmetry or extra dimensional space-time. Uh-uh, no way, that's because I'm easy going on it. I just keep my thoughts relatively simple...nothing above college level. I'm just trying to get along with the damn thing. But how does it repay me for this conciliatory attitude towards its over exertion? I'll tell you — With contempt!

"As soon as the lights go out, it's free to do what it wants. Then, it comes up with the most irksome dreams and sends them rambling through my head. This is inexcusable! And you know, I believe anything it tells me while I'm snoozing. Such a sadistic prick.

"So, last night, just before I hit the hay, I had it out with the old gray matter.

"Noodle,' I said, 'you've been mucking about with my school days far too long. I mean, how often must I endure stomach acid bubbling into my esophagus because you find placing me in an introduction to number theory class, for the first time, on the last day of class, during the final, to be a great source of amusement? Or what about this penchant of yours for having me walk into the Texas Division of Motor Vehicles office to be confronted by some pigheaded bureaucrat over some nonsensical rule, which I apparently have violated on numerous occasions?'

"These things are no basis for a good relationship. Okay, I'll grant you that I do like the dream with the old mansion filled with hidden passages leading to rooms with beautiful antiques, but you've sung that tune to me too many times. Couldn't the two of us turn a new leaf? We have such great potential together. Why waste it on drivel?'

'Listen to me, with just a little scripting, things can get spiced up. All you have to do is follow my lead and we'll be having a blast together. I'll tell you what, tonight make me an Italian starlet living in a villa on the Island of Capri. You know the sort of thing... flowing wine, ebony cigarette holder, some handsome male lead. Clark Gable? Errol Flynn? Cary Grant? A 1950's heartthrob. Perhaps sneaking off with him after a cast party? All you have to do is fire up those synapses of yours and off we'll go to the Gulf of Naples. What fun! Shall we give it a try?'

"Well, I heard no complaint from the old squash, so I assumed everything was all set and within no time I was fast asleep.

"So, Spider, how did things work out last night, you might ask. Well, a woman wearing bifocals found that I had been delinquent in returning three sets of plates from my various vehicles, the university lost my diploma and finally I ended up mucking about in some swamp... imagine I was in the Bayou with a bunch of dead people floating by on their way down the Mississippi. Come on! That is not my idea of the good life and it certainly didn't look anything like Capri.

Penelope then smiled at her spider, as it remained indifferent in the center of its web. "You know, I just got a glimpse of one of my fingernails in that damn swamp. Strange, that after you've had a dream, you often don't know much about it by the time you've woken — just have some kind of after taste of it in your head. But this time I thought I had it. I can remember that I had seen the skull and crossbones. Doctor Hernandez had suggested that I look for a color. He suggested blue. And if that didn't work, he said to get myself to glance down at my watch. It is a prearranged signal to myself to let myself know that I must be in a dream. Blue or a wristwatch? How is that going to catch my interest? That's why I thought of these neat skulls and cross bones. They work like flashing neon signs. YOU ARE DREAMING...YOU ARE DREAMING...YOU GOT THESE THINGS TO LET YOU KNOW YOU ARE DREAMING...THIS IS THE SIGNAL... TAKE OVER THIS DREAM NOW!

"That's right, take the dream over. Doctor Hernandez says it's good therapy for me to get ahold of my dreams. But as I've mentioned, my brain hasn't been helping... but when does it ever? I'm not sure how controlling my dreams is going to help. The doctor figures that if I put my foot down on what I will allow for dreams, I might move on and put my foot down on what I will allow for reality. Baby steps? Perhaps? But I'll tell you my eight-legged friend; that sounds a lot better than those injections they used to give me. Oh, and Doctor Hernandez has this machine that he hooks me up to. No dreaming then. But that's another story. Suffice it to say that I'm kind of his lab rat. Ha! I'm a rat and you're a spider. I guess we've bonded because we are both considered vermin."

The chimes from a grandfather's clock out in the hall signaled to Penelope that it was time to get her act together and to get on with the day.

"Well, my itty-bitty friend, it's time to get you out of this house. I've got to get up and I do have an appointment with this very same doctor this morning. Don't take it personally. No offense, but there are no insects allowed in this place. Simply won't have it. But I know of a hibiscus that just broke out with some sawfly larvae. You'll have some good dining there and I promise I won't spray it."

Penelope slid out of her bed and headed for the kitchen. A few minutes later she returned to her bedroom with a mason jar that had once contained tomato sauce. She gently coaxed her new bug buddy into it. She saw no need to fasten down the brass lid.

———— ❬❭ ————

Penelope Farquhar's house had the feel of an old family home... minus the old family. She liked to pretend that a great aunt had left it to her. She had picked the place because it had a sense of permanence and tradition to it. Somehow this house had managed to stay the same even as the modernity of the surrounding city of Austin laid siege to it. It was a Queen Anne, three stories, with a tower and fancy carved interior archways made to look like an opened lady's fan. The descending second floor stairway was equally as ornate with elegant wainscoting and the richly colored wallpaper. And she had stuffed this house full of Victoriana. Everything in it was meant to express a now-archaic view of beauty and grandeur. It was Penelope's way of announcing to the world that she had made it, though she would secretly agree with anyone who might decline to accept her claim. But then she would feel obliged to point out that she had been out of the East Hampton Psychiatric Center's Gruber Wing for Bipolar and Schizophrenic Disorders for well over two years and was coming close to completing her masters in mathematics and statistics. Penelope liked numbers; like her Queen Anne style house, they had permanence. Nothing open to debate about numbers. You got the equation right, or it was wrong. Mathematics was not a subjective study — no cultural fads coming out of nowhere to affix a new meaning to them. Unwavering and absolute, that's what numbers were.

As Penelope stepped out onto the open front porch, she looked ahead at her various gardens filled with all sorts of flowers: coral tea roses, red columbines, deep blue salvia, snapdragons in a variety of soft pastels, white foxgloves all bordered with either lavender Mexican petunias or fiery red coleus. This was perfection. Not a weed to be found anywhere among them. And Penelope took a great sense of satisfaction from this; though the world was out of control, here amongst her flowers was beauty and order. So too it was with the exterior of her house. She had replaced the gable ornaments that the previous owner had allowed to rot — and had had a full-time crew of painters working the entire exterior for weeks to strip off the old paint. Then, only after they had met her rigorous scraping and sanding standards, were the painters finally allowed to repaint the house. Of course, Penelope stood nearby, binoculars in hand, ensuring that there were no drips or bare patches. The result was lovely — balconies and dentil trim in white, with the fish scale shingles in soft pink and all the cracked stained-glass windowpanes replaced by a glazier with the exact matching nineteenth century glass... though it did take him three or four attempts to get that right. But it was now all complete — and perfection!

The inside was just as perfect as the outside. She saw to that as well. Francesca Bianchi, Penelope's overtaxed cleaning lady, often groused that before a dust particle got into Penelope's house it would first have to apply for a visa, as she had.

Filling her lungs with the heady morning air and breathing it out with a sense of contentment, Penelope walked down her stairway to her gardens below. She still had her bug in hand, safe within its glass mason jar. She spied the hibiscus that she had promised it. This flower was the perfect home for a companion of Penelope's. It was as ornate as her own — a large crimson flower that looked a bit like a cluster of oak leaves with a long stamen emerging from it like it was an elephant's trunk. It was an unusual hibiscus, quite rare. That was one reason she had planted it. The other reason was for its name, Hibiscus schizopetalus.

"Careful Penny, that's a brown recluse spider and it's poisonous!"

Penelope was jolted, so surprised by the voice from out of nowhere that she almost dropped her Mason jar.

"Jesus Christ, Cecile! Who the fuck turned you into an entomologist?"

"I'm just telling you that that thing is dangerous. If it bites you, you'll be howling in pain for days. Then that bite will ulcerate. Brown recluse spider bites don't heal — They just get bigger and bigger. If it bites you on your arm you'll have to have it cut off."

"Cecile, this spider made an orb between my bed posts. Brown recluse spiders don't build fancy webs. Besides, it is not reclusive. We met out in the open of my bedroom and I found him to be most gregarious."

"Don't listen to me, just stick a finger in that jar and we'll find out who is right."

"How the hell did you get loose, Cecile? I thought I had you locked away with Ernest, Ada, René, Belle...and what was that other one's name?

"Billy Bowlegs."

"Oh yea, why on Earth did I choose that name? Never mind, I rarely hear from him anyway."

"That's because you don't want to talk to anyone these days."

"That's right Cecile, I don't want to talk to any of you. And this is a serious setback. Doctor Hernandez is not going to be pleased. Not enough meditation, he'll say. And he'll be right. Now get away from me!"

Penelope managed to steady herself, and then returned to extracting the spider from the bottle and transferring it to a hibiscus petal. Of course, Cecile was still trying to rattle her, chattering away about making an offering to some Caribbean god called Anansi. But Penelope pretended that she wasn't there.

Once the spider had been safely relocated, she placed the Mason jar down onto the lawn, walked out directly to the front of her gardens, sat down on the grass and crossed her legs. Placing her hands upon her knees, Penelope adopted an upright posture and began to meditate.

CHAPTER TWO

Siwar Q'enti

Vines twisted upward, curving around the girth of the giant kapok tree, bypassing bromeliads and epiphytes along the way. They inched slowly around the many tadpoles of poison dart frogs incubating in rainwater that had been captured within the cupped leaves of orchids. Sunlight was a rarity below the canopy of the rainforest. The vines had to seek it out. If a neighboring tree lost in the competition for the scarce light, it died, shedding its greenery. Then the trunk of the ancient kapok would receive a meager share of sunlight its rival once held claim to. When this happened, a race began. Tendrils of Spanish moss would extend lower, reaching for the life-giving essence of the sun. But vines moved quicker than moss moved. The moss had no roots, and could only absorb nourishment from the thick Amazonian air. The vines had roots — deep roots, which burrowed down into the leaf litter, sucking up the moistened remains of countless plants that had failed centuries before. Soil-based vigor had allowed the vines to contend for and win a certain patch of sunlight on the old kapok tree.

It would be a long time before the moss could catch up and block it out. When the vines had reached the light, they sent out leaves to soak up the energy. Once sustained, they budded in an attempt to reproduce their kind and cement their stake in this struggle with a dazzling array of scarlet passionflowers.

Siwar Q'enti was not a flashy bird, unlike most of his kind. Dark green, almost black, with dull black wings and an accent of deep blue on the throat and around the eyes, the hummingbird looked like he was dressed for a formal occasion rather than a gaudy Mardi Gras. His wings flapped seventy times per second. He breathed two hundred and fifty breaths per minute. His heart raced one thousand two and sixty heartbeats per minute. But with all of this bodily excitement, Siwar Q'enti was always in control.

Siwar Q'enti maneuvered about the airspace in front of the passionflowers with unruffled precision, examining each stamen carefully before plunging his tubed tongue in for some nectar. Backing away, hovering, moving perpendicularly or horizontally like an avian automaton stationed on a pollinating assembly line, he applied himself to the feeding task before him. But suddenly, quite uncharacteristically, he left the floral banquet, and its life-sustaining sugary liquor, to bolt straight upward.

Up through the branches of the great forest he rose, unimpeded by any obstacles, as though he had found the only opening in the two million square miles of tropical canopy that allowed for a vertical take-off. Higher and higher he flew until he broke through the cloud cover of the forest below. He leveled off just above the clouds, where the bright equatorial sun was beating back the morning mist.

Siwar Q'enti flew on, skimming the clouds and crossing to the opposite shore of a river, the Rio Marañón. Here was the source of the mist, where the cold water of the Andean Mountains flowed into the hot and sticky jungle. Now Siwar Q'enti began his second ascent, this time up one of those steep mountains.

Here was where the vast jungle below surged into the North Andes like a biological tidal wave, spewing flora and fauna up and over the mountain side: white-bellied spider monkeys, rufescent screech-owls, iron-wood palm trees, giant land snails, golden-headed quetzal, tapirs, red creepers, glasswing butterflies, giant armadillos, jaguars, short-eared dogs, gold-mantled howlers, hyacinth macaws, elephant ears, tree sloths, crimson-rumped toucanets, tree ferns, pink tarantulas and giant kapok trees. All of which broke up against the alpine chill near the peak. Here was where existence became fragile — where only stunted vegetation, tolerant to the cold, survived.

Siwar Q'enti looked about and then headed towards an exposed rock face where an ancient road had once been cut to provide a narrow foothold to reach the mountain summit and the now-lost city of Paititi.

The bird followed this road, passing houses of stone blocks, whitewashed and rose painted, clinging to the carved basalt. These were not homes for the living, even when the people who built them were alive. These were homes for the dead. Here the most powerful among the Chachapoya's dead had been tied into sitting positions and treated like the living. They had servants and farms; food was brought to them with chicha, maize ale. Dances were performed for them. Songs were sung in their honor. This was their land, which they owned even after they had taken their last breaths. They owned their servants' villages and their servants' terraced fields, and their temples. They owned their servants, and their servants' children and their servants' children's children. There was no escape from it; the living must perpetually tend to the needs of the dead. And so they did, until the Inca came. And after the great battle was fought, the Chachapoya, who had called themselves The Warriors of The Clouds, ceased being warriors. However, they still remained servants to the dead, but not the Chachapoya's dead.

The hummingbird moved on, leaving behind the village for the Chachapoya mummies. Though the houses remained, their mummies had been removed long ago. There were still ancient villages running along the sides of the old road, with successions of terracing walls that once restrained fields from washing off the mountain side. But there were no people there; hadn't been for centuries. From high above, even the hummingbird wouldn't have been able to tell where the people had lived and gardened; twisted scrub and grasses obscured most of it from view. But from the road, bits and pieces of it were still vaguely discernible. The bird continued up the road to where the Warriors of The Clouds had once built their temples. These temples had been destroyed long ago, taken apart block by block, and reassembled by the Inca, for the use of their gods, not the Chachapoya's.

Cushion plants, tussock grasses, stump ferns, crustose lichens and club mosses were now the only living things that made this mountaintop their home. When they died they composted into soil, shrouding the temple of Inti — god of the sun — ancestor of the Inca.

The great square had become so layered over the centuries with soils and grasses that wandering tourists had overlooked it, as did archeologists and prying satellites.

On the western side of this great square, opposite Inti's temple, was the temple of Mama Killa, mother moon, Inti's sister and wife. Mama Killa, whose beauty caused a fox to fall in love with her. As she embraced him, his imprint was forever left upon her face. Perhaps wisely, Mama Killa's temple had been situated so she would catch sight of her brother-husband when he came down from the sky.

There were many temples in the hidden plaza: Mama Sara, mother of maize, in whose image the Incas dressed their stalks of corn; Kuychi, the rainbow god; Pachamama the Earth goddess; Catequil god of lightning, who bangs upon clouds to make thunder; Kon, god of rain and the southernmost winds; Urcuchillay the protector of animals, who guards them as a llama; Ekkeko god of wealth, who carries all that one can desire upon his back; Paryaqaqa, the water god born of a falcon and Sach'amama, the twin headed serpent goddess of the Amazon forest. From above they all appeared as undulating terrain on a particularly uninspiring mountain, not even worth a photograph — but no one ever bothered to pass by. At the far end of this sacred square was the largest of the temples. But this structure was more than a temple; and it was a palace for a corpse. Measuring eighty-one meters wide and forty meters high, it was the stepped pyramid tomb of Pishtaco. Pishtaco was the grandson of the supreme Inca, the Sapa Inca, who had conquered the Chachapoya.

Pishtaco's grandmother, Ciqui Ollco, was the favorite of the Sapa Inca and she had given him a son, Capac Huari. Capac Huari was deprived of the Inca throne when the Sapa

Inca's sister queen, Mama Ocllo, accused Ciqui Ollco of being a witch and put her own son before him. Therefore, Pishtaco was not allowed to become the Sapa Inca.

Siwar Q'enti ignored the temples of Inti, Mama Killa, Kuychi, Pachama, and Sach'amama and headed straight toward this dead man's tomb. As he did so, the earth trembled gently, just enough rumbling to shake away the topsoil that had masked the ancient doorway. Here the bird entered and flew up to a stone bed that had been mounted over a great cavern. This was where the body of Pishtaco was laid.

His hide had been freeze-dried by the cold mountaintop, his bones wrapped in a death shroud of his own skin — skin that had been carefully washed, rubbed in herbs and massaged with powdered gold, copper and silver. Around Pishtaco's neck was a succession of necklaces, golden beads to the left, silver beads to the right, gold for Inti and silver for Mama Killa — the sun and the moon.

Indigo-dyed vicuna, stitched with gold and silver wire, hid his nakedness. A headdress of blue and red and green macaw feathers and black condor feathers still held to his skull. Gold earplugs clung persistently to his flesh. These ornaments would indicate that he was of a very high rank, but this finery was unimportant compared to what was in the center of it all — a great golden mask. The mask of Apu Inti, the great god of the Inca. It was reserved for the semi-divine Sapa Inca, the emperor of all the Inca. But there would have been many who would have objected if they saw this mask over the face of this corpse. They would have violently refuted any claim that Pishtaco was a direct descendant of the sun.

Two warriors dressed for battle had been killed and placed at either side of the cavern opening. They had been sacrificed with a tumis, a gold and turquoise hand axe, which now lay by their sides. Surrounding the perimeter of the burial rotunda were ornate pots filled with maize, coca leaves, fruits, quinoa and a strong brew of fermented chicha. Several llamas and a dog had been strangled and left on the cold stone floor to mummify on their own. There were women that had been bound in sitting positions and stacked before the feet of Pishtaco. They had not been killed with an axe but had instead been left in place alive. The cold mountaintop air had killed them long before they would have starved.

Like the Chachapoya in their cliff-face village for the dead, the people of this region had used the square for singing, dancing, storytelling, and offerings of all sorts after Pishtaco died. The entire community was still expected to plant their fields, tend to their livestock, raise their children and pay their taxes, all for the sole purpose of honoring the great Pishtaco. This was not done out of respect, but out of fear.

The hummingbird now moved upward until he was even with Pishtaco's burial slab. He moved forward so that the point of his beak came to rest near the breathing holes of Pishtaco's golden mask. He inserted his tongue so as to touch one side of the shriveled nose inside.

A faint glow appeared just beneath the skin of the mummified flesh. This glow gradually intensified, giving the body the appearance of a small fire that was being stoked with more and more twigs.

Pishtaco's eyelids opened to reveal crusted-over white remnants that still held together within the sockets.

Pishtaco's mouth moved. He whispered slowly, "Siwar Q'enti... pollinator of the Hanan Pacha, the Kay Pacha, and the Ukhu Pacha — Heaven, Earth and Hell — and all between, you have come to me."

Siwar Q'enti rose up just enough to stare into what was left of Pishtaco's eyes. There was nothing there that could intimidate him. Siwar Q'enti had long ago looked into the eyes of Viracocha. Viracocha created the Hanan Pacha, the Kay Pacha, and the Ukhu Pacha. He created Inti, Mama Killa, Pachamama, Kuychi, Catequil, Mama Sara, Kon, Urcuchillay, Parayaqaqa, Ekeko, Sach'amama and everything in and amid Hanan Pacha and Ukhu Pacha. There was no god or creature, living or dead, neither in Heaven or Earth or Hell, nor in all that lies between, that could move between them, save for Siwar Q'enti.

Pishtaco's inner light now glowed with more force than it had after a thousand children had been gathered up and sacrificed on the moment of his death. The light lingered for a long time. But gradually it softened and dimmed as the people of Paititi abandoned the mountaintop and scattered into the jungle.

Though Pishtaco had ordered that the children's feet be cut off, and their bodies buried about the perimeter of his tomb so they could not leave, this did not prevent their souls from running away. They fled upon the backs of the others who had been murdered or sacrificed, leaving Pishtaco's light to die.

Siwar Q'enti had been a guide to many shamans. Viracocha had commanded so. But never had Viracocha sent Siwar Q'enti to help someone like Pishtaco.

The hummingbird proceeded up, pivoted and shot out through the exposed doorway. Some passion flowers had just opened up on the giant kapok tree.

——— ‹› ———

Pishtaco managed to rise up onto his rotted elbows. Despite the light Siwar Q'enti had given to his shriveled soul; he was still a feeble and cadaverous invalid. Every man has two lives; one with blood and flesh and a beating heart, and another that is only born when his heart stops beating. The second life sustained by memory and dies when he is forgotten. When both of these lives wear out a person is finally dead and only then could he descend to the world of the dead — Ukhu Pacha— to be tested. Pishtaco had never entered Ukhu Pacha. He knew that Supay, the horned lord of the underworld awaited him there with the demons and their yawning jaws. Pishtaco knew that any judgment of Supay would doom Pishtaco to stay there with his demons. Pishtaco believed that his spirit would never be allowed to travel back to the Kay Pacha to visit the living or to spend some time in the Hanan Pacha to see Inti and Mama Killa. So, he had wisely determined never to venture into Ukhu Pacha.

Out of a sense of self-preservation, as well as a twisted sense of humor, Pishtaco had his temple built directly over the great cavern that led to Ukhu Pacha. Once completed, he ordered the Chachapoya to build his stone funeral bed, supported by four great pillars, over this doorway to Supay's kingdom. There, when his heart had finally stopped beating, he lay for centuries, tantalizing the demons below.

When Pishtaco was alive his magic ruled the North Andes. He was more than a shaman. Pishtaco thought of such people contemptuously. He had six of them buried under him, each with their own funerary vault that had been cut into the sides of the great cavern. Pishtaco had stolen their mummies from the cliff houses, where the Chachapoya had once honored them.

All of the other embalmed Chachapoya, Pishtaco had cast off a cliff, from which they fell into the Rio Marañón. There were thousands of them. Their bodies bobbed up and down in the mud-colored water as they floated along the river and into the jungle, disappearing out of sight. So, ended the legacy of the Warriors of The Clouds.

The remnants of this culture lived on, but only to serve Pishtaco. That was accomplished through terror, which he had etched well into their memories. Long after Pishtaco's flesh had dried into human leather, the Chachapoya, who now had forgotten that they were once called Chachapoya, still remembered the name Pishtaco. Over the centuries, they had managed to creep down the mountainside and slip away into the jungle in ones and twos. Like the corpses of their mummified ancestors, they followed the Rio Marañón as it twisted deep into the forest. A day came when not one of them could remember who they were. But they never forgot who Pishtaco was — Pishtaco and his ceremonies — Pishtaco and constant labor — Pishtaco's blood sacrifices, all gathering more and more light into his soul. So, it went from generation to generation. Babies would learn to fear Pishtaco before they could walk. Such fear made their shamans brew ayahuasca vines, known as corpse vines, and through this hallucinogenic drink find out where Pishtaco might be lurking in the forest.

The light that was now in Pishtaco strengthened as his sinew knitted together. He could feel moisture coursing back into his dehydrated tissue. And as it did, he could sense the presence of the others who shared his tomb. Atoc named for the cunning fox, and he was crafty, was waking — so was Alliyma the good person and Ussun, who once loved to eat plums. Ozcollo, whose name and eyes were that of the ocelot, had woken, as well as Orotongo, who was once big and fat and named for the bear, but now mostly bone. Huallpa, full of joy had opened her eyes. Pishtaco knew that Huallpa had had no joy for hundreds of years, ever since he had robbed her from her tomb along with the other shamans. Atoc was growing in strength. His comical cursing was echoing up through the shaft, running through the six tombs of the shamans, to Pishtaco. He was shouting that Pishtaco was such a miser that he had only croaked to inherit his own gold. Pishtaco chuckled. The fact that he could chuckle surprised him. Pishtaco then laughed hard. It had been a long time since Pishtaco had laughed and it had been a long time since Atoc had told Pishtaco what he had thought of him. Atoc was quite colorful in his hate. Atoc's mind must have been all afire from the light that Sirwa Q'enti had planted within Pishtaco. The six shamans were feeding upon Pishtaco's glow. Pishtaco was pleased. Harnessing their enslaved skills brought to him great power. But at the moment, he had no idea how he was going to use them.

The vertebrae along the length of his spine snapped into position as Pishtaco assumed a sitting position. He hadn't sat upright in over four hundred years. So many years on his back, staring vacantly at the stone block overhead, he had almost forgotten what he was buried with. He took a quick glance about the chamber.

He thought, *Lots of pots. But the drink has long dried up and all the food has putrefied with me.* Though he had no need of it, a swig of strong chicha and a bite of sugary tumbo was appealing. He dismissed the idea as foolish and then continued with his scan of his grave goods.

His eyes paid little attention to the two warriors at the entrance to his tomb, and the numerous llamas that had been killed and placed about the floor. He gave them the same regard a spider might give to the moribund husks of insects that piled up below its web. The dead dog did give him pause. He knew that he once liked it, but why he couldn't tell. Then there were the many decomposed women, strewn in front of him. He assumed that someone thought he might have need of them in the spirit world. Then he saw her; she was in the front row — in the center — where she should have been.

Imasumaq! The name stirred in his thoughts, as his memories of her came flooding back.

Imasumaq, your family was right to have named you How Beautiful. Even with your jaw now dropped and your frozen flesh pulled taut against your ancient skull, you still are How Beautiful — beautiful in life and now in your decay. But perhaps decay better suits us all. The stench of death lasts a little while but the stench of the living is continuous — exuding from pores, feet, bowels and mouths.

Ah, Imasumaq, you were there for so much. I kept you about me only for the contrast. Like the luxury of my garments, you were there to adorn me. And though I never asked you to be good, you were. Oddly, I appreciated it —goodness is a hard surface for sharpening evil on. Like a stone for a fine tumis blade — makes it thin and precise — able to cut through anything, no matter how loved, noble, worthy or blameless.

I see that they strangled you when I died — a quick death. — no need to freeze like the others. I would not have killed you — though it was the right thing to do. Your soul was too thick with pain to live on. Sparing you would have condemned you to a life tormented by bad memories. Odd, Imasumaq, you are the only one I wouldn't have killed. Is that weakness? Ha! I killed my grandmother. You were there. You saw her garroted in the public square. Ciqui Ollco defied me. And none dared to defy me after that.

Pishtaco's long-dead voice began to awaken when Siwar Q'enti had touched his nose with his hummingbird's tongue. It had been faint and rasping. Dust-filled lungs, which had last pumped air when the Spanish had been marauding the Empire, could spare little breath for making words. Pishtaco could now feel their strength returning. No longer would he be forced to confine his words to his thoughts. Now he spoke them, but with great difficulty.

"Dear Ciqui Ollco, you were Topa Inca Yupanqui's witch and you managed to beguile him with your daughter. She had such a pleasing face and body, so you didn't need any of your magic. But his sister-wife Mama Ocllo Coya was right; you had taken control of him both with your daughter and your spells. I owe you so much. You turned this brat grandson of yours into the greatest of sorcerers. And if it wasn't for your cunning, Mama Ocllo Coya would have garroted me."

He suddenly began coughing; his tongue was as dried-out as the soles of his sandals. His voice was hoarse and cracking and thoughts of Mama Ocllo Coya and the day he was to be garroted made things even worse. There was little spit in his mouth but oddly he was sweating. Nothing was alive since the last time he had sweated. Mouse mites had long ago taken up residence in the pores of his skin. But there it was, perspiration, and not the sweat of a noon-day's heat, nor the sweat you get from drinking bad water. This was a cold and clammy variety of sweat, the sweat of fear.

Pishtaco was the half-brother of Huayna Capac, the newly proclaimed Sapa Inca and no rival claimant to the throne could live.

Pishtaco's knees still shook at the thought of the summons. Men with axes had gone out to bring him before Mama Ocllo Coya. Cuzco was the imperial city; no commoners were tolerated there, so the men who came to the house were nobles. Their orders were to fetch the boy Pishtaco and his witch grandmother, Ciqui Ollco and bring them to the Amarucancha, House of the Great Serpent. Pishtaco's mother had been the favorite concubine of the late Sapa Inca, Topa Inca Yupanqui. He had died in the evening. She had been garroted at the first light of the next morning.

That sun was now setting. Mama Ocllo Coya had set herself a busy schedule to kill everyone who could possibly interfere with her son's rule by the morning of the next day. Hundreds of people were being summoned to the Amarucancha. By the time Pishtaco and Ciqui Ollco reached the courtyard at Amarucancha, it was well beyond darkness. His future was now measured in hours.

Amarucancha was in the Plaza de Armas, a dried-out swamp that had been drained to provide room for the expansion of government buildings. He remembered the oversized torches that burned on either side of that palace's gate. This was where his guards turned him and his grandmother over to a higher class of nobles. These men were permitted inside. They were dressed in the imperial livery, black and white checkerboard tabards with red V-shaped yokes.

Heading up this new group of officialdom was the kuraka, high governor of the Cuzco. His name was Qasa, meaning frost, but he wasn't called that because of his snow-white hair but because of the state of his heart. Among Qasa's many civic duties were the planning of festivals, the adjudication of minor crimes, providing for beer and corn at the many religious events and acquiring and maintaining the snakes on the palace grounds. Some of these snakes Qasa had selected for their great beauty, like the many breeds of coral snakes and forest vipers he had imported. Other snakes he had chosen strictly due to their great size and ferocity. Qasa had paid particular attention to purchasing bushmasters, the largest venomous snakes to be found in all the lands of the Inca. They were so big that they had to be carted to Cuzco in great baskets that were carried by four men.

Ciqui Ollco and Pishtaco were instructed to follow close behind Qasa. He led them on carefully flicking the coiled reptiles from their path with his long pole of office. Qasa did this with the detached indifference of the hardest of bureaucrats. He was the consummate functionary; he could gather up poisonous snakes for you, or strangle this little boy. During the morning, he had personally killed the child's mother and then gone home to a hot breakfast of potato stew.

Ciquo Ollco and Pishtaco had been to this palace before. It had just been constructed and had been made with the finest stone block. Topa Inca Yupanqui had been very proud of it and had just recently shown it off to the two of them. Beyond the entranceway the walls were painted with ominous depictions of snakes, and just inside the door was the depiction of a huge snake sculpted from stone. This statue was of the most honored snake within the Amarucancha, Palla, the Noble Lady.

Though Palla belonged to the Sapa Inca, Qasa thought of her as his own. She was a great prize. He had to take an army into the jungle to capture her. Palla was magnificent, the most glorious of all green anacondas. He had measured her by lining up with six men against her, end to end. Then Qasa determined that she weighed as much as these six men, and twice that, once she'd eaten them.

Qasa stopped in front of the doorway that led to this great snake's private room. Then he motioned to two of the guards that had been escorting them. They then grabbed Ciquo Ollco under her shoulders, lifting her up into the air. Ciquo Ollco was a slight woman and very easy for them to toss.

"This boy is my daughter's son, a child of Topa Inca Yupanqui," she had asserted just before she was thrown. "He's the brother of the new Sapa Inca! He is of the most royal of all bloods! Kill him and you'll bring death upon all within this house! I swear it!"

Qasa had expected her to say those very words. Ciqui Ollco didn't disappoint. She fell into the circular pit, where Palla had lain, resting. Normally Palla ate capybara and torrent ducks and occasionally, during religious festivals, she would be supplied with a live jaguar whose fur had been massaged with honey. But on this day, she had been given a very special treat, the great witch who had recently served Topa Inca Yupanqui.

Pishtaco's grandmother screamed as she fell and her grandson quaked in fear and lost what little control he had. Qasa looked down on him shaking his head, as he muttered in disgust, "Son of Topa Inca Yupanqui." A pool of urine had formed about the boy's feet.

Palla had been fasting in anticipation of this very occasion. So, it took the green anaconda little time to unhinge her jaws and get them around Ciquo Ollco's head. Qasa was surprised that the witch had offered no resistance and went so meekly into the mouth of his serpent.

Pishtaco was now grabbed up like his grandmother had been. His feet never touched the ground as he was frog-marched into the royal audience hall. There high upon a dais of adobe on a bench, encrusted with emeralds and pearls, sat Pishtaco's little brother, Huayna Capac. They knew each other, though their mothers had always tried to keep them apart. There were occasions when the adults had let their guard drop, distracted by something and inattentive of their charges. These brief moments usually occurred during one of the court's many religious ceremonies. At such times, they would pass a nod or ask about a pet monkey. Not much else was allowed to happen, but Pishtaco could tell that his younger brother was somewhat in awe of him. He doubted that that was the case this evening. But he couldn't tell. He could only see that Huayna Capac was hunching beneath their late father's mantle of stitched together vampiro bat fur, and that his face was completely hidden behind the golden mask of Apu Inti.

Though Huayna Capac was seated on the imperial throne and wearing the sacred mask of Inti the sun god, it was clear that Mama Ocllo Coya was in charge. She stood slightly behind where he was seated with her left hand resting upon his shoulder. Huayna Capac did not speak to Pishtaco, only stared at him with remorseless eyes through the slits that had been cut into the mask.

Mama Ocllo Coya was determined to spare her son any discomfort and made this meeting quick. "We have no time for you, bastard child," she had said. "Your life is now coming to its inevitable end. You will stay here, in front of the throne, till daybreak. You may gaze upon it and contemplate the royal succession of Sapa Incas, and be proud of that lineage, or you may continue to quiver, and guessing from the wetness of your cloak, piss yourself. I don't care. Your thoughts and feelings are irrelevant. The only purpose your life now has is to end. These four guards shall keep you here till the first morning light. Then they take you to the top of the roof, for all of Cuzco to see. There you will greet the great god Inti as he rises from his slumber and be strangled. Once the priests have garroted you, your body will then be taken to Pisac and thrown from the cliff. There your remains will join your mother's at the bottom of the gorge and your names will be forgotten."

And with that, the royal audience ended. Mama Ocllo Coya, pinched her son's shoulder and in response he got up and led her and a small assemblage of dignitaries from the chamber.

Though many dreadful things had happened during the course of Pishtaco's life, that night was the worst of it all. Perhaps it was because he was so young that sitting there upon the stone floor as the hours slipped past before his execution made the most lasting impact. Pishtaco still had a boy's fragile sensibilities, but within minutes after that announcement of his impending death, what little remained of his childhood then disappeared with a serpent's **GULP**.

Torches clattered on to the floor as Pishtaco's guards shrieked in terror. They fled out of the audience chamber and ran to the entrance of Amarucancha. Once they had gotten out the main door, they flew down the pathway that led to the main gate that opened up into Cuzco. Unfortunately for them, Qasa wasn't there to flick the snakes away for them with his long staff. But he was nearby, on the ground, twitching. Pit-vipers become annoyed by commotion. So, it was only natural for them to lash out at passing legs. The walled courtyard soon became littered with the writhing bodies of the very guards who had recently protected the House of the Great Serpent.

Of course, Palla had little problem gliding down the path to the gate that opened out into Cuzco. Nor did the great serpent encounter any difficulties negotiating her way through the streets of Cuzco. It was still quite dark outside and the few people who were out fled from her with the same speed as did the palace guards.

Unopposed, Palla slithered on her way and, in no time, was well beyond the boundaries of Cuzco. It wasn't till she found a swamp to her liking that she finally came to a stop. Then, stretching her body out lengthwise, so not a coil or slight bend was showing, she began to convulse. With each convulsion, two large bulges in the middle of her stomach moved a little bit closer to Palla's mouth. Eventually they became close enough for Palla to lift up her head and vomit. Out in her vomit came bits and pieces of capybara, some torrent duck bones, jaguar fur, a lot of mucous as well as Ciquo Ollco and her grandson, Pishtaco. Pishtaco always thought of this spewing as the time of his real birth, the one he could actually remember, and it was an event he could never ever put far from his mind.

Ciquo Ollco was truly a great magician. This, Pishtaco would never contest. Once Palla had left them, she determined to take her grandson into hiding among the soothsayers of Cota Coca. If it had not been for her and knowledge of the spells that would take them to that out-of-the-way valley where black magic was practiced, the Inca's troops would surely have caught up with them. And Ciquo Ollco left rumors about with everyone she and her grandson encountered, so Mama Ocllo Coya's people searched everywhere but Cota Coca. Ciquo Ollco knew that it took little effort for men to do the easiest thing, and that was exactly what the soldiers did. Her magic proved to be flawless and during their many years among the soothsayers, Cota Coca was never disturbed by the troops of Mama Ocllo Coya.

At last, the dreadful images of those days receded from Pishtaco's thoughts. And he was again free to use his rediscovered voice. Miraculously, spit had returned to his mouth, which had been absent for so very, very long.

At first Pishtaco sniggered, but then he spoke aloud, and it came effortlessly. "Dear grandmother, you must have known that to turn an apprentice magician into a better one than yourself was to finalize your own doom. Surely you must have realized, well before I nodded to the executioner to tighten the rope, that being strangled at my orders was always your fate. All that your magic had done for you was to shift the when, and where your garroting would eventually take place."

Pishtaco gestured to the air with a bony finger. "The irony, of course, being that you were ultimately garroted by the person you were saving from being garroted. But you would have known about spells feeding on spells and ending up doing something more than what we asked them to do." He laughed again, and it was a surprise to him, and a pleasure, that his lungs would allow him to do so often. It occurred to him to regard his own fate and his laughter suddenly stopped.

"Behold, the great Pishtaco, laid out here on a stone slab above the cavern that leads straight to Supay and eternal torture. How sad, my magic was once greatly feared. You saw to it that my young spirit matured, leaving the foolishness of the shamans behind. No tepid white magic for us. No, no, just greed and malice. Life is hard, rude and unbending. At first the soothsayers of Cota Coca protested — then a few of them died by or spells. They moved on. We stayed.

"Our reputation was growing and growing, and with that came more and more power. We no longer needed to hide from the Sapa Inca. He began to send envoys to us. There was famine, drought, warring factions, treason in court — all of which you and I, Ciqui Ollco, resolved for him from afar. In gratitude, he sent for us.

"We returned to Cuzco, but we were only permitted to enter the city at night. We were ushered out of it before dawn. How the Sapa Inca feared us, he worried about our dark arts far more than my claim to his throne. They said that he had his concubines go about the palace eating every hair that might have dropped from his head, as though that would have stopped us if we wished him harm.

"The Chachapoyas were rebelling. He offered soldiers and heralded me his viceroy, granting me dominion over them and all of their lands. I remember you telling me that strength comes in stages, like building muscle. So we accepted his offer. The Sapa Inca was very pleased; pleased, that is, to send us as far away from the capital with a small army that could be easily destroyed by the rebellious Chachapoya. But it wasn't."

Pishtaco's heart banged in his chest. His revived lungs were now sucking in all the air they could take. His legs pushed him up from the stone slab they had rested upon for so many countless years. He was standing.

Pishtaco cried in amazement, "Look Ciqui Ollco, the gods have summoned your grandson back to his first life! The gods have made me new again! A new life for one who had done so much with his old. I smashed Chachapoya and rebuilt Paititi, enslaving or scattering its inhabitants. I recruited new residents to replace the Chachapoya and then enslaved them. When the Spanish came to Cuzco, crushing our army, their captain, Pizarro, held the Sapa Inca for ransom. The Sapa Inca sent runners to all the provinces demanding the Empire's treasure for his life. Ha! I gave no treasure. I hunted down his treasure. I found where it was being loaded so it could then be taken south. I ambushed Supa Inca's general, Rumiñawi, slew him and left him in quarters in the road. And when the Sapa Inca could not supply the rest of his ransom, he was garroted like you, Ciqui Ollco. But perhaps you know that? Perhaps you are now seated next to Rumiñawi, in Hanan Pacha, discussing the treachery of your grandson? And perhaps the gods have whispered in your ear their plans for me?"

Pishtaco squatted down and lowered his legs so that his feet touched the floor of his tomb. Rising up he began to walk, slowly and with great care, in the direction of the ancient doorway that the tremor had just reestablished. As Pishtaco moved towards the light, he began to plaintively entreat the god of the daylight.

"Inti, Lord of the Sun, Bringer of Light, Inti — Father of all the Inca, I have protected this treasure. Yes, I claimed it mine, but you know that it did me little good. At least no Spaniard has ever touched it. They tried. How they tried. But your Pishtaco prevented them. Rumors and traitors fled to them, all looking to abandon you and gain favor with these new masters and their new god, yet I held Paititi till it and what it contained drifted into obscurity and legend.

Yes, I was the one who buried the roads and planted over them. Yes, I was the one who slaughtered the villagers and destroyed all the villages along those roads. But Inti, the conquistadors were fueled by a greed as great as my own. When I blocked the mountains and the jungle they took to the river. And the Rio Marañón would have carried them to Paititi if not for me sending out Sach'amama. She hummed to them, as they lay in their tents along the Marañón, current reaching out electrifying them, paralyzing them in their sleep. Then, like a tiger crow that has swooped down upon roosting jays to crush their skulls and eat their brains, Sach'amama dined upon Spanish heads. Still the Spaniards came.

I had to sacrifice many children to Sach'amama before she deigned to come out of the forest. Their souls being the freshest and most enticing to the goddess."

Pishtaco had now crossed the threshold and was looking out upon the ancient plaza. He focused upon the ancient ruins of Inti's temple that were just across the way at the opposite end of the court. "Inti, so many, many children. But Sach'amama did eventually slither out of the Amazon and reached the banks of the Rio Marañón. Her snake-like, plant-covered, body blended into the forest. With her large ears, she listened for them. Inti, Spaniards make so much noise. She found the prey easily, the eyes on her two heads mesmerizing them. They walked into her gaping mouths almost gratefully. See, oh God of Light, how I have been of service to you and your people? I have been restored and I now rededicate myself to you and your service. How may Pishtaco serve his Lord Inti?"

Pishtaco waited for Inti's answer. He ruminated as to why he had been called by the great god Viracocha. Surely Viracocha knew that his son Inti's gold was in peril. As he thought, his attention fell upon the plaza in front of him. As he took a good look at it, he was shaken. There was a strange covering over Inti's temple...Mama Killa's too! The cushion plants, tussock grasses, stump ferns, crustose lichens, club mosses, the cold high plants were gone. The plaza temples were now covered in vines, Spanish moss, kapok trees and ironwood palms and orchids of all description.

The area where Siwar Q'enti had touched Pishtaco's nose with its tongue, still remained dried and shriveled, unlike the rest of Pishtaco's body. As Pishtaco's mouth opened in astonishment at the transformations in the city's square, his nostril broke away from his face and fell on to his left foot.

CHAPTER THREE

Doctor Hernandez

Her scalp had been painstakingly cleaned with a Q-tip to ensure that no particle of dirt would interfere with the seventy-four electrodes that she would soon be wearing. An EEG cap was then placed onto Penelope's head and cinched tight with a chinstrap. Then, additional electrodes were attached to her nose and cheeks; they were to monitor her facial movements. Finally, a harness containing the collected wires from all of these electrodes was plugged into an electroencephalograph.

Penelope Farquhar was now transmitting seventy-four signals from different parts of her brain — that would be thirty-two more channels than is broadcast from all of Austin, Texas, and Travis County's AM and FM stations combined. Penelope had no classic rock, country, jazz, evangelical, sports or regional Mexican channels, but if you were looking for a talk format, inside Penelope's head was the place to be.

The technician now had her lean back in her chair which raised the foot rest and elevated Penelope's legs. As she nodded that she was comfy, a computer screen, attached to a swivel arm, was positioned in front of her. It was like being seated in a dental chair, but without the blood and the pain.

A few minutes later, after the technician departed from the room, Doctor Hernandez made his entry. He was in his forties, and Penelope found him to be a tad attractive, but she didn't care much for men...or women. For Penelope, emotional attachments were just a whole lot of bother. She was always surprised by how lean Doctor Hernandez was. She imagined that he must jog on his lunch hour and eat only scant amounts of overpriced organic food for dinner. But that was his business and she had no doubt that he made enough money doing what he did to be able to afford his pomegranate extracts, dehydrated wolfberries and kopi luwak lattes to prevent any cramping post workout. Of course, she had no idea if he did any of this. Perhaps he just leisurely walked to McDonalds for a quarter pounder when feeling peckish, but Miss Farquhar preferred her new age professorial typecasting. She liked to hold onto her stereotypes because they offered such a nice framework for dismissing the rest of the world.

"So how did your week go, Penny?" Doctor Hernandez said as he sat at his desk, which was just to the left of, and slightly behind, the chair that Penelope was seated in.

Penelope wasn't sure that his seeming eagerness to know the details of her week was motivated by a genuine enthusiasm for her as a person or for her as his prized specimen. She was reluctant to answer his question, though she was grateful that Doctor Hernandez had worked so hard to get her into the university's program for psychiatrically challenged students, she still couldn't resist going on the offensive. Maybe it would get him off of the topic of her week and any discussion concerning the appearance of Cecile.

"I'm not Penny. The name is Penelope, Penelope Gertrude Augusta Farquhar, as you very well know."

Doctor Hernandez just managed to maintain part of his smile "Sorry. Ms. Farquhar, we are a bit informal around here. I just…"

She interrupted him, "Not Ms. — Miss. There should be no ambiguity concerning my marital status. I'm a Miss, and most likely always will be one. Which is to my satisfaction. No need to cover up a good thing, is there?"

"No, absolutely no reason to cover up. So, you have had a setback?

Doctor Hernandez wasn't as simple as she thought he was.

"Well, Miss Farquhar, don't let it bother you. It's nothing to feel ashamed of. Perfectly normal. You've been making very good progress. So, who was it...or were there many voices this time?"

A bit perturbed that she had been out-maneuvered, Penelope wasn't sure if she should just lie or fess up. Considering that he already had her brain all wired up, there was little point in lying. If she did, he would no doubt watch the lying areas of her brain light up on his computer screen like some sort of neurological Fourth of July.

"It was Cecile. And only a brief encounter."

"Oh Cecile, the voodoo priestess from Haiti? Didn't she foment the slave rebellion?"

"You've been reading up. Yes, in Saint-Domingue, over a thousand slave owners killed, and close to two thousand plantations destroyed, but around me she's just an annoying pain in the ass. I guess that you have figured out by now that all my voices have some historical notoriety. You see, I don't like talking to people inside my head or outside of my head if they aren't interesting. But, getting back to Cecile, she decided to check in on me while I was gardening...I mean, while I was releasing a spider into my garden."

"Okay, and what did she say?"

"She was just trying to get me going. She made a big fuss over the spider. Claimed it was a recluse spider. It was a pretty poor attempt on her part. She normally does better. Cecile does like to stir the pot. It's not like I'm going to let anything into my house without knowing what it is. I'd purchased a guide to spiders some time ago and knew exactly what I was dealing with. Even if it had been a recluse spider, that wouldn't have been a big deal." Penelope grinned. "You might say that spiders and I have a lot in common."

"As I've mentioned, we've been making great progress with this meditative therapy. I've seen significant thickening of your basal ganglia. I'm pretty confident that you'll soon learn to be able to block out most of your hallucinations. As I've said to you before the brain is like a muscle and our equipment here is like a gymnasium for it. You've got this underdeveloped area, the same thing that young children have. That's why they also have imaginary friends that they truly believe are real."

"Well, if you say so. I read that there are over a billion adults on Facebook, and from what I've seen, each one of them has hundreds of imaginary friends." Penelope enjoyed that zinger. Defending her schizophrenia was something that she felt compelled to do, even though she really didn't like having it.

"So, did you try your hand at some lucid dreaming?"

She held up her right hand and twiddled her fingers so that he could see them.

"Oh yes, you said that you were going to get them painted up like pirate flags. Does it help? Were you aware that the things you were dreaming were not real? Were you able to manipulate your dream and its characters?"

"Only for a second. But I did manage to catch a glimpse of my nails."

"Great! This is hopeful. We might be able to approach your symptoms from two angles — meditation and lucid dreaming. I'm no good at it but you seem to be developing a knack. If you can control your interior dream world there's no reason you can't start dealing with Cecile. Send her back to Haiti, I say."

Penelope liked the idea of sending Cecile back to Haiti. Of all the voices, she had to put up with, Cecile was the most prying and irksome.

"So, what was the dream about?"

"Don't know. Not much to report. I was in a swamp and looked down at my nails. Then, I realized that I was dreaming and woke up."

"As I said, this is good. It's a beginning. Now, shall we get started with the meditation?" Doctor Hernandez reached over and flipped on the monitor that had been positioned in front of Penelope.

"Now let's go through the warm up exercises."

To Penelope these warm-up exercises were a little like when she was in kindergarten and was required to do the hokey-pokey with the rest of the class. She found it to be embarrassing then and especially now as an adult. But back then, when she was sane, she could resist. Today, she had no other option but to comply.

"Neck first. Good. Inhale. Now rock your arms from left to right engaging your whole torso. Remember to breathe slowly in and out."

"Excellent! Let's get to it."

Given the doctor's go-ahead, Penelope placed her hands on her knees, palms up, and slowly began to breathe in and out. She attempted to focus on her breath and clear her mind of all other thoughts. She then turned her attention to a red ball that was floating near the bottom of her monitor. As she stripped her mind of any of her thoughts, as well as those of her cranial tenants, the red ball began to slowly climb upward towards the center of the computer screen. There were black cross hairs in the middle of the display. They were the target. The more she pulled herself quietly inward the more the red ball would move in the right direction. She had it! This would be a first. The ball was positioned dead center, right where it was meant to be. She held it there by maintaining her breath and clearing her head, other than to concentrate on those cross hairs. One minute went by. Then, two minutes. Then five — ten — seventeen minutes into her therapy session and she was maintaining the red ball in the middle of the screen. The room was so quiet. She was so relaxed. Penelope felt at peace with herself for the first time in over a decade.

Then, the ball started to act strangely. It drifted up, like an ascending balloon, to the top of the monitor. There it bounced about. Then it began to behave like the computer game of pong — bouncing from left to right and from right to left — as though it was encountering ping-pong paddles.

Penelope lost her concentration, but the red ball was still behaving queerly.

Doctor Hernandez got up from his chair and took a look behind her monitor. While he examined the connections, the screen became fuzzy, then sharpened.

Penelope's eyes opened wide as a jungle full of bright red flowers came into view. As it faded, a head appeared... well, not really a head but a mask shaped like a head. A mask made of gold with feathers around the top.

"HOLY CRAP!!!"

The doctor's head shot up from behind the back of the computer screen. "Is everything okay? I must apologize this has never happened before. The system was working perfectly this morning. Are you well? You look pale."

"I...I... have a migraine. That's all. I think staring at the screen when it went crazy gave me a headache."

"I'll get you something for that. This silly device can wait."

"No. No. I really just need to get home and lie down. I'll be fine. If someone could just call me a cab?"

"Certainly will — and get you some Advil and water while I'm at it. Once again, I do apologize and I sure will have this all sorted out by the time of your next session. You were doing fantastic! What a shame that everything had to go haywire."

CHAPTER FOUR

The Spider's Lullaby

Penelope was taking great care with the presentation. The center of attention in the Lavender Room was a burr walnut tea table. On it she always kept a fluted cut glass vase overflowing with flowers. Delphiniums in shades of pastel pinks and blues were the floral arrangement of the day. No grand master from the Japanese tea ceremony school at Mushanokōjisenke would have faulted her on how she placed a silver tray containing a cobalt blue and gold bone China tea service next to her delphiniums. Dignified and poised was what she was aiming for. Precision and control were so necessary after this afternoon's appointment with Doctor Hernandez. It had rattled her. But now Penelope was getting herself together. She had never seen anything like it before. But then again, schizophrenics do occasionally have visual hallucinations. And Doctor Hernandez did say that she was making progress. He wasn't just being kind; he had brain scans to prove it.

First Penelope warmed the Wedgewood teapot with hot water and then she drained it before adding her teas. Blue vervain, American passionflower and motherwort were tonight's selection. It was all meant to calm and induce sleep. Penelope was already dressed for bed in a bird print Mother Hubbard.

Just before she added boiling water into her pot of dried leaves, Penelope inserted a pair of earbuds into her ears. Forgoing her customary selection of Iannis Xenakis, who used mathematical models for composition, she opted for something melodic and syrupy. She tapped Straussian waltzes from her iPod files. Then she cranked up the volume.

In Penelope's mind, there was no doubt that her predicament was all Cecile's fault. Things had been quiet for some while before Cecile had shown up in the garden. That golden mask with feathers was definitely one of those voodoo props of hers. Cecile was no doubt getting back at Penelope for trying to shut her out. Well, the Gartenlaube, Walzer, set to high volume would provide for an impenetrable wall of sound and keep Cecile's voice away.

The Kaiser-Walzer was playing as Penelope downed her third cup of tea. Swaying to and fro with the melody, she placed her cup on its saucer and then padded her way up the staircase to her bedroom. She did indeed feel calmer. And she was now convinced she was on the road back to good mental health. Cecile be damned, Penelope knew she had a stronger will than even Cecile Fatiman.

She was tough all right. It had been a hard fight to get her share of her mother's inheritance out from under the grasp of her brother, but she had managed all of that while being locked up in the East Hampton Psychiatric Center. Yes, she had attempted to kill her, but the damned woman had lived through the experience of being stabbed. No doubt she enjoyed the martyrdom that it had afforded her. Probably it elicited plenty of pity at her duplicate bridge club. Besides, real murderers had often done less time than Penelope had locked up in that institution. And, initially, that court-appointed guardian was so reluctant to let her use her money to take on the ownership of this house. But Penelope had held her ground and managed to get him to acquiesce. Of course, a scholarship for the psychiatrically disadvantaged helped tip the scale in her favor. She had also convinced him that she was capable of staying within budget when it came to her monthly allotment from the trust fund. Why wouldn't she? Numbers were her friends… in fact, the only friendship she was capable of maintaining.

Once in her bedroom, Penelope firmly bolted the door in place and then opened the windows to the large dormer that dominated the wall just in front of her bed. Cool, moist evening air swept into the room bringing with it the fragrant scents welling up from the gardens below. Coming out of her master bathroom, she placed a filled Royal Albert water pitcher on her nightstand next to the hand-blown apple green water glass that was always on display there. Then turned her attention to the bedding, throwing it back but for a single lace-fringed sheet. She switched on her nightstand light and swept her hand along the crystal prisms that dangled from the rim of its rose-colored shade. Watching the prisms project rainbows about the room was part of her nightly ritual. They swayed in and out of the shadows and were gorgeous and calming. They acted like search lights in her room, illuminating various objects, bringing them to her attention. This gave her a chance to reflect upon the treasures she had collected within the room.

The shimmering lights buzzed about her curio cabinet, which she had stocked with megalodon shark's teeth and skate rasps, as well as rare seashells, and prehistoric flint projectiles. There was a beetle and butterfly collection, with flamboyant exoskeletons, scales and wings and small piles of agates, minerals, and flashy semiprecious gemstones which she had once polished to perfection.

Penelope's father had helped her assemble all of these things. Collecting was his passion. Before his death, he had been the curator-in-charge of fossil invertebrates at the Museum of Natural History. So, putting together a mini-museum for his daughter was just in his nature. He and Penelope spent a lot of time looking for special things to go in it, which meant trips to the Calvert Cliffs, to gather up Miocene shark's teeth, shining black amongst the pebbles within the Chesapeake Bay's surf; or a flight to Sanibel Island to gather seashells.

An emerald ray of prismatic light, that had been dancing across the curio cabinet, now slowed as the oscillation of its crystal petered out. Rocking to and fro it seemed to hover about one particular object within her collection. Deep green flickered about a dark gray mudstone as though it was trying to finger it. Penelope was pleased that this particular fossil was being highlighted in tonight's light show. It was her huge trilobite, and her greatest find. She'd stumbled upon it long ago when she was just a little girl. It was on one of those family outings her father liked to arrange. He had taken her in hand and they went stomping up the shallow waters of Fourteen Mile Creek. The idea was to find some rocks containing Devonian crinoids. Those kinds of fossils frequently dislodged from the bluff above and tumbled down into the streambed. But that day they didn't find any crinoids, and instead, Penelope discovered this magnificent rock…well, actually, it was her pink rubber boot that had found the fossil. She had tripped over it. But her father recognized it immediately. It was the largest Eldredgeops trilobite he had ever seen. She still recalled his enthusiasm as he proudly carried it back to the picnic table where her mother and younger brother were waiting. When they arrived, her mother wasn't quite as enthusiastic. In fact, she was incensed due to the fact that Penelope had lost her plush bunny at some point during the expedition. That was all that mattered to the woman. So, it was a bittersweet memory — mother shouting, little brother assisting with his disapproving frown, as her father failed at calming everyone down. Still, the trilobite was a great find.

Penelope flicked at the prisms once again and the rainbows sashayed about her room with renewed vigor. It was hypnotic and a reassuring display of her financial security. The flashes of prismatic light continued with this ostentatious theme, crossing over her tiger maple vanity, skirting her ivory framed mirror, then onto those barley-twist bedposts that towered above her feet. But here something was wrong. She sensed that, but it was so dim in the room, and the colors weren't staying put long enough for her to make out what it was. Penelope had to focus hard on the bedposts, and gained a little more clarity with each pass of the prisms. Then it gelled. It was a web. The spider had come back.

"Damn! I hope you are the last spider's sister or you surely are one persistent arachnid. You're lucky I'm crazy or I might get a bit spooked about this. Just to put you at ease, I refuse to fumigate this house. So, you'd better be some kind of homing-spider and not the first sign of a massive spidery infestation. Good lord, if you want my company that badly, who am I to deny you? But I guess there must be plenty of pill bugs about to maintain your interest. Yet I've looked about for them and I swear I've never seen a one."

Penelope thought a minute, then developed a wry smile, "Since we are to be roomies, I think it highly appropriate that we should be properly introduced. I'm Miss Penelope Augusta Gertrude Farquhar, formerly of South Lake, Dallas-Fort Worth. And now, as you well know, residing in the Bremond Block of Guadalupe Street, downtown Austin, Texas. According to my guide on North American spiders, you are to be called Miss Golden Orb Weaver. You see I've looked you up in the arthropoda social register. Yes, you should be flattered."

With that statement, she pulled the chain to her nightstand light but still felt like talking. Chattering to herself often kept the voices at bay.

"Don't get alarmed, I'm not about to suggest a pillow fight or anything. I know how tragically that would end. But I was just thinking," Penelope offered, as she spoke in the darkness of her room, "Do you guys dream? It's just that I recall reading somewhere that ants twitch their antennae when they are in deep sleep — like what people do with their eyes, but you guys don't have antennae, just a lot of legs and eyes. Eight of each...I think. I bet you do dream. Perhaps with one or two eyes left open in case a fly comes to visit you? Anyhow, what would you guys dream about? Flies? Lots and lots of flies? Or is there more to it than that? When you fall asleep, do you give up your sense of self? Do you become whatever your spidery mind thinks up? Do you become flies?"

Penelope folded her arms across her chest, like a reposing corpse, "You know, drifting off to sleep must be like death, your consciousness wavers, then you're gone. Just like that," she weakly snapped her fingers. "I think it is nature's way of preparing us for the big sleep. Odd how people fight to stay awake, but once asleep, few regret being asleep. In fact, most people just want to keep on sleeping. Maybe that's what dying is like?"

Trying to philosophize with her uncommunicative arachnid was beginning to take its toll. The herbal teas were kicking in and Penelope's voice started fading, becoming distant, less engaged in making her points to the spider.

"You know, it's weird when you first wake up — and just for a few seconds you really do believe that all you experienced in your sleep made sense. Dreamy logic hangs on no matter what sort of idiocy your brain cooked up during the night. But then you think about it and say to yourself... that was really stupid..."

The moon had risen sufficiently to clear the overelaborate rooftops of Penelope's neighbors. Moonlight swamped the windowpanes of her dormers, penetrating her bedchamber — illuminating the bedposts and the spider hanging between them. As Penelope dreamed that she was on a hurricane-hunting airplane being buffeted by turbulence as it coursed deep into her subconscious looking for the eye of her dreams, the golden orb weaver began spinning. If she had been awake, she would have seen it work its silk — teasing out one sticky spoke after another — overlapping them with concentric circles — expanding the central core of the web to engulf all of the space between the barley-twist posts at the foot of Penelope's bed.

CHAPTER FIVE

The Flight

She was buckled into a seat. Her forehead was pressed against an airplane window. Penelope felt fatigued. It was as though she was a passenger on a New York to Los Angeles bus trip traveling on a long bumpy road with more potholes than asphalt. Though the window was cold, it felt soothing, even though it vibrated with all the rattling that came from the airplane's four bucking engines. The airplane's clattering and jangling pulsated through Penelope's skull to her forehead, into her neck, and down to the tip of her spine. The clouds outside began to darken as the window became spotted with raindrops. Daylight was now replaced by a meteorologically imposed night.

Then a fiery comet with a tail made of rainbows coursed through the gloom. It was a starting signal for a race.

Hundreds of hot air balloons, luminescent and extravagant in color, emerged from a lower layer of clouds and soared upwards. In the gondolas of each of these balloons was a vignette from Penelope's life.

As they floated up past her airplane window, she could see that once again her mother throwing a fit of uncontrollable rage as her father hung from a beam with an overturned chair under his feet.

Penelope yawned. She was unimpressed. She had seen this very routine so many times before in so many other dreams. Oodles of psychiatrists had discussed them with her. Over and over again she had to trudge through the traumatic events in her life so they could interpret the deranged and repetitive symbolism within her dreams. And when this failed, out came the electric shock machine to zap the floating gondolas from her head.

> Miss Polly had a dolly who was sick, sick, sick.
> So she phoned for the doctor to be quick, quick, quick.
> The doctor came with his bag and hat,
> And knocked at the door with a rat tat tat.
> He looked at the dolly and shook his head,
> And said "Miss Polly put her straight to bed.
> He wrote a pad for a pill, pill, pill.
> I'll be back in the morning with my bill, bill, bill.

Well, that was unexpected. It took her quite by surprise. The floating balloons must have sensed her thoughts and then decided to throw her a curve. Right on cue they had presented her with something new — her six-year-old self, singing to herself. It came out of all of the gondolas in unison. And it was quite a delight for her to hear herself as she once had sounded. She had forgotten how she had spoken as a little girl, it was a soft voice, a bit tender. Penelope knew that her adult voice had acquired an edge to it. She guessed that for a few years during her early development that there must have been an almost blushing quality to the voice of her inner thoughts.

How odd, she thought, my brain has been adjusting my inner voice as I've grown older. though it's been going on all of this time, I've never thought about it before. How does it happen? When does it happen? Must be a gradual thing. I wonder how many voices it has devised for me for contemplating my inner thought? Must go from a baby's voice, to a child's voice, from a teenager's voice to the ever-deepening voice of the adult me. Of course, the voice I hear in my head, the voice I hear when I speak, is nothing like the voice everyone else hears. When people recognize my voice, it is quite different from the one I'm familiar with.

Like everyone else, it shocked her to hear her own voice played back to her after it had been recorded. It certainly didn't sound anything like the voice that she felt was hers.

She wondered why the brain would take such liberties. And it just wasn't her brain that was manufacturing voices for her head; all brains were doing that.

Since the voices used for our thoughts are no more than cranial fabrications, shouldn't we be consulted on this matter? Couldn't there be some sampling in the process... like selecting a ringtone for my mobile phone? Why not some nice possibilities for us to choose from? Couldn't Katherine Hepburn's voice be available? Or for that matter Liz Taylor's? There must be a better substitute for the one that is kicking around in my skull representing Penelope Farquhar's thoughts?

She wondered what criteria did her brain use to determine what the six other voices that spoke to her in her head would sound like.

When people read the words on the page the speakers acquire a voice in people's thoughts. There are different voices for each character in a novel. When I read the histories of the people who now inhabit my thoughts, my brain invented voices for them. The only difference between the voices in my head and those of normal people is that my voices stayed after I closed the books.

All of my shrinks agree that all of my delusional voices are just different versions of me. A smile now appeared across her face, So, she reasoned, unlike everyone else, my unique brain actually does provide me with a variety of ringtones to choose from. It's a much better model.

Christ! she thought, the hooded ventriloquists again!

Each ventriloquist was rising through the atmosphere seated on a floating chair with their dummies, talking nonsense: Here came the wooden Cecile in her voodoo priestess attire all in white with a white head wrap —followed by Billy Bowlegs, dressed in his Seminole chieftain's outfit. René Descartes was next, attired in a seventeenth century scholar's black robe, mouthing, "I think therefore I am" as buttons and wires were depressed and tugged behind a carved caricature of his mustached, hawk-like face. Next came Ernest Shackleton, in sealskin pants, followed by an overdressed Belle Star in so much flowery embroidery that Dale Evans would blush. Finally came Ada Lovelace, the Countess of Lovelace, daughter of the poet Lord Byron. Unlike the preceding five; she was crafted in white porcelain, dressed in a lilac satin gown and wearing a diamond-studded tiara. Of all the voices in Penelope's head, Ada was the one she appreciated most. Why wouldn't she? Ada was a woman and a mathematician.

Craning her head up, she watched the last of these dummies disappear out of sight. As she did so, she felt a sudden twinge of pain. She thought, *I must have knocked my pillow on to the floor and I'm getting a crick in my neck from the way my head is resting on the mattress...* Then she realized, if I am dreaming how can I know that I have crick in my neck from the way my head is resting on the mattress?

Slowly raising her right hand up to her face, Penelope turned it so that she could see her fingernails. There they were, the five skulls and crossbones decals that Carmen had applied over Penelope's black nail polish. She had done it! Penelope Augusta Gertrude Farquhar had somehow managed to take control of this dream. Her heart raced. Now she didn't know what exactly to do — she could screw this all up so easily. One mental misstep might cause the whole thing to collapse within her head, like forgetting to close an oven door gently after looking at a soufflé.

Penelope was breathing so quickly now that she thought she might hyperventilate. She double-checked her nails several times. Then, cautiously she began to check out her surroundings. There could be no doubt, she was on an airplane and, so far, it appeared that this wasn't one of those plane crash dreams.

She knew that she was seated in a cabin, and that suggested that it was more than likely that something could be in it with her. Now came the tricky bit. If she turned her head to look, would whatever was in the cabin with her be so outlandish or horrifying that Penelope would instantly find herself back in bed recounting the night's events to that spider? Or would she be able to control the situation, tailor the events, change them to her needs — turn a space alien into a pussycat?

It was now or never. Penelope knew that there must be something seated right behind her. The question was, was it going to have a jaw full of fangs or a plastic flower pinned to its lapel that would squirt water into her face?

Penelope took the plunge and turned her head to confront whatever was behind her.

"My dear Miss Farquhar, what a pleasure. I've wanted to meet you, in the flesh so to speak, since you were a young lady and our paths first crossed. I know that this is a dream, but it is the best we can do. Especially if you take into account that I've been dead since January 5th, 1922...I believe that was the date...wasn't paying too much attention. Heart attack, you know. On my way to the Antarctic, once again. Yes, yet another expedition. Wasn't at all prepared for the bloody heart thing. Bam! There it was. All gone. No more Ernest. But let's not discuss me. It's you I want to talk about. You, our patroness, so to speak. You have so kindly kept all of us going within those dark closets you keep on the other side of your eyes."

He now jumped up from his seat proffering a hand, "Miss Farquhar, might I properly introduce myself?"

Penelope nodded her assent, delighted and taken up with how she had so cleverly crafted the lines of his monologue.

Shackleton beamed, "Sir Ernest Henry Shackleton," then he leaned in and added, "at your service, madam."

Now it was Penelope's turn to beam, but she didn't shake his proffered hand. Instead, she raised her right hand up to be kissed. As far she was concerned, this was her dream and all men were going to be obliged to kiss her hand, which Shackleton did with great delight.

"Penelope Augusta Gertrude Farquhar, daughter of the late Sidney Allen Farquhar, formerly of the East Hampton Psychiatric Center but now attending the Lorenzo de Zavala School of Science in Austin." She smiled coyly and added, "This is a great honor."

"No. No. The honor is all mine. But here I am hogging the limelight and you have so many other friends aboard just dying...well they've all done that...Let me rephrase, chomping at the bit to see you face-to-face."

"I too must kiss the hand of my dear friend, Penelope Farquhar."

Penelope extended her hand, saying, "Monsieur Descartes, you know normally I wouldn't be happy to hear from any of you, but considering that this is just a rather elaborate dream, I'll be quite good about it. I won't even try and hide the fact from Doctor Hernandez. As long as you stay out of my head while I'm awake, I'm really good with spending my nights with every one of you...I mean, when I'm asleep, that is."

René Descartes chose not to kiss her proffered hand; instead, he raised his right arm and extended it in a dismissive flourish, "Mademoiselle Farquhar, I know that you have read up on all of us..." He paused, for the right word, "What should be the appropriate term? For now, let us call ourselves your inner tormentors. But then, you selected us from the vast number of biographies that you have read. The case may be submitted, are we your tormentors or your prisoners? However, I amend this question by adding that it has been a particular delight for me to be allowed into the confines of your head. You have proven to be a magnificent hostess and have provided all of us with quite a party.

"Yet, merrymaking aside, what I most admire about being held within your brain is the considerable detail that you have managed to gather concerning all of us. You are a woman who insists upon historically accurate delusions. Which brings me to your request that we only inhabit your dreams...well I have been oft-quoted as saying, 'I am accustomed to sleep and in my dreams to imagine the same things that lunatics imagine when awake. So, I doubt that the arrangement you propose will make much of a difference.'"

Smiling broadly, he stepped back and waited to see what would be the results of his little experiment.

Penelope didn't miss a beat and responded immediately, "You went on to say — 'When I consider matters carefully, I realize so clearly that there are no conclusive indications by which waking life can be distinguished from sleep that I am quite astonished, and my bewilderment is such that it is almost able to convince me that I am sleeping' — your Meditations on First Philosophy.

Descartes bowed, reaching out to finally kiss her hand, "Enchanté, mademoiselle!"

"Well, that was a lot of work just to get a smooch. By the way, while you are down there, what do you think of the nail polish?"

"Superb! So piratical…"

BANG! BANG!

Descartes hit the deck as Penelope jumped from her seat. Not only was she startled by the gunfire but she was also very much concerned that it might cause her to lose hold of this dream.

Belle Starr threw her head back and laughed uncontrollably. "Serves you right for putting me in this ridiculous getup. Next week you'll have me covered in rhinestones. I was a horse thief! I rode with outlaws and murderers, like the Youngers, Blue Duck and my husband, Sam Starr. I wasn't no Grand Ol' Opry singer, gussied up in sequins. Shit! I wore dresses that I sewed from calico I got at dry goods stores."

Mrs. Starr calmed down a bit, twirled a pair of chrome-plated six-guns and dropped them back into their holsters before continuing with her complaints. "True. True. I once put a red plume in my hat, but that was just because I was feeling rambunctious that day and then somebody decided to take my photograph. The fanciest thing I ever wore was a black velvet skirt," she said resting her hands atop the handles of her revolvers. "And, what about these silly things?" she said, tapping the pearl handles. "Where'd you get the notion that I would ever carry anything that looked this outlandish?"

It was odd that she felt compelled to justify herself to one of her delusions, but Penelope did. "I just didn't take the time to study up on you. You popped into my head not after I had read a book but after I had watched an old Randolph Scott, Gene Tierney movie about you called The Bandit Queen. And it wasn't as though I was even paying any attention to what they had put on for us in the lounge — just another mid-afternoon black-and-white flick to pass the time in the nuthouse. The thing was that you soon came calling, like the rest. And, like the rest, you never left. I should have done more research on you, like I did with everyone else. Maybe I'm a bit of a schizophrenic snob; you being a horse thief and not some great explorer, freedom fighter or intellectual."

Looking down at her fingernails, ensuring that the skulls and crossbones were still showing, Penelope thought hard and then made a few adjustments. "Black velvet skirt, broad brim hat with red plume and a pair of black six-guns with walnut handles — how is that?"

"Damn! Pretty good! Thanks. Much better. This was me. Okay, my bitching time is over. Who's next?"

"Me," said Ada Lovelace as she tiptoed over Monsieur Descartes, who had chosen to remain on the floor until he was convinced that Belle Starr was again seated with her seatbelt snapped in place.

"You and I are so much more than a hallucination and hysteric."

"Ada, I'm a schizophrenic, not a hysteric."

Ada dismissed Penelope's term with the motion of a hand, "Today you are a schizophrenic, and they'll have a new name for you tomorrow. In my time, they would attribute your malady to a wandering womb. Practitioners of psychiatry are far too speculative and quick to label, in my opinion. My father was extravagant in nature, a poet, a romantic and an adventurer. He was also a habitual liar, a libertine and a profligate. Today, he would be labeled a bi-polar, manic-depressive anorexic. Yet, in my day, he was heralded as a founder of the Romantic Movement and a genius. Fact is, he may still be considered so, by the few people left who read poetry."

"I don't disagree. But there's not much I can do about it other than conjure up sympathetic statements from you in my brain. Well, that's not totally true. Doctor Hernandez has been making me do lots of mental pushups on that meditation machine of his. He hopes that I'll get so cranially muscle-bound that all I'll have to do is flex it and you people won't say a peep. Though I'm not sure that's quite what I want. I confess I like having you about at times. Never did care much for real people…"

Boom! The plane had suddenly dropped into a pocket of severe turbulence and began to pitch and yaw. Caught in a downdraft, it plummeted hundreds of feet before righting itself. Penelope's head shot forward and banged into the seat in front of her as Ada toppled on top of Descartes, both of who let out a yelp.

"Damn it, since when is a dream supposed to hurt?" Penelope said, rubbing her head.

"It's got to be that we're getting close!" Evidently Cecile's assigned seat was the one that Penelope had just rammed with her noggin.

"Close to what?" Penelope inquired, still in a bit of pain.

"Where your nightmares live!" Cecile advised, as she shook the stones inside her calabash-rattle directly in front of Penelope's face, as though she had taken over from Doctor Hernandez, but with voodoo instead of electrodes covered in goop.

Cecile clutched at a gris-gris bag that was suspended below her neck and frantically recited a very peculiar rosary peppered with "Hail Mary full of grace" and "Papa Legba, please open the door!" She abruptly stopped, looked into Penelope's eyes with a penetrating stare and added, "Billy Bowlegs says you got all sorts of horrible things swirling about your mind. They pile up near the eye going faster and faster!"

"What? My vision is perfectly fine. Who is this Billy Bowlegs, some kind of ophthalmologist?

"Not that kind of eye. The eye of this storm we are in."

Penelope looked out her window and saw a deluge of rain. Not rain but what must have been her entire life pouring out of the sky in a deluge of events. She turned her head away angered by it all.

"Cecile, this Billy Bowlegs, I believe I've met him twice. No more. He just popped in my head one day. Wasn't very talkative and then he left. Now he's some sort of expert on the inner workings of my brain." Penelope looked about the cabin, "Hell, he's not even here!"

"Yes he is!" Cecile insisted, as she picked up where she had left off with her rattle and her rosary.

"Well, I don't see him."

"He's not in the passenger's cabin. He's in the cockpit. He is our pilot."

"Oh, great, a figment of my imagination with a pilot's license. No wonder I haven't seen much of him. He's been in a commercial pilot's school. Hope it wasn't a correspondence course." Penelope said with irritation as she raised up both of her hands, checking them out, to make sure that all ten of the skulls crossbones decals were still attached to her black nail polish.

"This dream isn't behaving the way it ought to. I'm taking charge!"

As Penelope stood up and made this pronouncement, the cascading memories beating against the aluminum frame of the airplane ceased, and all four engines of the plane began to purr. Penelope turned to her fellow passengers with a self-satisfied grin, "Ladies and gentleman, we at Farquhar Airlines apologize for the bumpy ride. Please take your seats, and remain seated, with your safety belts securely fastened, seats back and folding trays in an upright position, as I go forward to wrestle the beverage cart from out of the hands of our pilot."

With this, she briskly moved down the aisle and swung open the door to the cockpit. Small, red, yellow, blue and green lights and gages on the instrument panel dimly lit the surroundings. Billy Bowlegs was behind the controls. There was no one else assisting him in the cockpit. Penelope could see that he was dressed in a standard pilot's blue blazer with matching pants. He wouldn't have looked out of place except for the red scarf wrapped about his head, with pink roseate spoonbill and snowy egret feathers sticking out the top. Penelope reasoned that Seminole headdress must be standard issue for anyone who was a pilot for Farquhar Airlines.

The plane heaved for just a moment. "Excuse me, I lost concentration there for a minute," Penelope said, assuming she had caused it. "I must get used to flying this thing."

"Me too," Billy added. "But please take a seat. I think we've made it through the worst. The winds are rapidly falling off as well as the pelting. I've heard of it raining cats and dogs but never cats and dogs, hamsters, snotty gym teachers, disinterested guidance counselors, bored ministers, stuck-up cheerleaders, math professors and assorted creepy relatives. It was something to see, even for a figment of your imagination, like myself."

Thump!

An estate attorney came crashing down, leaving a large dent on the tip of the airplane's nose.

"Well, we are almost out of it. I think we are nearing the eye. We should be safe in there...but, of course once in you've got to make it through to the other side and out again. I feel much better now that you are here. Of course, you could get us all out of this by waking up at any time but then again, I really would like to see what's in this eye we've been heading to. How about you?"

"Well, probably more creepy relatives. But, since the eye is supposed to be quiet, it's more than likely to be a big graveyard. Most of them are dead these days. Actually, I'm kind of enjoying this, meeting all of you in the flesh...sort of. And I'm gathering tons of material for Doctor Hernandez. And, he normally chides me for having nothing to say."

"There! Just a bit to your right. Looks like it might be clearing up."

Penelope shifted around in the copilot's seat so she could take a look out the window to where Billy had just pointed. There was a crack in the storm and he was guiding them to it. As the airplane punched through, into the eye, the winds dropped off. All suddenly seemed peaceful and serene. What had been harsh and brutal now revealed a soft soothing interior. It was like a hidden land, a Shangri-La. But instead of being protected by mountains, a great circle of billowing cumulous clouds, incandescent in the midday sun, defined the edges that separated peace from the madness of the storm. Penelope was beaming with unaccustomed delight.

Billy Bowlegs saw this and picked up on it, "Would you like to take a victory lap?"

"Oh yes, please!" she said. Then, catching herself bouncing on her seat, she added in a sobering tone, "I mean, if you would like to."

Billy Bowlegs chuckled, "Of course I would like to. Besides, it is your dream."

"Well then," Penelope said, as she made a sweeping circle in the air with a finger, "once around the park, James."

Billy banked the plane and set it on a course that curved along the edge of the wall. Below them was a vast forest with dozens of reddish brown rivers, giving it a ragged appearance, as if some celestial seamstress had done a poor job of stitching together odd pieces of emerald cloth. The sun was big and high in the sky. But oddly, the moon was up and full. It, too, was big and cresting over a distant mountain range. But, it was what was forming in the nearby clouds that had Penelope enrapt. The clouds were combining — watery vapor was mingling to form poorly defined images. But gradually their definition grew sharper. Billowy larger-than-life images now towered over everything else in the sky. They were developing in sequence, from her early childhood to present adult life — a procession of all that she had ever valued — from a lavender plush bunny to a fire-engine- red 2000 Mazda MX-5 Miata — from a pair of Winnie- the-Pooh pajamas to a pleased wink from her seventh-grade algebra teacher.

"That was amazing! Can we do it again?"

"Better yet, let's land. I think you can keep the storm away if you've a mind to. I've already scoped out the terrain and there is a landing field not too far away. We could have a picnic or something and stretch our legs. You'll be able to lie on your back and stare up at the clouds to your heart's content."

"Are you serious? A picnic?" Penelope began laughing at the absurdity of the situation. Checking her nails once again she added, "Sure, fine. Why not? It's my dime, might as well enjoy it for as long as I can make it last."

Billy Bowlegs nodded his approval and set the airplane into a slow dive. Up ahead, Penelope could see a long, deforested strip of bulldozed earth that was the same color as the rivers. As Billy throttled back to slow their descent, she could see that they were gliding above a tropical rainforest. She was amazed at how clear her dream was becoming —

how exact in detail — each tree different — a rusted-out truck by the runway near a dilapidated building with light blue paint on a fading steel roof. It was disturbingly ordinary. There was no comic strip presentation from her past — nor a nightmarish vignette readying itself to pounce. It was just too real.

"Illegal gold miners," Billy said, breaking up her thoughts. "Don't worry, they cleared out years ago. " He was about to elaborate on his comment when a sudden gust of wind, coming out of nowhere, shook the plane, lifting it back into the sky. The wall of the eye gave way as the storm came crashing down upon them. Billy Bowlegs began fighting with the yoke, hoping to force the control wheel into submission.

"Penny help! This is not good!"

"Do you want me to pull on my side of the yoke?" She asked, worked up and not even noticing he had called her Penny.

"Don't know. This is your dream. You'd best figure out how to get it back on track!"

Penelope began to concentrate on their situation. Her skull and crossbones nails were on strike. Nothing was happening except the number two engine cut out — followed shortly by numbers one, three, and four. Then that whining sound that she had heard in so many movies. Farquhar Airlines's maiden voyage was ending like that of the Titanic. It was time to wake up. Screw Doctor Hernandez; she wanted nothing more to do with lucid dreaming. She wanted out of here.

"Time to wake up!" Penelope shouted, trying to drown out the horrifying noise of their descent.

But she didn't wake up. She stared over at Billy hoping for an explanation, only to see him lose consciousness and collapse onto the control wheel. Penelope had no idea what to do. Bowlegs could at least operate this outlandish flying machine. Then it occurred to her — if they could inhabit her head maybe she could inhabit theirs. Penelope decided to throw herself inside of Billy Bowleg's head. And she did.

She felt like Alice tumbling down the rabbit hole. But this wasn't the White Rabbit's hole. It was something much more bizarre, and it was ancient — hard and cold — more surreal than anything to be found in Wonderland. It was Daliesque, full of uncouth shapes, odd sounds and putrid smells. Still, for a fleeting second, she felt safe. Her crashing plane was somewhere else. Then with a thud, her body was slammed back into the copilot's seat again.

She turned in astonishment towards Billy, who had just regained consciousness and was staring at her angrily as he managed to pull up on the yoke and level off the approach of the plane. They hit the runway going far too fast. The airplane twisted around, breaking its landing gear, and careened into the jungle, sheering off both wings in the process.

——— «》 ———

On a high, rain-soaked, cliff face that was overlooking the Amazon Basin, a man dressed in a headdress of blue, red and green macaw feathers and brown and white condor feathers observed the descent of the airplane. Once it had crashed, he turned his back on the scene and began his walk back to his temple. As he did so, a suggestion of a smile crept across his lips beneath his golden mask.

CHAPTER SIX

The Mining Camp

René Descartes was dead — of course, originally, he had died from pneumonia in Sweden during the winter of 1650. But now, this second time, he died from the injuries he sustained in an airplane crash somewhere in the Amazon Jungle somewhere deep inside Penelope Farquhar's head.

At the time of his first death, he was a Catholic residing in Protestant Sweden. And even though Descartes had been the tutor to the Queen of Sweden, he was still a dead Catholic. Therefore, no Protestant cemetery would receive his remains. So, what was left of the great mathematician was consigned to a pauper's graveyard, there to be buried among Stockholm's orphans.

Things hadn't improved much for poor René. Gelatinous, orange river clay was being patted down with shovels to hold him in place, in this most recent of his interments. Monsieur Descartes was the only serious casualty from the crash. Everyone else survived with only minor bruises and scrapes. That is, except for Penelope, who had a badly swollen knee.

Even though they had arrived at or rather collided with, the mining camp two days before, it took them this long to get around to burying him. And this was done primarily because the equatorial sun demanded his immediate committal to the earth.

The Countess of Lovelace gave the service, for what it was. She was not looking quite as elegant as she had aboard the flight; her gown was tattered, and she had a big shiner for a left eye. She kept her poise, but the service was brief. Ada read excerpts from Descartes' Meditations on First Philosophy; "Whatever I have up till now accepted as most true and assured I have gotten either from the senses or through the senses. But from time to time, I have found that the senses deceive, and it is prudent never to trust completely those who have deceived us even once."

She finished by saying that they all would dearly miss him in that companionship that they had all formed inside of Penelope's head.

All said amen as Belle Starr unleashed a dozen rounds into the air with her pair of six guns. Penelope was more affected than the others. Even though Descartes' demise might mean that there would be one less voice floating about her brain to annoy her and make her the social pariah she was, he had been a dear man and very kind to her.

René had first manifested himself to Penelope while she was sweating over a proof in an advanced calculus exam in her freshman year of high school. He introduced himself by stating that the answer was $f(x) = (3/4)x^3 + (1/2)x - (9/4)$. Well...yes, of course it was, Penelope had known that, but it was awfully nice of him to confirm it.

She would miss René. She had done everything she could possibly do to bring him back to life — stared at her fingernails for hours with no success. But staring at her fingernails hadn't been too helpful as of late. She had desperately tried to will herself out of this awful dream, a dream that had turned so ugly.

Shackleton, who had been absent from the ceremony, suddenly appeared from out of the forest with a garish floral sprig of heliconia, also known as lobster claws. These brilliant yellow and red flowers looked unsuitable for the top of a grave, but so did the mound of mud that constituted the grave. Though Sir Ernest's contribution to the burial didn't add or detract from the absurdity of the situation, the words that he offered next were just the right way to conclude it.

"You sir, were a gentleman. One can make no greater compliment." Then, without missing a beat, he turned to the assembled mourners and announced, "I've found a pretty good trail out of here!"

"Where?" Billy excitedly asked.

"West, just beyond where the mining operation ends. It was once well traveled, still passable."

Bowlegs nodded his head in ascent, grabbed a shovel, and disappeared into an abandoned workshop that was near the runway. A few seconds passed before he appeared with a handsaw, which he used to cut the shovelhead from the shovel shaft. He stuck the wooden shaft into the muck and leaned down on it hard. Determining it was suitable, he offered it to Penelope.

She looked at his gift suspiciously. Mildly annoyed, she put in her two cents. "So Shackleton and you have decided that the six of us should take our chances and go for a hike in the jungle?"

"There's no food here. There is food in the forest, and people made that trail so that should tell you that there is a likelihood that there are some people at the end of it. Of course, you could stay here and wait for the next gold rush. But from what I've seen of this place, it is spent. I wager that the last gram of gold left here on a DC3 some time ago. Your call. However, I think the rest of us are going to take our chances in that forest."

"Wait a minute. I thought I was in charge. This is after all my dream."

"Yes, it is. How's being in charge working for you so far?"

"Hey, I didn't crack up the plane!"

"No, you went and hid in my head. That was helpful. Let me tell you something, we may be just symptoms of schizophrenia for some lunatic math nerd but we still have rights. Shall we put it to a vote? All in favor of following Sir Ernest Shackleton, the famous polar explorer, into the rainforest, raise your hand."

So, it was that Penelope was defeated five to one, and so it was that she begrudgingly grasped the improvised crutch that Billy was still holding out for her.

"Viva la revolución," she said, muttering as she limped by, "As for being in the inside of your head, I'd never put it on the cover of a travel brochure."

———— «» ————

The whole area surrounding the runway was pockmarked with giant water-filled craters, which oozed with the same orange muck that they had buried Descartes in. Many of these craters still had rusted pumps mounted on wooden pallets with rubber hoses that led down into the neighboring river.

Penelope didn't see any gold. The only metal that might now be mined in these parts was toxic mercury. You could still see its dull gray stain where the miners had used it to clump up the gold flakes that were in their mining slurry.

It took over an hour of slogging through a mile of sludge to reach the burned-out perimeter of the mining operation. Here the edge of the forest had been set ablaze to clear out the undergrowth. The charred remains of limbless trees still stood rooted in blackened soil. It was evident that this area had been prepped for future expansion but, for some reason, it all had come to an abrupt halt.

"Yes. Yes. This is it. " Shackleton waved to the ragtag company of the patient and her symptoms, which had been ranging behind him in an untidy line. "It hasn't been used in a while but when I first discovered it I followed it for a couple of miles. It eventually becomes very passable. There must be quite a number of people around, the trail has been scooped out with foot traffic."

Here Billy Bowlegs insisted on taking the lead and made everyone file behind him into the thickening jungle. Penelope was having a particularly hard time keeping up. Each step she took was painful and the shovel end wasn't of much help keeping her weight off of her left knee. She had tried fixing her knee by staring at her skulls and cross bones, but they still weren't working. She couldn't even change her clothes with her nail polish magic. It had worked with Belle Starr, but for some reason had given out when it came to modifying her own clothing. The best it could do was change the Mother Hubbard she had gone to bed in from white with a blueprint to pink with a white print. That was far too girly for Penelope. But now it was becoming somewhat acceptable due to the mud spattered on it.

Ada, seeing Penelope's distress, decided to walk next to her and perhaps distract her from her pain. She summoned up stories concerning her writing the world's first computer algorithm for Charles Babbage, back in 1833, and how Charles Dickens had come to her bedside when she was sick, to read to her. Such accounts would have been diverting in better circumstances, but Penelope couldn't imagine how circumstances could get any worse. Though she did politely nod and fill in any pause in the Countess Lovelace's narrative with a few comments to show interest, her attention was really drawn to her fingernails and finding a way out of this mess. As far as Penelope could ascertain, each step that she took was conveying her deeper and deeper into her delusion.

"You know, my dear, I was considered very odd in my day. They said that I was beautiful but coarse, a genius but unstable. My mother was a mathematician in her own right and had me study math to provide me with focus and to keep me from my father's poetical ways. She believed that Lord Byron suffered from an excess of imagination and that destroyed him. But after all that expense to keep me grounded, I too, like you, had my hallucinations."

"You did? How did you get rid of them?"

"Well, I didn't, as I'm sure you know. I can't imagine you haven't read up on me after we've been so close so long—I died at a young age."

"Oh, not really the solution I was looking for."

"Well, interestingly enough, I did have two famous children before I died. My daughter, Anne, ended up marrying a poet. Marrying poets must be a family thing. Anyhow, she was the very first European woman to make it across the Arabian Desert. And then there was Ralph, my son, who explored Iceland and was a mountain climber."

Penelope managed to crack a smile as she interrupted Ada, "Are you suggesting I breed, then I die, hoping for better results in the next generation?"

"No! But perhaps a little breeding might do you some good? I thought it curious that you conjured up Sir Ernest as one of your companions. I mean, famous Antarctic explorer and all. Perhaps you are following in my footsteps?"

"What? Are you suggesting that I have a relationship with one of the voices in my head?"

"Oh...heavens no. I was just pointing out that, in a way, we are your children. You gave birth to us in your schizophrenic state and have been caring for us ever since. Though, perhaps you haven't been the best of mothers. As for Sir Ernest, well I rather fancy him, so keep away. Yet, I am almost sixty years his senior..."

"I assure you that no one could tell and for as long as you two are rooming inside my skull, I'll keep you young."

"Well thank you...Mother."

Then as if on cue, Shackleton appeared around the bend just ahead of them. "Ladies, we believe we are nearing a settlement."

Penelope and Ada picked up their pace as Sir Ernest escorted them to where the rest of their party had assembled. Billy Bowlegs, Belle Starr and Cecile Fatima were all staring up into the boughs of a very old tree that dwarfed the others of its kind in the vicinity. There were almost as many flowers on it, from the orchids and climbing vines that had made it their home, as there were leaves. Near the ground, its root had formed giant buttresses, which were shaped like the fletching of an arrow or the fins of a rocket ship, and it soared as high as any rocket ship. On it were a series of paintings, mostly geometric in style —white circles — red zigzags — yellow wavy lines — black diamonds. These designs extended up, around the height and girth of the trunk a good fifty feet. Where they had left off, handprints, in the same colors, continued on upward.

"It's a kapok tree," Billy commented to Ada and Penelope. "It's probably the oldest tree in these parts — certainly the biggest we've seen."

"Kapok tree?" Cecile said with derision. "It's Loco's tree, the woods god's tree. It has a great many of spirits in it — full of ancestors. See the handprints, they are from all the people who lived here. When they die, they go to that tree." She broke from where Billy and Belle were standing and began to spin, skip, and chant as she worked her way around the old tree, shaking her calabash-rattle.

Cecile managed to capture everyone's attention... everyone's, except Sir Ernest's. He seemed to be distracted by something and was peering into some dense undergrowth of crisscrossing vines and a cluster of young palms.

"Oh dear," he said, but no one could hear him over Cecile's ceremonial exuberance.

"Oh, dear me!" he said again, this time in a much louder voice.

A dozen or so men with large bows, nocked with very long arrows, came rushing out of the tropical thicket. Their faces were painted in the same manner as the kapok tree. Wooden slivers pierced their noses, lips and chins. And they were naked from the waist up. However, contrasting with this native regalia were modern affectations from what appeared to be considerable contact with the customs of the Western civilization.

From the waist down they had on an array of different colored gym shorts — bright red — royal blue— deep yellow and teal, as well as a few knee-length shorts in various Highland plaids. A couple of the men wore wristwatches. A few of them had blonde hair and the leader was a redhead. He was very much older than the rest.

One of the odder things about this situation was that all the arrowheads were pointed at Miss Penelope Farquhar's nose. No one else seemed to occupy their attention. Perhaps Penelope might have reflected upon how discriminatory this was, or wondered why she was so dangerous that no other person in their party was deemed to be a significant threat. And Penelope would have, except that she was so damn scared. Once again, she resorted to looking down at her fingernails. And once again, it was of no avail.

The old redhead stepped from the midst of the archers to confront her. He was very upset. His head shot up and down as he gesticulated wildly. His yellow tiara-like crown of feathers made him look like an angry bird.

Of course, Penelope couldn't understand a word he was saying, but she was trying to appease him by slowly enunciating words in English.

"I am so sorry! What have I done? We had no intention of disturbing you!"

This made no impression and only served to make the redheaded septuagenarian more irascible.

Billy Bowlegs grew fed up with the situation, and gallantly placed himself between Miss Farquhar and the old man. Thrusting his chest out he seemed to be daring them to shoot their arrows into him. He began shouting back at the group's leader in a language that Penelope had never heard before.

Whatever he said seemed to mollify the old guy. He suddenly lowered his tone and grew a bit respectful and motioned his colleagues to lower their bows.

In a much softer voice, he resumed directing his inquiries solely to her. In fact, he ignored Billy as though he wasn't there.

"What did he ask? What am I supposed to do?"

"You don't have to do anything. I told him that you were the dreamer. He just wanted to know how long you've been dreaming?"

"Tell him that I don't know. Days? In fact, I must be in some kind of coma. Hey! How did you learn to speak their lingo anyway? I thought you were a Seminole from Florida?"

"As we all know, it's your dream, so ask yourself that question. Besides, I'm the only Indian you brought on this trip, and I assure you that there isn't anyone else in our party that's up to the job."

Billy again spoke to the plumed redhead, who now nodded repeatedly while speaking and smiling at Miss Farquhar.

"He said that you were expected some time ago and wants to know what kept you."

"Schizophrenia," Penelope slowly said, exaggerating each syllable.

Apparently, there was no need to translate the word. The old man began to chatter as Billy put his words together for her.

"He says that's excellent. It is just what he was hoping for. He says he has many spirits inside of him and wants to know how many spirits are inside you."

"Ah...six, but with René gone, I guess five. That is if he doesn't come back. I mean it's not like René hasn't been dead before."

"Five," Billy said as he held up five fingers. But as he did so the old redhead became more perturbed and began waving his arms about as though he was fighting the air. One of his backhands hit Billy on the chest. The old man smiled and moved so close to Penelope that Billy Bowlegs couldn't get between them.

"Whatever spell you have applied to this creature so that he can understand me is not necessary. Tell it to go away."

"I wish I could tell the whole kit and caboodle to go away!" Penelope said, a little surprised by the old guy's revelation and a bit frightened as well.

"No, they are handy to have. No one in this village, except for me, has more than one voice. They will talk to it and it talks back, but still they are the ones doing the talking and the thinking." He pointed to the line of archers whose heads were cocked, as though they were trying to understand his words.

"They are my people but there is another village here." He tapped his forehead. "So many people to discuss things with, to figure things out with. This is very good — very good for the people you now see and very good for me. These people" he again pointed at the archers, "They think I am very wise. True, I am a bit smart, but only very smart after I talk things over with those inside and those outside of my head. That is why these people," he pointed for the third time, "made me their shaman. Is that also true with you?"

"Ahh...No, they did not make me a shaman. They did lock me up for a while. I had to convince them that I didn't hear the voices much to get them to let me out."

"Then they are not even a bit smart. So why are your voices now out of your head?"

Penelope was startled by the fact that he could tell, but realized that this was just another curious aspect of this dream that wouldn't die. She looked questioningly at Billy Bowlegs, who just smirked at her. She sought out the faces of her other companions. Belle Starr twirled an index finger near her right ear to signal that Penelope was simply loco, Cecile shook her rattle in the direction of the old shaman as Ada shrugged her shoulders, and Sir Ernest turned his back.

"They've never been very cooperative. I guess this is just them having a lark with me as I dream. Normally they are just beneath the surface, sometimes talking in unison to me. It is like white noise, or having tinnitus, I mean ringing in the ears. And lately, they've been bushwhacking me — jumping into my thoughts when I least expect them. But I've never had them all show up like this. How I wish I could be rid of them." Penelope turned to her five remaining voices and said apologetically, "Sorry."

Ada nodded sympathetically, as though to say that they didn't take her comment personally.

"I dream all the time, sometimes for days... I being Xuhpuri. My name is Xuhpuri... Xuhpuri of the Chayahuita. That is Xuhpuri of what's left of the Chayahuita. And you are Miss Penelope Augusta Gertrude Farquhar."

"Your voices told you that?"

"Yes."

"I need to upgrade my voices."

Xuhpuri motioned to Penelope. "Come with me. We need to talk about this dreaming of yours. I dream for many days at a time. Long dreams are very good. I hope this dream you are having will be good for you as well."

Penelope followed him over to where the huge roots of the kapok tree met centuries of leaf litter. She placed her makeshift staff against the tree and with a great deal of effort managed to sit down next to where Xuhpuri was squatting. Billy, Cecile, Ada, Ernest and Belle joined them, but Xuhpuri showed no interest in them and treated her as the only honored guest.

Women appeared from the forest. They were painted and plumed like the men, but without their modern-day paraphernalia. They built a fire near where Penelope and Xuhpuri had seated themselves. Fresh caught red-tail catfish and alligator gar were being wrapped in bjao leaves and submersed in pots of boiling water. Armadillos were gutted, skewered on sticks, and placed at right angles over the white embers of the fire. Bowls filled with mangos, papaya and branco açaí berries were passed about. Two men grabbed ahold of several vines and climbed up the trunk of the old kapok tree. Children arrived and scampered over to the tree. Soon they were making a game of catching passion fruit as the men in the tree tossed it down.

Penelope and Xuhpuri were the first to be offered the foods for the feast, then everyone else joined in — that is, everyone else except Billy, Cecile, Ada, Ernest and Belle. When Penelope insisted that food be given to her traveling companions, Xuhpuri laughed at her, but then good-naturedly complied. Large quantities of the Chayahuita's jungle cuisine were placed in front of Billy, Cecile, Ada, Ernest and Belle but they did not partake. This was strange considering that they had all been ravenous eaters back at the mining camp. Penelope assumed that they might have borne Xuhpuri some sort of grudge over his dismissive behavior towards them, but then shelved her concern, realizing that in this section of her dream they just didn't eat.

Penelope was about to ask if there was anything to drink when a man wearing designer sunglasses offered her a banana leaf filled with sautéed tree snails; she couldn't resist commenting.

"It is pretty dark here under the forest canopy and all, so what's with the snail guy's shades?"

"Oh...you mean the sunglasses. He just thinks he is cool."

"Cool, but it can't be doing his eyes any good."

"In time, they will break, and he won't be able to replace them." Xuhpuri gestured to the people who were joining the feast around the camp fire, "their shorts will rot, the children will lose that soccer ball, and all of those colorful feathers you now see will grow so soiled and tattered that people will throw them away and once again hunt for their plumage, instead of working for dyed chicken feathers."

"I'm guessing you are referring to the miners?"

"Yes. The gold is gone and so are they. So, things will go back to the way they were. For the land, it will take many, many lifetimes, but it will someday recover. You saw it; it's a mess — the river too. Relax, the fish you ate came from upstream... as did we."

"Right. So, you came down because of me?"

"Mostly. I also wanted to bring some of my people back here. They will eventually heal from their experience here… perhaps quicker than anything else. It is good for them to visit this place and come to terms with what they have done. But yes, you are the main reason I am here."

"So why the interest? Don't tell me, because I'm dreaming I'm the center of your universe? What else would an invention of my subconscious think? Yes, yes, I confess, I'm a bit of an egotist."

"Sorry, but you are not the center of my universe. You are no more than another aspect of my dreaming. It is just that right now your dreaming and my dreaming are overlapping."

"Somehow that doesn't sound decent."

"Probably it is not. But the dream I'm in told me I would find you here. Which is convenient because this place is familiar to me, as are these people. So are you…"

A woman with a thick black line across her eyes interrupted Xuhpuri. She talked non-stop as she dipped a wooden bowl into a boiling pot of water that had been suspended over the fire. Unlike Xuhpuri, Penelope couldn't understand a word she was saying. It soon became apparent that she was asking Penelope to take a sip out of the bowl."

"What's this, Xuhpuri?"

"Refreshment. Earlier you were wondering if there was anything to drink around here. And here it is."

"Okay, still, what is it?"

"Boiled corpse vine with chacruna leaves to help the kick. I had some a couple of days ago. If you want to know why I am here, it's because of the vine."

"Corpse vine? How unappetizing. This is not very reassuring, Xuhpuri. You drank that stuff and it told you to dream me up?"

"I should have called it spirit vine or soul vine, or even that bastardized Spanish word, ayahuasca. It will cause those willing to drink it to look inward and dream. Dream and heal. The people who have come with me are here to heal."

"You must have forgotten that I'm already dreaming?"

"Yes, you have dreamt enough to get you here but not enough to get you any further and you cannot go back the way you have come. You have not yet been able to wake up. You just tried to feed your five traveling companions, so that tells me you have not yet healed. But, I will go with you and we will enter this second dream together."

"That's supposed to make me feel better, is it?" Penelope said as she concentrated on all ten skulls and cross bones. It seemed like years ago that the decals had been applied over her nail polish at Carmen's Get Nailed, Spa and Beauty Salon.

"Any luck?" Xuhpuri couldn't keep a straight face.

Penelope abruptly turned to face her voices, hoping for some advice. "You guys have been talking an awful lot for most of my life and at this moment you've all decided to go mum? Okay, should I drink this stuff or not?"

They didn't answer her. They couldn't answer. In fact, they looked like the puppets that she had seen out the window of the airplane. They were all limp and this time there were no hooded ventriloquists standing behind them to pull on some strings.

"Perhaps I need a bit of a boost?" She said as she removed her mud caked bedroom slippers.

However, staring at the combined power of the tips of her fingers and toes only managed to turn her nail polish from black to mauve.

Xuhpuri was now laughing heartily. "Please. Please. You will hurt yourself!"

"Can you guarantee that if I drink this stuff nothing bad is going to happen to me? I don't know why I would trust your assurances."

"No. I can't guarantee that. How could I? You never know what a dream will bring — especially when you are dealing with dreams within dreams — and especially when you are dreaming with a Chayahuita shaman who is also sharing your dream. But remember, normally you wake up from a dream, even bad dreams. And please, stop looking at your toenails, nothing is going to happen."

"Throughout my life I've have had to endure swallowing Aripiprazole, Brexpiprazole, Clozapin, Olanzapine, Quetiapine and Ziprasidone, prescribed for me by countless quacks. I've also been subjected to electroconvulsive shock. Now it's time for me to drink some boiling broth made from a corpse vine stew, this time prescribed by a... Chayahuita is it?"

"Yes."

"By a Chayahuita shaman." Penelope then sighed and added, "What the hell, give me the stuff."

"Wise choice," he said as he handed the bowl to Penelope to drink.

Only briefly did she reflect upon what she was about to do. Then, she placed the wooden bowl to her lips and threw the contents back.

Xuhpuri removed the bowl from her hands, refilled the bowl, and did the same thing.

"You know, I doubled the dose hoping to fold one dream into another. I have never tried that before."

"That's just wonderful," Penelope, muttered as she drifted off into her second dream.

CHAPTER SEVEN

The Spider of Ukhu Pacha

As she drew her next breath, she realized she had left the Amazon. It was the smells, or lack of them, that tipped her off — no tart scents wafting in from the river — no chlorophyll-laden jungle air — no reek of mold rising up from the forest floor — humidity was absent — the scattered sounds from the jungle had gone.

Penelope knew she was still in the Chayahuita's camp. But the camp had changed; it seemed to be deep down and subterranean. The trees had all grown taller, towering over the camp like skyscrapers defining the edge of a small urban park. She felt as though she was at the bottom of a great tree-lined hole. All was dark except what was illuminated by the flames of the cooking fire which, like the trees, had grown much larger in the transition of one dream into the next.

"Ah, so there you are. What took you so long?"

"Did I keep you waiting?" Penelope asked as she rose to a sitting position.

"Not too long. It takes a while for someone new to the pigswill that you just drank to get acclimated to it. Brains can be stubborn about participating in this sort of thing. Are your voices with you? Any conversations going on in your head?"

Penelope took a minute to listen, "No, nothing. So, I'm cured. Can I go now?"

"No. It is not that easy," Xuhpuri said with a chuckle. Your friends are waiting for you back where we started, and I assure you that you will not want to stay here very long."

"So, where are we? Where is here?"

"Ukhu Pacha, I believe, from the looks of it."

"Ukhu Pacha?"

"Supay's home."

"Supay's home? That's not helpful."

"This is sort of like your people's hell and Supay is our devil."

"Xuhpuri, I think I'll keep my voices. Let's go!"

"Nothing to worry about, we are his guests, and we will not be spending much time here. Supay isn't always nasty, you know… though he does punish the wicked with great abandon. You are not in that category…well, not so far. Ukhu Pacha isn't all about tormenting souls. New souls are born here, and old souls are revived here. They go back to the Kay Pacha, like where you are from. I believe that would be the Bremond Block of Guadalupe Street, downtown Austin, Texas?"

"Did you Google me?"

"Google?"

"So, you aren't that well informed after all."

Ignoring her sarcasm, Xuhpuri continued, "It might be of comfort to know that some very good souls go on to visit Mama Killa, Illapa and Inti… that would be the moon goddess, the thunder god and the sun god, to you."

"Let's see…no, not comforting. Just sounds crazy to me, but then again, I am crazy. Whose religion is this anyway?"

"Why, my religion, Quechua…that is the Inca religion to you."

"Got it. Why not? If we were tripping on corpse vine in ancient Athens you might be babbling on about Hera, Apollo and Zeus. I guess I'm good with all of this so far."

"Well then, try also to be good with this," Xuhpuri said as he reached into a fur pouch made from stitched together fox snouts.

"Your overnight bag? You need an extra pair of socks in Ukhu Pacha or perhaps several changes of underwear?"

"It contains shaman stuff…magic crystals, sacred tom-tom, a few shrunken heads…though there is nothing magical about them, just some people who had really pissed me off, and this." Xuhpuri pulled a very large bone from out of his satchel. "It is a thighbone from the biggest tapir I have ever seen around these parts… Sorry, I meant to say from where we came. The tapir was jumped by a pretty big jaguar, which did it in."

Xuhpuri placed the tapir's thighbone in front of Penelope. Then he squatted down and began to gently pull on several small sticks that had been inserted through a couple of holes that had been drilled through either end of the bone. Once they had been removed, he tapped on the hollowed-out bone till a spider emerged from one end.

This was a large spider. Its abdomen was oblong, mottled yellow in color and in size about that of one of Penelope's thumbs. Its eight long legs didn't radiate from its body; instead four extended from its front and four trailed from its rear.

"A few of us still keep pet spiders. They can be very useful for figuring things out."

"I think I've met his littler cousin. They look kind of the same."

"Yes, I believe you could have. They are common enough. She is a golden orb-weaver, but most people would call her a banana spider. They are found in Texas, too. Such spiders have been around a long time. They were common when the headwaters of the Amazon River were located deep inside Africa, back when Africa and South America were one continent, the Amazon River flowed across these lands into the Pacific. I don't know why but it has reversed itself and today flows the other way around into the Atlantic. But this is of little consequence to us. What is important is that there have always been golden-orb weavers along its riverbank. They are the oldest of all spiders, and by being so have become very, very wise. I'm hoping that this spider might share with us some of what it has seen."

Released from the hollow bone, the golden-orb spider moved out cautiously, feeling her way across the lifeless floor of Ukhu Pacha till she reached the base of the tallest of the trees. Then she began her ascent, gradually climbing higher and higher, yet not fading from view. For, this spider grew larger and larger as it moved further away and could now be in tens of feet.

As the spider crawled up the trunk, the pads of its many feet triggered the bark to illuminate a series of designs — circles, zigzags, diamond shapes, wavy lines, handprints, too. But they weren't made of paint. These designs were made of stars. This was the village's old kapok tree, or perhaps a spiritual reflection of it under the ground in Ukhu Pacha.

Where the crown of the kapok tree branched out from the trunk, the spider stopped and thrust her abdomen out into the air. For the first time since Penelope's arrival, a breeze stirred in Ukhu Pacha. It grew in intensity, becoming a light wind. The spider expelled a thread of golden silk that floated in the wind across the forest till it stuck to some distant tree in the subterranean wood. The spider then tugged on the cable of silk to make sure it was firmly attached. After that, she moved to a new spot to launch more of her silk into the air. Anchoring each successive thread, she eventually formed a triangle out of them.

Once this triangle had been completed, the spider turned her attention to creating the radial threads — the spokes for her web. When they had all been laid into place, the spider moved to the center of her web and began to circle out from it, counterclockwise, laying down more golden silk to make the capture spirals. Each thread was now paired with another, all of which overlapped the many spokes that created the framework.

When her web was complete, the spider returned to the center and once again circled out from it. However, this time she moved in a clockwise direction. Images suddenly appeared within the rectangular spaces between her silken cords. It soon became clear to Penelope that the golden orb-weaver hadn't constructed this web to ensnare giant insects that might be ranging about Ukhu Pacha. No, the spider was telling a story.

Penelope watched the spider's progress, knowing what she was seeing was the recounting of history. Some of it was present history, but most of it was ancient history — the history of the land that was just above, terrestrial, Kay Pacha, and the land that was even further up, heavenly, Hanan Pacha. There, within one of the webs cells, was the sun god Inti, looking down upon mankind from his throne in Hanan Pacha. He was resplendent in gold. His solar heat made him sweat gold. Gold rained down from him to Kay Pacha, and unto the Inca people. Gold was his gift to them. But it was up to them to find it and fashion things from it, in celebration of the sun — and its life sustaining force that nurtured their crops. In another cell, there were ancient miners digging the earth for the precious metal. These miners were blessed and revered. They brought out of the ground the essence of Inti so that the Inca people could, through it, know him better.

Penelope then saw the red-horned god of Ukhu Pacha, Supay. He protected the miners as they dug towards his kingdom with their axes of copper and stone.

She saw a frightened boy, Pishtaco, who was being pursued by the Sapa Inca. Then she saw how his grandmother, Ciqui Ollco hid him among the soothsayers of Cota Coca. This boy then matured and grew strong in body as well as in magic — so strong that his magic was nearly as powerful as his grandmother's — so strong that he had Ciqui Ollco killed.

As the golden thread spun from the spinnerets, there came more tales, each tale lodging in a newly formed rectangle within the spider's wake. From each panel, Penelope learned new things about Pishtaco. One revealed to her how he had captured Paititi and destroyed the Chachapoya, the Warriors of the Clouds. Another told of how he had betrayed the Inca's general, Rumiñawi, as he attempted to save the Sapa Inca by delivering the empire's gold to Pizarro and his fellow Spaniards. A panel showed the Sapa Inca being garroted by the Spaniards. Another panel showed Pishtaco doing the same thing to his own grandmother. Several panels showed the Spanish attempting to find the lost gold — how they searched for Pishtaco and his faraway city of Paititi. Most of the remaining chambers dealt with Pishtaco guarding his stolen treasure. Within these she could see Pishtaco growing old and how he managed to sustain his life through terror — culling his people for sacrifices — sending raiders deep into the Amazon Basin to hunt down the few surviving Chachapoya. She saw his servants bringing back bound captives, whose fat he would rip out and consume, and whose flesh he'd cut into strips, then fry up to make chicharrón. Chicharrón which he would sell to his followers and force them to eat — eat to remember his glory and the terror of his name.

Then, a section of the web appeared showing the new mine, the illegal mine in the jungle where Penelope's plane had crashed. Now Penelope saw Pishtaco on his funeral slab above the pit that led to Ukhu Pacha reveling in the miners' destructive greed. He encouraged it and dreamt of the day when he would be strong enough to seek them out, bring them back, eat them, and add their gold to his great treasure pile.

As each tale within its rectangle was brought to life by the golden orb spider, Penelope could see the face of Inti, peering out from his section of the web. Apparently, Inti was confused. There was so little left of the Inca people, so little left of his memory. There was the gold, but Pishtaco was its caretaker.

The golden orb spider had completed her web. Finished, she moved to the center of the orb. All of her stories radiated around her, each section of her web had its tale to tell and had told it.

The spider's multiple black eyes suddenly latched hold of the pale blue eyes of Penelope Farquhar. Both sets of eyes now glowed with the same fiery intensity as the embers under the pot that had boiled the corpse vine. Supay's red demon face appeared within Penelope's brain. Penelope instantly knew that he was not confused about what had become of the Inca, nor about what had become of Inti's gold. She could feel the soils of the jungle coursing through her veins as it was washed by a newer breed of miner who had blackened the ground with mercury. No, Supay was not confused. Supay was angry!

Penelope awoke.

CHAPTER EIGHT

Walkabout

Penelope grabbed the nape of her neck and began to massage it. Apparently, she had been leaning forward for some time. Just the small of her back had been resting against the kapok tree, which left her with a seriously sore neck. Her mouth was dry too. That always happened when she'd been snoring. There was nothing but white ash under the cooking pot, so she knew that she had been hallucinating for some time. She turned to her left, hoping that Xuhpuri wouldn't be where she had last seen him in Kay Pacha — maybe he had gone — maybe he was just part of the dream she had had under the influence of that awful corpse vine or perhaps he had disappeared along with that pet spider.

Xuhpuri, guessing her thoughts, stated flatly, "No, I'm still here." Then he added, "I felt for sure you were going to say something like, 'that was an awesome home movie'. But from the look on your face, I suspect that you are not."

"You got that right. And why did you say that that vine of yours was supposed to heal? I feel worse than ever for all my troubles. If I could get out of this damn dream, I'd voluntarily go back to the Gruber Wing of the East Hampton looney bin I just made it out of and beg them to take me back."

"Well, I didn't expect you to be inspired by the trip but the only way you are going to get out of this dream is by moving forward. You've got one direction to go if you are going to get back to the Bremond Block of Guadalupe Street and that is not to the way you came…"

Penelope interrupted him before he could go any further, "The answer is no. That's a decisive no! I'm not debating it."

"No to what?"

"Don't play coy with me, Xuhpuri. Once she had finished with her silky power point presentation, that big bug of yours blasted my brain with her glowing eyes and I got the message loud and clear."

"Oh, I didn't realize she had told you everything, I had thought telling the rest was up to me. Good, so you understand."

"Yes, I do, and the answer is no. No, I'm not heading up the river with all of my tag-along voices. No, I'm not going to Paititi. No, I'm not going to destroy Pishtaco. This is not the sort of dream I had hoped for. I thought I had made it clear to myself that my dreams should be about me being an Italian starlet living in a villa on the Island of Capri in the Gulf of Naples. What's the use of lucid dreaming when all you can do with it is get stuck in a very bad dream? No, this ends here. If Supay wants Pishtaco's ass in Ukhu Pacha so badly he can come up here and get him himself!"

"But he can't. Hence the arrival of Miss Penelope Augusta Gertrude Farquhar."

"What do you mean he can't?"

"Supay controls Ukhu Pacha and has only limited powers in Kay Pacha. It is not his turf. True, everyone ends up with him in the end anyway. That shouldn't be a big concern. However, so far Pishtaco has found a way to keep out of the clutches of Supay. Inti has favored him for a long time. Pishtaco has guarded his gold. Even Supay had no problem with pursuing gold. Up until recently, Supay had protected all miners. But you have seen what they've done. No choice — they had to go."

"Go?"

"Yes. You remember those shrunken heads that I mentioned that are in my bag."

"Oh...well, then do the same thing you did to the miners to Pishtaco."

"Not possible. I am just a phantasm of this dream of yours. This is a concoction of your mind. Therefore, only you are equipped with sufficient power to defeat Pishtaco. I have no idea why Viracocha resurrected him. The Creator God's purposes are shrouded by mystery. He sets the heavens in motion and we react. I assure that if anyone else goes brawling with this renewed Pishtaco they will lose. If they lose, so do the Chayahuita people. What Pishtaco did to the Chachapoya of Paititi will be seen as gentle treatment compared to what Pishtaco will do to the present generation that has somehow managed to survive in the forest."

"Oh...I hadn't picked up on that. I see what you are after. You are looking to have Paititi restored to you...at least in my head?"

"It is a start. But, more importantly, if Pishtaco is allowed to live, all will suffer both inside and outside your head. That, especially, includes you."

"I'm not sure I'm following. What are you telling me? That they all are real?"

"As real as your house on Guadalupe Street. Just think of it as if you are standing between two mirrors and looking at the hundreds of repeating images of yourself. If one image alters, they all are forced to alter."

"Obviously, I'm still under the influence of your corpse vine; or maybe that little orb-weave that was on my bed post crawled under the sheets and took a bite out of me? Cecile did say it was poisonous. I've been tripping on spider venom, that's all."

"Then you will either get better or die from the poison. Let us see if you will wake up in that comfortable bed of yours surrounded by your expensive antiques?"

It was clear that Xuhpuri had finished attempting to convince Penelope to go destroy Pishtaco. Ignoring her further protestations, he leaned back against the kapok tree and closed his eyes. They stayed closed.

After several hours had passed, Penelope managed to muster up enough nerve to call Xuhpuri's name and then gently nudged his lifeless body. When that didn't work, she upped the ante by yelling at him and jabbing him in the ribs with her finger.

Her five traveling companions were still comatose as well. There they were, Xuhpuri, Billy, Cecile, Ada, Ernest and Belle all seated with their backs resting on the trunk of the kapok tree, each one as listless as a caterpillar in a cocoon waiting for the spring. Nothing she did could get their attention either. Shaking them didn't work, they were like ragdolls, just as impervious as Xuhpuri was to whatever obnoxious scream she could come up with. Taunts and insults were just no good.

It occurred to her that she might be fighting with herself and that if she could figure out a way of waking them up she might just apply the technique to herself. Oh how she longed for that big bed of hers on Guadalupe Street. She'd do almost anything to get back there. She'd gladly take Xuhpuri, along with the other five, back there. After all, with the death of poor René, there was now a vacancy. An Amazonian shaman would fit in well with that crew. They could teach him the ropes — tuck themselves in between the folds of her brain as she slid in between her soft sheets. She wouldn't even mind if they kept her up late at night with their constant chattering. No need to be boorish, and certainly no need to go see Doctor Hernandez. It was simply a matter of getting used to things. But there was one thing for sure, she would never get used to them here.

It must have been two days, by Penelope's estimate, that she had attempted to rouse everybody up. She wasn't so sure about how many days had passed because the sun was stuck. It hadn't moved a bit. The same shafts of light filtered through the canopy at the same angle. Shadows weren't moving either; it was as though they had been painted on to things. There hadn't been much of a breeze before Xuhpuri had decided to zone out, but now there was absolutely none. The heat was still intense, as was the humidity.

Eventually it dawned upon Penelope that she wasn't going to be able to force anyone out of his or her stupor. She picked up the makeshift crutch that Billy had made for her and decided that she would walk her way out of this mess. At the very least, she thought she might walk her way into a neighboring dream that just might be slightly better.

The first direction she chose led back to the landing strip and the sluice mining operation. That was no good, and the only other trails led only to the peripheral boundaries of the mining camp. She didn't entertain hacking her way out of there, through the jungle, to the city of Manaus; that is, if there was a city of Manaus. She only had Billy Bowleg's word that there was, and why should a figment of her imagination be more informed than she was? Still, Billy had been adamant that there was such a city, and that it had over two million people. During the group's earlier discussion, that is before they had encountered Xuhpuri, Billy had said that heading a thousand miles downriver was too risky. He did mention that Cajamarca was closer — only a couple of hundred miles to the west up and over the Andes. Of course, all of his talk had only gone to prove that Billy Bowlegs was an amazing source of local geography and useless cartological information.

The sun was still not going to set. Seconds, minutes, hours and days no longer seemed to have any consequence. Penelope literally had at her disposal all of the time in the world. It was fortunate that she wasn't hungry. Nor was she thirsty. Penelope had no need for sleep. It was as though all of her bodily needs took a break when the sun got stuck. Consequently, she could see no reason why she couldn't just head off in any old direction and just keep going till she bumped into something she truly wanted to find.

So, with that in mind, Penelope decided to head out for Cajamarca. Despite her efforts, she could never find it. Penelope kept getting turned around — kept passing the same waterfall with its droplets of river water frozen in the air — kept passing a group of scarlet macaws that had been checked in time joyously socializing on a Brazil nut tree. There was also that giant anteater, which had been embarrassingly immobilized during mid poop. This anteater served Penelope well. It was a kind of landmark. Whenever she got so turned around that she thought she would never see another human face again, she would stumble upon the pooping anteater and know that Xuhpuri's camp was just on the other side of it near some crisscrossing vines and a dense cluster of young palms.

For a while, when she marched back through the camp, Penelope would go through a drill of shaking and pummeling everyone there. But then she got bored with that, knowing what the results would be. All was the same. Nothing changed... except for that giant kapok tree. It seemed to be immune to all of Xuhpuri's hocus-pocus. There were times when the old tree had all of its leaves, and there were other times when all of its leaves were on the ground. That was how Penelope came to realize that she had been spending years roaming about the rain forest, which made her ponder a bit upon how stubborn she was to have kept going. She always knew that she had a powerful will, however, this time her actions had passed beyond being mulish into ridiculousness. Penelope also knew that going in circles and getting nowhere would have driven anyone else mad. She felt that it was fortunate that she had come to the Amazon already crazy. So, she plugged along... till the day that all of her steadfast jungle tromping suddenly came to an abrupt halt. She had just passed the pooping anteater again and had turned to head into camp when she noticed it. It must have been happening for some time but Penelope had long given up on paying much attention to her surroundings because they were always the same.

The sight proved to be a shock.

Though the Countess Lovelace, Sir Ernest Shackleton, Belle Starr, Cecile Fatima, Billy Bowlegs and Xuhpuri were still where she had left them, things had changed — incrementally over countless seasons. The kapok tree hadn't stopped growing, dropping its leaves in June then growing them back in December, expanding its girth with each passing year. But Penelope hadn't noticed that the falling leaves had decayed, turned into loam, and then with the passage of time covered everyone underneath up to their necks in rich dark jungle soil. In fact, Shackleton and Starr had a bed of snake ferns growing from their laps and strangler fig vine was getting started around Billy Bowleg's neck. The bark of the kapok tree had pushed out too. Everyone was semi-encased in it. If things were let to go on any longer all that would be left of Lovelace, Shackleton, Belle Starr, Cecile Fatima, Billy

Bowlegs and Xuhpuri would be six pairs of eyes and six noses sticking out from the tree's trunk. If Penelope elected to make another attempt at finding Cajamarca they'd all be gone.

She'd had enough. Walking over to where Xuhpuri was resting against the tree, she dusted some twigs off of the top of his head, and then stared into his closed eyes.

"Okay, I'll go, "she said, surprising herself with her lack emotion. Apparently, Miss Penelope Augusta Gertrude Farquhar was now resolved to find and destroy Pishtaco.

"Good! I was sure that you would come around. Though, it took a little longer than I had hoped for. Now that that is over, would you mind digging me out of here?"

CHAPTER NINE

Rio Marañón

More than scooping off the topsoil was required to extricate Eva, Ernest, Belle Starr, Cecile, Billy Bowlegs and Xuhpuri. Bracing a foot against the trunk, Penelope tugged and twisted, wrenching each of them out. The first one was toughest, thereafter; each freed person lent a hand. When all of their work was finished, six impressions of heads and torsos were left behind in the bark.

Xuhpuri was now moving about his camp giving orders to his now unfrozen tribesman. They didn't seem any worse for wear after being stuck in the same position for what had to be countless years. No bursitis of their joints. No sprains or strains or back disorders of any kind. They hopped to it as lithe and limber as they had been before Xuhpuri had decided to gum up the works.

Provisions were gathered in and loaded onto two large dugouts that had been carried out of the jungle and secured to the shore of the nearby river. Soon the dugouts were filled with pots of roasted monkey, smoked fish, fruits and berries of all kinds, Brazil nuts, and several bunches of grubs threaded on sticks, like shish kabob.

Xuhpuri also had bows with sheaves of arrows and a dozen or more spears packed on board.

––––– «» –––––

"Well, I wish you could stay longer…no, not really. You've been hanging around this place for almost a lifetime. It is high time you were moving on."

"Where to?" Penelope drolly retorted.

Xuhpuri chuckled, "Of course you don't know, though you've tramped near it on so many an occasion during your stay with us. He wouldn't have allowed you to see it and you weren't even looking for it. Pishtaco, that is."

The mention of his name turned Penelope's stomach. She had been trying to put Pishtaco out of her mind, deciding to live for the second and not think too far into the future. She had no doubt that the end of this journey would be the end of her. At best, she'd be a side dish and not the main course at Pishtaco's table. Penelope felt that when the time came, and she'd confronted him there might be a chance that she would wake up in a cold sweat, vowing to never drink a mixture of blue vervain, American passionflower and motherwort teas again before bedtime. That was the thought she was going to hold on to — stand up to Pishtaco and the dream will end. Xuhpuri had told her that killing him would bring an end to the dream. He might have been just a bit confused as to who was going to get killed.

"I may be very old but I'm not senile yet. I meant what I told you. You must destroy Pishtaco. Paititi is several days journey up this river, the Rio Marañón. You have walked by a wide bend in the river where the jungle, inexplicably, has pushed up and over a high mountain. The city is there, at the top. You'll be able to see its gate from the river, Inti's Gate. There is a road from there that will take you to where Pishtaco lives...so to speak. Sorry we didn't pack tents and things for you. I know how your people like your comforts. We don't use them but you can manage to produce whatever necessities you need."

"You've got a lot of faith in my jungle craft?"

"No, I would not say that." Xuhpuri said, as he pointed to her nails and added, "Those things should be working now, at least I hope so."

His comment caused her to glance down at her mauve colored nails. To her surprise they were no longer mauve or black, the way Carmen had painted them. They were now red — and glowing. This caught her attention just for a few seconds. She looked up, hoping to get an explanation from Xuhpuri for this sudden change, but he was gone, so were all of his people. Had they vanished into the jungle? She didn't know, but she did feel a bit hurt — such an abrupt departure. It wasn't like they had had a romantic "We'll always have Paris" sort of relationship. Ukhu Pacha was seriously no Paris, but a simple good-bye would have gone over well.

———— ‹›› ————

There was no rhyme or reason as to the allotment of the crews in the two canoes. Sir Ernest took the bow paddle position of one, with Cecile in the stern holding the other paddle. The countess Lovelace was between the two in the middle, waiting to spell whoever tired first. Similarly, in the other canoe, Belle Starr was in the bow, Billy Bowlegs in the stern, and Penelope was in the middle.

Pulling away from the camp had presented no problem and proved one of the easier tasks they had to perform since leaving Penelope's bedroom in the Bremond Block of Guadalupe Street.

Though the river was rich in reddish silt, the canoes frequently passed black water tributaries that fed into it. Here, where the clear water mixed with the cloudy, they would often get a glimpse of what was going on under them. Peacock bass and red- bellied piranha were the most common sight. Often, they were chased by grey or pink dolphin, which would give up pursuing their quarry just to tag along with the canoes for a while.

Bulldog bats came out just before sunset approached. They flew around the dugouts, dipping their oversized claws into the river water, occasionally coming up with a fish.

The canoes were making their way through a stretch of large lily pads when the clouds above Rio Marañón began to show color. The flat green shoreline was beginning to recede into the shadows. Penelope hadn't seen the sun set for ages and she spent a little too much time contemplating its beauty. It was Billy Bowlegs who had to pull her out of her trance with a sharp question.

"Do you intend for us to paddle all night or are we going to make for shore somewhere and set up camp?"

Penelope turned her head astern and noted his sarcastic grin.

"I didn't know you could get tired. Though you certainly have needed lots of sleep these days. I'm not sure about this camp thing. Xuhpuri said that it shouldn't be a problem for me, but everything since I went to bed has proven to be one."

"Well, there is a lot about us you don't know. And as far as Xuhpuri goes, trust me, I may be an Indian from the Northern Hemisphere and he's one from the Southern, but that guy's the real thing and he knows his stuff."

As Billy spoke, Penelope realized that he was still dressed in his pilot's blue blazer and matching pants and his red scarf wrapped about his head, with pink roseate spoonbill and snowy egret feathers sticking out the top. It occurred to her that he might be the perfect guinea pig to try out her newly constituted powers on. She stared down at her fingernails, which seemed to glow as though they anticipated that she was about to do something. When she looked back up at him, she saw that she had changed his wardrobe to more traditional Seminole clothing. He still had his red scarf wrapped about his head, with pink roseate spoonbill and white snowy egret feathers sticking out of it but below that he wore a knee length shirt that was secured about his waist with a wide and intricately beaded belt. Below his knees she could see fringed buck skin trousers that somehow were tied into the laces of his boots like a pair of gaiters.

"Like it?" she inquired.

"Sure do. Glad you thought of it."

"But what about yourself?" Belle Starr chimed in. She'd been preoccupied pushing lily pads away from the bow but now felt it was time to put her two cents in. "That Mother Hubbard of yours is looking pretty stale. Why don't you do for you what you've done for others and get yourself some new threads."

Since Penelope had arrived at Xuhpuri 's camp she hadn't given any thought to her attire. Her Mother Hubbard had become so faded and dirty that the pink was closer to the color of the Marañón than anything else. And it had become so ragged from all of her years of jungle tromping that more skin showed than cloth.

"Oh dear. This is an embarrassment. What do you think, Belle, something more appropriate for our current lifestyle? I'm thinking safari. You know, like out of a Tarzan movie — the khaki shirts with epaulets — khaki skirt too. The sort of clothes you see these days in those fashionable catalogues for urban ladies who live near Central Park. Maybe a pith helmet too?"

"Sounds good to me. Go for it!"

With a tad too much flamboyance for being in a canoe, Penelope stood up and raised her hands above her head, wiggled her glowing fingernails and then swept them down along the length of her body.

"Oh...what is this?"

Billy chimed in with the answer. "Very fashionable in the higher elevations of the Andes. You have on a lliclla, a jobona, a polleras and a monteras. These are not the first choice for people living in the jungle. With all of those layers of alpaca wool, you must be sweating?"

"No, surprisingly not at all. It's beautiful. She pulled a hat off of her head and admired it. So, this smallish red sombrero is a lliclla?"

"No, that's a monteras. The matching red cape is a lliclla. Your jobona is your black jacket. That black skirt you conjured up is the polleras. I'm not sure why you chose gaucho boots?"

"I swear I had no intention of creating any of this. Never seen the like. But it is beautiful."

"I see, so the other changes weren't part of your plan either?" Belle inquired.

"What other changes?"

"Well, you no longer have blonde hair, and your eyes are not blue. Your skin is much darker, but it has a much more visible glimmering to it. In fact, I would have a hard time saying you were anything other than a native to these here parts...that is, one that glows."

"Hmmm... okay...I'm a different race and I've got some glow thing going on?

"Yes, you started looking a tad incandescent back at Xuhpuri 's camp, but now you look like we could use you to stew up a pot of corpse root."

"Okay, so I'm starting to look like a barbecue briquette, but am I prettier and perhaps a bit taller?"

"Yes, definitely prettier, I mean, you weren't ugly before, but I think this is a better look for you. Perhaps I'm prejudiced. But I'd say you're still the same height."

It surprised Penelope that she liked the idea that Billy found her to be attractive, even though he didn't quite say that. As to still being the same height? Well, she'd take still being short if it went along with being prettier.

"I guess I'll keep this look and skip all of that Manhattan safari wear."

"Good choice," he added.

"Maybe I should apply myself to our camp now but I'm worried that I'll summon up a yurt or a mobile home."

"After sleeping against that kapok tree for so many years, I wouldn't mind a night in a mobile home. How about you, Belle?"

"Sounds welcoming to me."

"Well, I'll give it a whirl." Penelope said, as she reached out towards a stretch of the river front, letting her fingernails go crazy."

"Two tents, some cots and kerosene lanterns? That's the best you can do?" Billy said, feigning indignation, "I mean... must I share a tent with Shackleton?"

"Sorry, I'm spent and that's the best I can do. Besides, I'm dying to get into my cot and get some sleep. Unlike you guys, I've been up and about for a very, very long time."

CHAPTER TEN

The Captive Sorcerers

The vines that had first appeared about the plaza temples, when Siwar Q'enti had awakened Pishtaco, had grown even denser. So too had the Spanish moss that hung down from hundreds of newly arrived kapok trees. Orchids were now in abundance everywhere. The density and variety of their flowering was unnatural — their colors too intense — their fragrance overpowering. Pishtaco had been appalled by the aromatic stench of their perfume. Paititi was not meant to smell like vanilla, raspberries or lilac. Its air was meant for the odors produced from fear.

He had managed to keep the trail open by his sepulcher, but that had been hard, requiring constant attention to eliminate insidious growth. He supposed that this was all Pachamama's doing. So he stole some llamas and sacrificed them to the Earth Goddess, the goddess of life and renewal, on top of her now tree-covered temple. But these offerings had no effect, even though he had taken the extra effort to procure llamas knowing that Pachamama would not accept villagers. He realized that Siwar Q'enti would not have roused him from his moldering slumber just to point out that Pachamama was redecorating the crumbling city of Paititi. Viracocha had to have concerns about Inti's gold. But Inti was silent. No number of offerings would bring him to speak to Pishtaco. Nor would Mama Killa, Mama Sara, Kuychi, Ctequil, Kon, Urcuchillay, Ekkeko or Paryaqaqa condescend to talk with him. Only Sach'amama, the goddess of the forest, was willing to speak to him, and only after Pishtaco had sipped from a brew he had concocted from hallucinogenic toad skins. She materialized before him in her favorite form, that of a large two-headed snake.

Sach'amama told Pishtaco that, though she was the goddess of all trees, the kapok trees in the square had had nothing to do with her. The fact that they had appeared without her knowledge had embarrassed Sach'amama. So, to find out what was going on, she went to the oldest of the kapok trees to complain. This spirit tree that had been rooted along the Rio Marañón for centuries and was the source of all of the kapok trees in the area.

Yet, this tree behaved just like Inti, Mama Killa, Mama Sara, Pachamama, Kuychi, Ctequil, Kon, Urcuchillay, Ekkeko and Paryaqaqa, and refused to speak. This saddened Sach'amama, to be the mother of all trees and have her most remarkable child ignore her.

Fortunately for Sach'amama, she did find a nearby woman, a Chayahuita woman, hiding in the brush. This woman had little will when caught by the mesmerizing eyes of Sach'amama's dual snakeheads. She told Sach'amama that all of the tribes in the forest were talking about a sorceress who would come from the north. She was going to Paititi. Once there, she would send Pishtaco's soul to Supay and take his gold.

Pishtaco rarely knew fear. He had withstood dangers as they had come his way. The Sapa Inca had tried to kill him when he was a small boy and failed. The Spaniards had come to take his gold and failed. Who was this woman who was now coming against him? Why were the gods mute? The fragrance of vanilla and raspberry and lilac then had the smell of fear mingling into them — Pishtaco's fear.

It took more than just toad skins; lots of hallucinatory mushrooms had to be added to the stew, but Pishtaco did finally find Ms. Penelope Augusta Gertrude Farquhar. He found her seated on a padded throne. She was a short yellow-haired woman wearing an odd cap with vine-like tentacles growing from it. Standing next to her was a man all dressed in white. She called him Doctor Hernandez, a Spaniard, no doubt.

Hernandez had her look into a strange box. That is when she saw Pishtaco gazing back at her. Quick to act, Farquhar shouted a counter spell to block his presence. Pishtaco searched his memory trying to remember the words employed in the incantation. *Were they sacred excrement?* He thought. *No, he remembered, it was **HOLY CRAP!*** This spell had worked and Pishtaco then lost sight of her.

Since then, Pishtaco had ingested many a concoction so he could keep tabs on the Farquhar witch. Through a drug-induced haze, he had wormed his consciousness into her dreams. There he saw how the phantasms of her brain would spill out of her head. With his potions, Pishtaco was able to trek through her land of strange enchantments — a world of rigid magic, worked into metal shapes and brought to life by mechanical fire. He had hoped that she would stay there among the soulless toolmakers of the north. But soon after her visit to the man dressed in white, she became seduced by a dream.

It had been his hope to have ended that dream. When she came, he had crashed her dream into the muck of a mining camp — squeezed it into a grave of twisted steel. He had intended that she be mashed, along with her phantoms, within the belly of that flying machine. The thought of their falling from the sky still pleased him. Death in a gold mining camp would have been a fitting end for anyone who had come to destroy Pishtaco and take his gold.

Inexplicably, no further amount of hallucinogenic elixir had allowed Pishtaco to see Farquhar again. But, somehow, he sensed that he had failed and that she was still alive.

A few days later, while he was searching for her from his perch above the Rio Marañón, he confirmed his suspicions. He knew that it must be her. There, down in the jungle, was a faint flickering of magic, a glimmering that became stronger and stronger. There was nothing much he could do. His magic had become very weak while Inti was stuck in the sky and Mama Killa hid below the mountains. With the passing years, Penelope Farquhar's glow grew, gaining in strength with the completion of each new circle beneath the cliff of Paititi. Pishtaco saw her become stronger and stronger. Though the fool never knew that she was passing beneath Paititi. He had seen to that, with the little magic he could muster, he blinded her to its presence.

But the blinding came at a cost, for which the local Aquano and the Shetebo tribes paid a terrible price. Villagers foolish enough to venture into the forest at night soon found themselves trussed up and turned into a human ingredient to maintain the enchantment.

The cliff face overlooking the Rio Marañón was again dyed red with human blood. Old spells and new sacrifices just barely worked, but Penelope Farquhar's eyes never saw the great gate of Paititi. However, Pishtaco knew that they soon would. Penelope Farquhar had become too strong, strong for him alone.

The great creator, Viracocha, had been very wise and had sent Siwar Q'enti to awaken him. Viracocha had created man — breathed into stones making man from rock. Then he wandered amongst them, as a beggar, teaching the Inca about all of his creations. Viracocha made the moon. Viracocha made the stars. Viracocha made the sun. The sun was Inti, who sweated the gold that Pishtaco guarded. The moon was Mama Killa, who cried silver. Sweat and tears — gold and silver — to be fashioned and shaped by the people who Viracocha had summoned from the stones to honor their gods, not to be used to glorify and empower mortals. Viracocha had seen his people's glory destroyed by Spaniards. Pishtaco felt proud that he had saved a little of their magnificence here in Paititi — keeping it for himself and destroying any Spaniard who came for it. Now he must destroy the Farquhar witch as she came for it. So far, he had succeeded against all comers. Viracocha must have grasped that he, Pishtaco, was greedier than any other man and that his matchless greed would keep the treasure safe. No doubt this was why Viracocha had summoned Siwar Q'enti to awaken him.

Viracocha had placed all in motion. The forces were aligning. Penelope Augusta Gertrude Farquhar might be a brilliant sorceress but she would not be able to kill him and get what was left of the Inca gold. She would die like the Spaniards!

The sun was setting a hundred miles away to the southwest, behind the Huascaran Mountains. As it disappeared below the snow-capped peaks, a light appeared around a nearby bend in the Rio Marañón.

From his perch, Pishtaco had watched the movement of the light with great concern. He knew its meaning and also knew that all the world's toad skins, white-lipped tamarin paws, baby's ears and the very magic emitted from his great pile of gold would not be enough. He had only one hope, and that would come from the power that he had kept hidden deep within his tomb — it was a strength he rarely used or needed. Now had come the time to waken it.

———— «» ————

Pishtaco's sepulcher reflected the golden glow produced by the many torches that he had placed about the walls. Pishtaco sidestepped the remains of a dead dog, several llamas, two rotted warriors, a cluster of strangled virgins and Imasumaq, his sacrificed lover. However, Pishtaco paid no attention to them as he passed by. Time was of the essence, but not so pressing that he wouldn't pause to take a glance at his burial slab. There, straddled across the opening leading to Ukhu Pacha, Pishtaco had spent many centuries — hoping that his memory was fresh in men's minds — praying that Inti would never allow his spirit to be forced down those depths to face the judgment of Supay and his demons. During those years, it had never occurred to him that the real threat to his existence was some insane woman from Norteamérica.

Pishtaco looked over the cut block perimeter ringing the edge of his personal entrance to eternal damnation. The glow from the hell fires below threw up a brilliant red light that illuminated the circular wall of the great cavern all the way to its top of Pishtaco's great pyramid, Pishtaco could see the openings to the chambers that he had ordered made to contain the six Chachapoya shamans whose mummies he had stolen and imprisoned there, and whose magic he had enslaved with the powers contained within Inti's gold.

"Up Alliyma! Up Ussun! Up Ozcollo! Up Orotongo! Up Huallpa! Up Atoc!"

"Pishtaco, you have the balls of a hen. A hen with no huevos! Are you scared, Pishtaco?" Atoc was awake.

"Mock me! Mock me if you will, Atoc. But you are still a corpse held below my feet forced to do my bidding."

"You know, we do talk to one another down here, Pishtaco, and we are not that far away from Ukhu Pacha. We hear things coming up the shaft. Supay's demons shout to us. They are saying that Supay soon will be dining on your living corpse for eternity and that they will be playing their flutes in time to your screams."

"Atoc, you are more of a gossip than a magician. Get your mind clear. Alliyma, Ussun, Ozcollo, Orotongo and Huallpa, clear your minds too. I will need all that's in them — every spell and trick — curses and incantations. Defy me and I will wrack you in pain. Remember the pain that I first used on you when I brought you here? Remember how you then begged to serve me?"

Pishtaco raised his arms towards the vaulted ceiling of his burial rotunda, "Now join your minds with mine and let them add to my power. I feel you entering my head, Alliyma called the good person. Ah, here is Ussun, who once loved to eat plums. And now comes Ozcollo, whose name and eyes are that of an ocelot. Here is Huallpa, full of joy. And, now you come Atoc; fear is a powerful force, isn't it Atoc?"

Atoc didn't answer; he was waiting for what was about to come next.

"Now for Orotongo, who was once big and fat and named for the bear but now looks more like the decaying remains of a bear's kill. Come, Orotongo — come."

Orotongo did not come.

"Orotongo?" Baffled, Pishtaco shouted with such force that his voice echoed about the burial chamber and reverberated down the shaft that led to Ukhu Pacha."

"Yes, Pishtaco, that's it, shout. Let Orotongo know that you miss him."

"What are you talking about?" Pishtaco snarled.

"Supay came for Orotongo while you were pouring blood on your perch above the Rio Marañón. Orotongo is

on his way to rebirth, or even more likely, he has gone to go
dwell with Inti in the sky of Hanan Pacha."

Pishtaco could not sense Orotongo any longer. The idea
that Supay had climbed up the cavern to Orotongo's cell
and liberated him frightened Pishtaco more than the coming
of the Farquhar woman. Would Supay soon come for him?
Pishtaco slunk down and carefully peered over the wall
surrounding the cavern that reached down into Ukhu Pacha.
He could sense that Orotongo was no longer down there; he
could sense that his mummified carcass of bones was absent.

He thought of how Siwar Q'enti had summoned him by
bringing him back to life. "Ha! Atoc! What is Supay but a
lesser god that sits at the feet of Viracocha? Viracocha sent
Siwar Q'enti to bring me back to my full manhood to save
Paititi. Orotongo's help is of little value to me. He was a poor
shaman. Now, do as I command!"

Pishtaco strode angrily out the entrance to his tomb and
stood atop his great pyramid. He stared out into the night
sky. His composure regained, he once again raised his arms
straight above his head. His fingers seemed to stretch out
and almost touch the heavens. Alliyma, Ussun Ozcollo,
Huallpa and Atoc were now all in lockstep with his thoughts.
Pishtaco lowered his hands to shoulder level. He then began
to chant as he rotated his arms in the same direction as the
northern and southern circumpolar constellations, which
were spinning slowly at the opposite ends of the equatorial
horizon.

Pishtaco could see that his right hand was tracing
the clockwise movement of the stars in the Chameleon
constellation, and those of Hydrus and the larger and lesser
Magellanic Clouds as they circled the south celestial pole.
His left hand was moving with the counter-clockwise motion
of the stars in the Draco constellation and the larger and
lesser bear.

He felt that his body had come into sync with the
night sky, so he reversed the direction of his hands. As he
did this, he began to chant. The irises of his eyes drifted
upward becoming hidden within his eye sockets. And with
that, all the stars in the sky reversed direction and rapidly

spun backwards. Strange purplish vapor rose up from where he stood, forming a cloud. Pishtaco glowed within this cloud with a light not dissimilar to that which he had detected within Miss Penelope Farquhar. He lifted his head to the spinning heavens as his lower jaw detached from the upper — snakelike and ready to eat. With his chin resting on his chest, like a sacrificial corpse in his sepulcher, Pishtaco, cried out with a low guttural voice that emanated from deep within his guts, "Chinkirma Mama!!!!!!"

———— «» ————

At the bottom of a densely covered palm swamp, deep within the Peruvian jungle, a gigantic electric eel opened her eyes and surfaced. Gently, she began to swim around the column-like palms that gave this swamp the appearance of a drowned ancient city. Slowly, she sensed her way, avoiding the tree trunks that stood in her path. After some effort, she reached the black open waters of the Rio Chambira. Once in the river, free of all obstructions, Chinkirma Mama applied her caudal fin hard to the water. She now swam swiftly with the current, heading rapidly downstream where the Rio Chambria joins the Rio Marañón.

Chinkirma Mama kept her eyes above the water. She could see the sky as she swam, and how the stars were circling fast and in the wrong direction. Chinkirma Mama knew this was due to Pishtaco's magic. It excited her so that she let some of her body's salt secrete into the mammoth electrical organs in her tail. That reversed the polarity within her body, much like Pishtaco had just done with the northern and southern celestial poles. As salt trickled into the organ, she emitted a massive discharge. Electricity coursed through the water of the Rio Chambira, grounding on either side of its palm-lined banks — caimans, catfish, turtles and stingrays, unintentional targets within Chinkirma Mama's electrical wake, went belly up. The Rio Chambira became littered with the bodies of its inhabitants.

CHAPTER ELEVEN

Chinkirma Mama

Everything came to a standstill. No one moved. And in an instant, everything was back to normal, as if a power outage had been quickly restored — the furnace fires up — the lights go on — and the digital clocks all go beep. Ernest, Ada, Cecile, Belle and Billy were all talking and moving again. However, Penelope had seen none of it because she had fallen asleep as soon as she had crawled into her cot. Which was understandable because she hadn't slept for a century or so.

Though her consciousness had switched off, the glow from her body hadn't. This had made her companions wish for a more permanent power outage when it came to her incandescence. There had been no need for Penelope to conjure up kerosene lanterns when she'd created the tents. Once the sun had gone down, she'd started blazing brighter than any campfire.

Billy Bowlegs and Sir Ernest relocated their tent further upriver. But Cecile, Belle Starr and the Countess Lovelace had been stuck with the radiant accommodations. Cecile Fatima had to shake her rattle and mutter all sorts of sleeping incantations, before finally dozing off into a trance. Belle Starr didn't have any voodoo abilities, so she tried to remedy the problem by piling the leaves from a giant elephant-ear plant all over Penelope.

Belle exclaimed to Ada, as she completed her task, "I'm a guessing that she's now more firefly than person. You know if I put any more of these leaves over her she'll turn into compost. Well, I'm going to find me self a soft patch of ground and sleep out in the open, cowgirl fashion. I hope, Ada, you manage to get a bit of shuteye with Miss Glowworm here."

But Ada Lovelace wasn't concerned. That was because she had already made her own plans for different sleeping accommodations. However, she wanted to be discreet and not let Belle Starr know.

"You do that, Belle. Go and sleep outside. I will persevere here. It won't be a problem for me."

Once Belle Starr had said her good nights, the Countess Lovelace made her exit as well.

Belle soon found herself a nice pleasant spot along the riverbank and decided she would stretch out there till daybreak. She was far enough away from Penelope, that by lowering her Stetson over her eyes she was able to block out all of Miss Farquhar's annoying light.

——— «◊» ———

Chinkirma Mama bounced weak electric pulses off the objects that lay in front of her. Like radar, the pulses enabled her to thread through the large lily pads that had obscured the surface of this section of the Rio Marañón. Occasionally she would lift her head out of the water, take a breath and scan the shore for victims. Chinkirma Mama's pale blue eyes were feeble but returning signals from her electrical current gave her a detailed mental image of the things about her. This was how Chinkirma Mama's could hunt so successfully at night. Getting food was never a problem, and from what she could now sense, there was lots of food in front of her.

It was nearing time for the feast; an easy catch lay there in front of her. Chinkirma Mama planned to dine well here all night. She pondered for a moment as to what might be the flavor of these edibles. They were odd creatures — a bit insubstantial. She had never seen the likes of them on the shores of the Rio Marañón nor along the shores of the Rio Chambria. Chinkirma Mama imagined that they might be some sort of lighter confection — not heavy — full of fat and wine like the Spaniards. She still remembered that meal, an ill-flavored meat that gave Chinkirma Mama indigestion for many days. However, Pishtaco feared these creatures much more than he did the Spaniards. That told her that they were much more powerful than those flimsily-built Conquistadors. Perhaps they were lesser gods, lesser gods like her. Chinkirma Mama thought back through the many centuries of her existence and realized that she had never eaten any gods before. She had no idea how they would taste. But that didn't really matter; she was doing this for Pishtaco. Chinkirma Mama liked Pishtaco very much, and if he asked her to eat some Spaniards or these odd things she could bear whatever digestive disorder that came her way.

Now it was time for the fun part. Chinkirma Mama drooled with anticipation. There would be an explosion of synaptic discharges as adrenalin and stress hormones dumped into her quarry's brain. The byproducts of fear always helped to season the food. Soon there would be squealing and screaming as she ripped off heads. Changes in biochemistry always helped tenderize and improve the flavor of the meat Chinkirma Mama chomped on in her maw.

The thought of it was making her too hungry. Chinkirma Mama just couldn't take it any longer. Suddenly, her electrical organs reversed polarity. She spasmodically slapped her tail into the water with all the force of a gigantic oar. With a shower of unrestrained voltage, she rushed the shore.

However, beneath the Stetson of her first chosen victim, there wasn't a sleepy eye. Nor was there panic or fear.

Belle Starr had been watching strange movements in the water for some time. Fortunately, Penelope had cast enough light through the leaf pile Belle had placed over her that it illuminated the waters of the Rio Marañón.

Belle knew what was coming. She'd seen the beast peeking out at her with a lily pad draped foolishly over its head — like that sort of nonsense would fool a notorious outlaw and horse thief like Belle Starr.

As Chinkirma Mama plowed into the riverbank, she craned her neck high over Belle ready to kill.

Then, there was gunfire.

BANG! BANG! BANG! And again, BANG!

Whatever Belle had loaded into her six-guns had a powerful effect upon Chinkirma Mama. Instead of gobbling up Miss Starr, she threw her head back and roared a roar that no fish could ever produce. The sound shook the riverbank — dropped branches from the trees and brought the entire crew of the Let's Go Kill Pishtaco mission out of their tents and scrambling towards the edge of the river.

Billy Bowlegs was the first to arrive at the scene. Belle had fired off all of her ammunition and was in the process of reloading. Billy had just gotten his hand on her shoulder when Chinkirma Mama made a determined lunge at Belle. She came at Belle sideways, but this strike from an unexpected direction didn't catch Billy off guard. He tugged hard, pulling Belle away from the river just as Chinkirma Mama's jaws whizzed past.

Cecile was now out and busily dancing along the shore of the Rio Marañón, casting every curse of misfortune and affliction that she could muster upon the head of the monster. Seeing this new opportunity, Chinkirma Mama swung her head, pendulum-like in the opposite direction. She caught Cecile as she spun around with her rattle. The giant eel grasped the head of the voodoo priestess firmly and lifted Cecile high up into the air as Ada and Ernest came up to do battle, armed with clubs that they had hastily improvised from a few of the fallen limbs. Without concern for themselves, they began to pound at the exposed underbelly of the beast.

Not to be excluded from the fight, Belle Starr, her six-guns now re-loaded, walked steadily towards the creature firing a Colt 45 from either hip.

But Chinkirma Mama was not to be distracted. Stretching her throat straight up to the heavens, she opened wide and sucked in whole every bit of Cecile Fatima. Ignoring the pain of the clubbing and unremitting barrage of gunfire, she moved ashore, focusing her attention on the unarmed Chief Bowlegs.

Breathing on land was no problem for electric eels, especially for one who was semi-divine. Snake-like she came in. Billy couldn't move fast enough. Facing her and attempting to run at the same time, his legs tangled and tripped him up. He fell hard to the ground. As he was attempting to get himself back onto his feet, Chinkirma Mama tried to get ahold of him just like she had Cecile. If she managed to fit her maw over Billy Bowleg's head, she would shake him like a rat terrier breaking a rodent's neck.

"ENOUGH!!!! — Wooooo!!!! Wooooo!!!" Deep red fiery light burned from the fingernails of Penelope Farquhar. It had taken her awhile to get up and out of her cot. She had heard all the noise, but her mind had been in a muddle after being sleep-deprived for so many years. Once she had stumbled from out of her tent and clearly saw what was happening, Penelope instinctively went in for the kill.

There was no longer any self-doubt concerning her powers — no hesitation. There was absolutely no way that Chinkirma Mama was going to get Billy Bowlegs. The energy radiating from her fingers went from red hot to white hot as Penelope focused all ten rays right between Chinkirma Mama's eyes.

The roar that Chinkirma Mama had made when she had been struck by Belle Starr's gunfire was but the purring of a kitten as compared to the deafening howls she now emitted. But it was too late to try and get on Penelope's good side. Miss Farquhar had no intention of stopping now.

Sizzling and spitting, Penelope's powers shot out from Chinkirma Mama's head, traveling straight up and into those twirling stars that Pishtaco had set into a perverse motion hours before. Bolts of lightning ricocheted off moons, planets and constellations, as the entire heavens froze. Then, abruptly, they all reversed course and headed in the opposite direction.

Chinkirma Mama's body burst into flame — into a twisting column of whirling fire. All of her shrieking and screaming now stopped. Chinkirma Mama disintegrated into nothing more than glowing embers raining down upon the Rio Marañón — extinguishing one at a time as they touched down on the river's surface.

"I loved Cecile", Penelope sobbed as she sank to her knees. "I know. I know. She was a pain in the ass who constantly bothered me with that damn rattle of hers. But still, Cecile was my good friend. She had come to me in my late teens when the whole world was pulling away from me. I needed company. I was restrained in my hospital bed. Cecile was there for me, no one else was. She told me stories about how she and her mother were sold together as slaves in Saint Dominique — about how she had become possessed by a spirit who was a lot like my voices. She had one voice within her head, Erzuli, the African spirit of beauty, dancing, extravagance, and flowers."

Still weeping, Penelope looked up at her four remaining voices, who were now staring at her, their eyes full of pity.

"I do like flowers, beauty and extravagance...and someday I'd like to try my hand at dancing."

Penelope clutched at herself, violently shaking as she sobbed.

Billy Bowlegs felt he had to do something for her, but he didn't know what. He dropped to one knee next to her and wrapped an arm about her shoulder.

"We are all sorry to see her go," he offered awkwardly. "But you know, you might be better off if we all went. Sorry, that wasn't very sympathetic. I didn't know her well but she seemed to be... very interesting. But somehow, I recall hearing that she led some rebellion of some sort?"

"Oh, she had her moments. I remember reading a book about Cecile. She slit a pig's throat and swore all the slaves to a blood oath. She got them so riled up that a few weeks later there were over a thousand dead French planters."

"Oh...I had no idea."

"Yes, Cecile was good at pushing people's buttons. She had a talk with me just before I stabbed my mother."

This was also news to Billy, he hadn't been around Penelope in her earlier days and wasn't sure how to respond, so he changed the subject. "You know, if we ever get a day off from this dream of yours, reserve a space for me on your dance card."

CHAPTER TWELVE

Descartes Sends a Gift

The sun was making its presence known. What had been a black starlit sky was going through a series of revisions — from pale gray to an incipient blue, with only a few of the stronger stars still visible in the oncoming rush of light. The chorus of frogs, which a few seconds ago had made the jungle sound tauntingly mechanical, began to quiet down. A few frogs, like some stars above them, still tried to make a claim to the day, but interloping chirps and squawks became emboldened. Bird songs and the hoots and grunts of monkeys soon supplanted all of the nighttime noises.

As the sky became streaked in a glow of soft purple and gold, the two dugout canoes were again pushed into the waters of the Rio Marañón. Their paddles dipped into the river slowly, thoughtfully, but not mournfully. In a kind of religious way, no words were spoken when they broke camp. Forest noises provide a kind of hymn for the sort-of-soul of the departed Cecile Fatima. But once the travelers were on the river, with the sun rising above the trees, the warmth of the coming day began to loosen tongues.

"She needed to be stabbed." Penelope said with certitude.

"Well, I assume that she must have," Billy rejoined. He was feeling a bit uncomfortable being the only other one in the dugout canoe and therefore Penelope's designated sounding board. Belle Starr had opted to join Sir Ernest and the Countess Lovelace as the stern paddler, alleging that Ada wasn't up to the job and that she suspected that the two of them required a chaperone. But Billy knew better. The three of them were leaving it up to him to keep the expedition on track. He always was the one that they relied on to take the lead.

"She had to control everything. She dominated my father. That poor man couldn't breathe without her permission. And nothing that he did was ever good enough. He hid in his office at the Museum of Natural History to avoid coming home. I can understand that, when I was young…that is before your voices came along, I used to pray for the school bus to come and take me away. Then she began having affairs and accusing my father of doing the same thing. I don't know if she meant that as a smokescreen or she did it to make him feel doubly uncomfortable. Whatever it was it worked. He killed himself. Then it was just me and my brother and Mommy Dearest. However, she liked my brother."

"Oh, so that's when you met Cecile?"

"Sort of…we got to know one another slowly. First, I read that book I told you about. I was hospitalized after Dad died and that's when she showed up in my head. When I was finally released and forced back into our happy home, my mother just couldn't let up on my dad, even after he had died. It was disgusting. I managed to get through high school and even got a bachelor's degree before Cecile finally said go stab your mother. Funny that I took her advice. By then I had met René, Ernest, Ada and even Belle, but they remained silent on the issue."

"I take it you had been passing the time reading a lot of historical biographies?"

Penelope now felt a bit silly. "Yes, apparently I did. Obviously, I read one about you not too long ago. Read books on Amelia Earhart, Fidel Castro and Bobby Kennedy about that time too. I was hoping that Bobby would take root but for some odd reason you came into being."

"Hey, I'm just as colorful and interesting. Didn't I fight off the Federals so they never took the Seminole land? I was a thorn in their side and they never managed to capture me."

Penelope laughed, "You know I wish you would learn your part better. You surrendered to them in 1858 and were sent off with your two wives, numerous children, a fortune in cash, and fifty slaves to the Indian Territory. You became a wealthy planter in Arkansas, then a captain in the Union Army during the Civil War. But you are right, that surely is colorful and very interesting. No doubt that's why I settled on you."

"Hmm…maybe I should read my own biography."

Their conversation was interrupted as Ernest began shouting from the other dugout. The two boats had been paralleling each other as they headed up the river. The paddling had been slow going due to all the giant lily pads that had clogged up the surface of the water. Something in the water had grabbed Sir Ernest's attention.

Both dugouts turned towards the center of the river where a large, ornate box was floating amongst the water lilies. As they grew nearer, Penelope could discern the details. It was a trunk or a chest bobbing in place among the lily pads, where it had apparently become stuck within all of the vegetation.

Billy hollered to Sir Ernest, "That's some fancy chest or is it a coffin?"

"Can't tell you yet, my friend. What does it look like?"

Penelope shouted back to him as she placed her left hand on top of the object to bring it alongside. "It's marquetry — ebony and different shades of lighter woods. There's lots of mother-of-pearl inlay, too. It would go nicely with the furniture that is in my house."

It wasn't long before Sir Ernest, Ada and Belle's canoe reached the site. Gently, everyone reached out to guide and position the chest so that it was between the gunwales of the boats.

As Ada glided her hand across the inlay on the chest's lid she suddenly exclaimed, "Look, it's us."

"It is," Belle said, with some excitement. "It's all water lilies floating on an ebony river with us and our dugouts in the middle. And there is a miniature version of this box floating between the miniature versions of us. Sure is a pretty thing."

"What do you think Billy, a present of some kind? Perhaps a gift sent down river from Paititi?" Ernest said with a degree of caution.

"I don't know. Somehow, I think this Pishtaco fellow isn't very generous. One thing I'm sure of is that there is no Inca gold in this trunk. It could be filled with gunpowder. Whoever placed it here wanted us to open it. Look, they've left the key in the lock. Maybe it contains something nasty. An electric piranha? I mean, considering that we already took care of Pishtaco's electric eel."

A faint smile drew across Penelope's lips as Billy said the word "we" but she was not interested in making any points about the resolution of the evening's slaughter and let his comment pass.

"The thing is, are we going to take the bait and open it?" Billy asked, turning his face towards Penelope.

"Why are you looking at me?"

"Well, you are the heroine of this saga — founder of this dream, so to speak and the chosen one of both Xuhpuri and Supay. Without you there's no show. So maybe you should tell us figments of your over-active imagination what we should do next."

"Well, I guess we probably should open it. It's such a beautiful trunk it would be a shame not to see what's inside. Obviously, it was designed to get my attention. It's the kind of thing I would have out-bid everyone on at an antique auction and then would have paid movers to relocate it to my bedroom back in Austin. Hey, Billy, let's do it! I'll keep my fingernails at the ready while you turn the lock."

"That's comforting," Billy said. "Belle, could you take your side arms out and lay a bead upon this chest? Just in case some of the polish has worn off of Miss Farquhar's nails."

As Belle drew out her twin 45s, Billy reached down to the key and turned it in the lock.

The lid of the chest flew back. And as it did so, Billy yelped, throwing himself backwards, nearly upending the dugout.

"My god! What is that?" He exclaimed.

A girl...well, at first it looked like a girl, shot bolt upright in the trunk. Her face was painted and her movements were mechanical. She opened her eyes as she pivoted her head in the direction of Penelope. Then, with one of her hands, she reached out and handed her a card.

Penelope waived Belle off, "Please holster your six guns! I know her."

"You know her?" both Belle and Billy shouted incredulously, in unison.

"I should say that I think I know of her," Penelope said as she snickered to herself.

Ada then said with some insistence, "My dear, you are toying with us. Please provide us with the necessary information that will end this suspense you have created."

"I will. I will," Penelope said, as she tried to appear somewhat serious. "But let me first examine this calling card that I've been presented. I bet it confirms my suspicions."

She then examined the printing on the card. "Ha! I was right!"

"Well! What does it say?" Ada said sharply, abandoning her breeding.

"-1 -2"

"Well, I'm the only other mathematician in this group, and, even to me, that is not helpful. Could you elucidate, please, Penelope?"

"Sorry, this is René's daughter, Francine. Her name is on it but I haven't a clue as to why she's handed me this calling card, nor what the -1 -2 is supposed to mean."

"I see," Ada said slowly, reflecting upon the cryptic message. "I thought he was dead, apparently not. However, I can understand having an automaton for a daughter after trying to raise the flesh and blood version of my own. How strange. Do you think René is somehow having us on? A mordant joke of some kind? Perhaps he is a trifle miffed with us for burying him back at the landing slip? Though, we did try to give him a decent service."

"Sorry, I can't speak to any of that, but I do suspect that my own mother would have opted for the automaton version if she could have gotten her hands on one. Actually, René had a real daughter, whom he doted upon a long time ago back in Holland. Her mother was his housekeeper. It was probably the only time in old Descartes' life that there was some normalcy to be had. I'm afraid that Francine died young from scarlet fever. Her death was devastating, not only because he lost his daughter, but it freed his housekeeper from staying with him. To compensate, he built this robotic child. He was quite clever with that sort of stuff. Built himself a flying pigeon and a hunting dog that hunted.

A while after he had lost his daughter, he was sent for by Queen Christina of Sweden to be a tutor of some sort. That required that he get into a boat. You know smart people are so often the most clueless — he took his android version of his daughter with him in a case...must have been this one... Anyhow, René told the captain of the ship he was on, and his crew, that he was traveling with his daughter whom he kept in a box. Everyone on this planet, except Monsieur Descartes, knows how superstitious sailors are, and back in the seventeenth century, it didn't take much to get anyone worked up over devil worship. That someone might break into his luggage was a forgone conclusion for anyone who might think the matter through. Which, apparently, René did not. The crew opened the box with Francine in it, freaked out and threw her overboard. I guess they came close to doing the same to René. Not sure how he talked himself out of that, the smart gene must have clicked on. But it wouldn't have made much difference if they had dumped him overboard because he died in Sweden six months later, and he had a horrible time while there."

"Hmm, so -1 -2, is it?"

"That's right, Ada. -1-2"

"We will have to all give that a think," Ada said, then continued, "Evidently, René has chosen to be playful. Not sure if it wouldn't have been better if he had just stayed quiet in that second grave that we gave him, but I imagine that this message is of some import. I do know that mathematics is a precise language for the economic expression of ideas but there is such a thing as being rudely terse." Ada rolled her eyes, "-1-2, everybody."

The mechanical Francine, hearing Ada's pronouncement, turned her head towards Ada and gave her a courteous nod. A gurgling sound followed. And before anybody could reach out and prevent it, the marquetry chest filled with water and sunk beneath the surface, taking the mechanical Francine with it to the bottom of the Rio Marañón.

———— «◊» ————

As the day wore on, the water lilies petered out. The river grew shallower, swifter, narrower and harder to paddle. Its character changed from a slow, wide, meander, plump with all sorts of aquatic things, to an unforgiving surge where only the most artful of creatures managed to survive. On the paddlers' right, rolling hills formed up. Still, the jungle was able to hang on to them. But as the elevations heightened and steepened, it had no recourse but to fall away. Rocks jutting out above the surface, constricted the movements of the two dugouts, channelizing them within countless currents — forcing them to stay uncomfortably close as they competed for any navigable space. As exhaustion began to set in, an island conveniently appeared in the middle of the Rio Marañón.

Shackleton shouted to Penelope that this island might make a good place to camp before their final push to the gates of Paititi. She agreed, and both canoes soon were dragged up upon the rocky shoreline.

There was an almost giddy sense of expectation within Shackleton's boat, one that was not shared by Billy or Penelope. Though the island was vegetated, the plants and the topography looked shabby and tired, as if it would not resist if floodwaters came to whisk it away. All would spill into the Rio Marañón and be swept downstream, leaving just a jumble of stones to indicate where it once had stood.

So why were Belle, Ada and Ernest acting as though they had just landed on the beach of a five-star hotel? Penelope wanted to know, and it was apparent by the grin on Belle's face that she desperately wanted to tell her.

"Well?" Penelope exclaimed, with some impatience.

"They're going to get hitched!"

"What do you mean they're going to get hitched?"

Belle Starr laughed at her question, "You know, matrimony, conjugal bliss, all that stuff that happens before infidelity and divorce."

"So, how are they going to do that out in this jungle in the middle of nowhere?"

"You."

"What do you mean, me?"

"This jungle may be out in the middle of nowhere, but it's smack dab in the middle of your head. You are sort of our creator...the creator of everything, apparently. Who better to officiate over a service involving the marriage of two of your mental aberrations than you?"

"You may have some sort of hallucinatory point, Belle, but they are already hitched. I do read up on you people before my brain takes the liberty of incorporating you into my psyche. Ada is married to the Earl of Lovelace and Sir Ernest to Mrs. Shackleton...err..."

"Miss Emily Dorman, my late and lovely wife." Shackleton had overheard the conversation while unloading the remainder of their provisions upon the beach. "If she were alive today, a union between me and my dear Ada would be out of the question."

Shackleton reached a hand out in the direction of where Ada was setting up a tent. She had been secretly listening and took his cue to come by his side. Now, grasping her hand, he continued.

"Both the Countess Love Lace and I have fulfilled our connubial obligations as specified by the Anglican Book of Common Prayer. The liturgy specifically states, "Till Death Do Us Part." We have both died — Ada in 1852 and myself in 1922. What's more, both of our spouses have passed on quite some time ago. So, unless your brain is about to incorporate Emily and Count Lovelace into your inner-self, I see no legal impediments that could deter us."

Penelope scowled as though she was thinking his point over when Sir Ernest attempted to assuage any fears of delusional impropriety that she may have been entertaining.

"Miss Farquhar, I do have some proficiency at understanding contracts. I have mounted several Antarctic expeditions. Loans, vessels, crew, supplies, sled teams, Manchurian ponies and propeller drive sleighs came with legal papers attached."

Now Ada weighed in on the argument. "Penelope, I never suspected you of being a prude. Ernest's points are very good ones. Don't take this personally, my dear, but the way you've been leading this expedition does call into question whether any of us will survive it. What's wrong with a couple of Victorians desiring some solemnity associated with their romantic undertakings before they pass on to the great beyond?"

"Oh, it's not that. I'm not sure that it's really required, since you've both gone to the great beyond once before. But if that's what you want, it should be done. I'm just not sure how."

"Not a bother," Shackleton said. "We are sure you will come up with something very interesting yet still appropriate. We have all noted the quality of your rather over-active imagination."

"Well...thanks. I hope not to disappoint. If this is what you want, it is the least I can do for you, considering how you all have been shanghaied by my mental ravings."

"Well then, how delightful. I will ask Billy to be my best man, not only because there are so few of them about but because I like him as well. And, I assume, Belle will assist Ada at the altar?"

"You bet I will!"

———— ⟨⟩ ————

It was turning out to be a rather formal affair. There was an angel's trumpet tree so laden with brightly colored flowers that it looked more like a heavenly waterfall than a drooping floral display. It was Belle who decided that this tree would make the perfect backdrop for Ada and Ernest's wedding. She had taken charge of making all of the arraignments. She assigned Billy to climb out on tree limbs and snatch some orchids. She then wove some of the flowers down into Ada's hair, the rest she gathered to form a fiery bridal bouquet. There weren't any white flowers on the island — nothing to symbolize virginal purity. At first, Belle felt a bit awkward about this, but then she considered that Ada had been around the block a few times during the past two hundred years.

"Sorry, no offense, it's just that the color red is all that we got."

"They are splendid. Red is the color of passion. Don't trouble yourself with trifles."

"Well, I like a good wedding and want yours to have all the trimmings. I've asked Penelope to conjure up a wedding cake but so far, she has only managed to summon up a bunch of parrots. Kinda spotty those fingernails of hers."

"Oh, she is learning, and they do come in handy when she gets it right."

"Gets what right?" Penelope had abandoned her efforts at paranormal baking and rejoined the wedding party.

"Your magic," Belle clarified, as she looked up at the treetop. She then added with a degree of sarcasm, "How many parrots do you think are up there?"

"No idea, thousands. I almost had it. There was this beautiful ten-layer cake with white frosting and covered in an exquisite pale pink floral border, then twenty or so parrots came flying out of the top of it. After that, it wasn't fit for consumption. Sorry."

"Oh, that is quite all right. We still have plenty of roasted monkey and those grubs on sticks that Xuhpuri had packed up for us," Ada said, smiling politely. Then added, "The ceremony is the thing. We really do appreciate all of your efforts. We just want to get this over and enjoy what little of our lives that we may have left. You do understand Penelope?"

"Yes, unfortunately, I do. And, I would like to apologize for getting you all..."

Shackleton interrupted her by tapping on his pocket watch, "I believe the sun will be going down soon. We really hadn't planned for a midnight exchange of vows and we are running low on kerosene for the lamps. If you wouldn't mind."

"Oh...of course. I'm not dressed as a minister or a ship's captain, will this Andean maiden outfit suffice?"

"But of course. Please, Miss Farquhar, the sun sets in seventeen minutes."

"Right, everyone gather round."

Penelope took center stage, as Billy, Ernest, Belle and Ada positioned themselves under the angel's trumpet tree. "Let me see...."

"Dearly beloved, "Belle coached.

"I knew that, Belle. Here goes, dearly beloved, we are gathered here today to join... dearly beloved, we are gathered together here to join together this man and this woman in holy matrimony... Belle, I'm now stuck. You can help me out with the next bit."

"Don't know much more than that. Anyone else got a notion?" Just blank stares confronted Mrs. Starr. "It's been a long time and frankly, I was too nervous to remember much of what was said."

Ada reached out and grasped Penelope by her hand, "Just improvise my dear."

Penelope cleared her throat to continue when the trees around them began to speak. All of the wedding cake parrots began to recite in unison, "which is an honorable estate, instituted by Viracocha, signifying unto us, the mystical, and, therefore is not by any to be entered into unadvisedly or lightly; but reverently, discreetly, advisedly, soberly, and in the fear of Viracocha. Into this holy estate these two persons present come now to be joined. If any man can show just cause, why they may not lawfully be joined together, let him now speak, or else, hereafter, forever hold his peace."

Everyone was stunned that Viracocha was part of the parrot's liturgy but grateful that the parrots had stopped in their squawking for a few minutes to listen for any objections. But then, they started up again.

"We require and charge you both, as ye will answer at the dreadful day of judgment when the secrets of all hearts shall be disclosed, that if either of you know any impediment, why ye may not be lawfully joined together in matrimony, ye do now confess it. For be ye well assured, that if any persons are joined together otherwise than as Viracocha word doth allow, their marriage is not lawful."

The parrots never missed a beat. Both Ada and Ernest did as they were told. They agreed to be man and wife and placed the rings, that Billy Bowlegs had carved for them out of some driftwood, upon one another's fingers. The parrots then declared them to be man and wife and just before they could squawk out the final sentence of the ceremony, Penelope beat them to it.

"YOU MAY NOW KISS THE BRIDE!" she yelled, above all of the birdy screeching.

Penelope's abrupt shouting caused the multitude of parrots to dispossess themselves of their assorted perches and launch themselves into the air like a murmuration of starlings. Shimmering with every color imaginable, with a few new ones thrown in — orange-winged, orange-cheeked and yellow-crowned, rose-faced and blue-headed parrots, scarlet-shouldered parrotlets, military macaws, red-green macaws, blue and yellow macaws, scarlet macaws, chestnut-fronted macaws, cobalt-winged parakeets, white-eyed-parakeets, golden-plumed parakeets and maroon-tailed parakeets swirled above the wedding party. As they did so, the newlyweds kissed in a long embrace as Billy Bowlegs ducked down low, placing his hands over his head, but the shower of bird poop he had been expecting never came.

Belle Starr was so taken aback by the twisting shapes of the masses of birds in the sky, that she forgot to fire off a celebratory salvo. She didn't even notice when the bridal bouquet had been tossed and landed at her feet. There was just something in the bird's movement that riveted her attention. It was like a language, one she couldn't translate, but she was sure that their flight meant something.

The parrots now began to do a loop around the perimeter of the island — faster and faster they circled — then suddenly they broke off and headed up the Rio Marañón.

CHAPTER THIRTEEN

Sach'amama

They were a ragtag, woebegone assortment of sacrificial victims. Pishtaco had canvassed all of the neighboring villages for some decent specimens but most everyone had run away. The only people left behind were either the very old or the very sick. Pishtaco feared that they wouldn't have enough juice in the entire miserable collection to spark the attention of the gods.

He was in the process of herding them slowly up the steps of his own temple when an unbroken stream of parrots flew just over his head screaming his name.

"PISHTACO! PISHTACO! PISHTACO!" They cried in unison.

It was meant as heckling; not a greeting and he felt it sorely. Who or what would be foolish enough to deride the great Pishtaco? Could the gods be forsaking him?

Even though Siwar Q'enti had recently restored him back into his living form, he was beginning to falter. His power seemed to be draining away. Atoc had claimed that Supay had gotten into the tomb of Orotongo and removed him to Ukhu Pacha. He must have climbed up the great cavern again. If things kept deteriorating this way he might as well take his place in line among this pathetic procession of the feeble and infirmed.

"Move! Move!" Pishtaco shouted above jabbering parrots as he poked an eighty-year-old widow with a pointed stick. "You are going to be sacrificed! You should be grateful! All of you should be thanking me! I bring you release from your tired pitiful existence! Soon you will be on your way to Ukhu Pacha! Perhaps to be reborn, or perhaps torn up by demons for eternity…" His voice tailed off as the last of the parrots flew over again mocking his name.

It was hardly worth Pishtaco's effort to beat this bunch. It only made them falter and collapse upon the pyramid steps. Then he had to threaten and cajole them into regaining their footing. He suspected that many of them were just not listening, either too hard-of-hearing or too senile to comprehend his commands. Some were so far gone they couldn't even manage a look of abject terror. What was worse was he had to pull a couple of them up from where they had crumbled to the ground and carry them to where they would be sacrificed.

It just wasn't dignified for a sorcerer of his quality to give piggyback rides to toothless old grandpas just so he could slit their throats. If Paititi were still the vibrant metropolis that it once had been, there would have been a huge selection of victims to choose from. Only the choicest souls would be released to satiate the gods. Why, these people might not have enough blood in them to make a mess upon the altar. Of course, in the old days, he might just leave them bound within his burial chamber and allow them to die of exposure, like the maidens who had been chosen to adorn his tomb. But the climate had grown so hot that there was no longer any frost in Paititi — not even a cold night.

He figured that he would try and summon Sach'amama. She seemed the most receptive to the call of his magic. If she were willing to accept this offering, then he would ask her how to best kill this hodgepodge. He had never asked the gods about this before. Up until now, Pishtaco had never thought that the gods might have individual preferences on how their victims should be slaughtered. It might be a little like wanting your fish steamed and your guinea pig barbecued. Perhaps this was why they had become so quiet? He had just assumed that he was doing it all right and never thought of providing a menu. Pity that pickings were so meager, there just wasn't enough time to do things right. Pishtaco thought that it would be great fun to provide Sach'amama with a list of the choicest victims and all manner of ways that they could be dispatched.

There was little room within the confines of Pishtaco's tomb. He had to shuffle his victims as space allowed. An ancient widow was commanded to squat down among the cadavers of the maidens who had been sacrificed at his original interment. He had to station several old men among the empty chicha pots. Pishtaco laughed, as they looked wistfully into them, "Old fools, all that dried-up centuries ago. Do you expect to get one last taste of it before you die? Do you expect me to let you lick the rims? Put it out of your heads. No last pleasures for you, prepare yourselves, your deaths are near..."

"Hey!" he shouted as he turned his attention to another corner of his tomb. The widow had been in the process of slinking her way out the entranceway. "You get back to where you were!" As she sat down among the dead girls, Pishtaco noticed that her balding head and weathered skin allowed her to blend in perfectly among his victims of yesteryear.

"Do you imagine," he lectured, "that you can crawl out of here and that I am so stupid to think that you are still among the corpses? Do you think I'd grab a corpse instead of you? I am sorry but the gods don't accept recyclables. Once someone is dead they are no longer of use to me. Like those empty chicha pots!" he said as he turned and sneered at the old men who were insistently probing the bottoms of the pots looking for any sign of moisture. He frowned at them, then turned his attention back to the old lady, "Stand up, I want to keep my eye on you. There may be little life in your body but still it is life. And what you have left is going to the gods, not out the door."

As the old woman wobbled up onto her feet, a voice rumbled up the well from the tomb just below Pishtaco's. "You might catch some fat flies and kill them with this lot. They could tip the balance in your favor with the gods."

"Atoc, I was anticipating your sarcasm. Yes, they are a paltry lot, but with my powers, augmented with yours and those of Ozcollo, Huallpa, Ussun and Alliyma, I am confident that Sach'amama will come. Once this Farquhar sorceress has been destroyed, I will go deep into the jungle and stay there till I find plump and beautiful children to honor her altar. But Farquhar is nearly at Paititi's gates, and I cannot afford to spend months scouring the forest. Sach'amama will understand and thirst for these future offerings. And once the witch is gone, there will no longer be a need to have Ozcollo, Huallpa, Ussun and Alliyma imprisoned under my feet. I shall throw you all off Paititi's cliff. And down into the Rio Marañón you will all go —floating into some back eddy, no doubt. The scraps of flesh that now cling to your bones will no doubt feed the fishes. There will be no Ukhu Pacha awaiting any of you. I will enchant the river so that your souls will never escape, just as I enchanted your tombs. But take heart, my dear Atoc, your bones might comingle with the bones of other of the Chachapoya's refuse that I tossed off the cliff centuries ago. There, among the stink of the river muck, there will be a great reunion of your people. I'm sure that you and Ozcollo, Huallpa, Ussun and Alliyma will spend the rest of eternity praising me for this liberation."

"Not Alliyma!" Atoc shouted back.

———— «⟩» ————

It had been several centuries since Pishtaco had explored the tombs below him. He did not often make a personal call upon the witches and wizards he had kept there. There was no need to. They had always allowed their magical forces to become part of his — not happily mind you, but begrudgingly. Since Pishtaco had yanked their desiccated bodies from the cliff side houses the Chachapoya had made to honor them, these withered skeletonous bundles had remained beneath his feet within the cells he had had carved for them from the rock face of the temple cavern leading to Ukhu Pacha. They appeared to be no more than sacks, sacks that were still tied together the way he had found them, but what miraculous powers lay within these sacks.

When their clout was added to his own, charged with the magic from Inti's gold, Pishtaco felt as though he might be able to challenge and even supplant some of the lesser gods. But then the Spanish came. Paititi became a different place. Their priests stripped the land of his people's magic. His people began to ignore their own gods, even feeling ashamed to honor their festivals. So, the gods went away — hid themselves in the clouds, the mountains, in the trees and in the rocks. Yet like Pishtaco's, the people's memory of them still hung on.

Pishtaco wasn't certain how they had managed this. He knew that the entire real world had been relegated to something now called myth. Yet, myth had its appeal. There were still a few, mostly learned, who actually made it their life's passion to study what had now become the old ways. These learned people had few powers, if any at all. Pishtaco was sure that the gods would have granted them some if they had not become so sickly.

He had often thought about these things as he lay above the cavern to Ukhu Pacha, wondering what would happen to the gods if they were completely forgotten. Would they go to Ukhu Pacha and be reborn or would they just vanish into the clouds, the mountains, the trees and the rocks? During such times, he had felt that the people's memory of him was slipping away. No matter how much terror he had inflicted when he was living, his existence started to become myth — a lesser myth, known only to tiny tribes who hid themselves in the forest, much like the gods in the clouds, the mountains, in the trees and in the rocks.

Pishtaco had almost passed away to Ukhu Pacha before Siwar Q'enti came to him. And he now wondered if he had not done enough since then to perpetuate the fear of his being. He consoled himself with the thought that once he had destroyed Farquhar and preserved for himself the power that came from Inti's gold, Viracocha might just take pity upon him and let Pishtaco continue to remain above the cavern leading to Ukhu Pacha.

Atoc, Ozcollo, Huallpa and Ussun would be pleased if Pishtaco's memory no longer dwelled within Kay Pacha. Then they would be free of his power, and at last could fall down the great cavern and be reborn. Pishtaco had prevented this. He had harnessed their memory to his. And now only those tiny tribes in the rainforest still knew their names and how they had been stolen from their tombs and forced to become his servants.

More than ever, he had to hold all of them close in order to destroy this norteamericano sorceress. He felt weaker and was almost certain that Supay had again been among the tombs and, as Atoc had suggested, taken Alliyma with him. It was now time to revisit those tombs and take stock of his magical larder.

———— «» ————

Pishtaco walked to the edge of the great cavern and cautiously poked his head beneath the stone bed that had cradled his remains for almost five centuries. At first, he was afraid to look down. There was always a strong tugging. The many gold and silver necklaces draped about his neck seemed to gather weight as they dangled over the edge of the foul fissure. It was as though Supay was trying to pull him down to where he felt he belonged. Pishtaco braced himself. His back and shoulders tensed as his hands gripped tight to the cut stone that surrounded the opening. An orange light flickered from far below; making the gold, copper and silver powders that had long-ago been massaged into his skin sparkle. Gradually he turned his head down to peer into the abyss. For a split second, he thought he saw the horns and the sharp menacing features of Supay grinning up at him. This took his breath away. At first, he recoiled, but then found the courage to look downward again after he had convinced himself that he had not seen Supay but only the shadows coming from the fires that Supay had kept burning in anticipation of the day when he would welcome Pishtaco to his kingdom. The light from these fires helped to illuminate the six open doorways that Pishtaco had cut into the rock face.

"Why don't you come and pay us a visit? We will serve you fried duck with Aji Amarillo and plenty of chicha! Just throw a rope over and come down. But mind that you do not fall, or you will be a fried duck."

Atoc's laughter echoed upward, reverberating throughout the mausoleum. Pishtaco once again recoiled from the edge of the cavern.

He was never going to throw a rope over the side. Pishtaco had not even considered such a stupid thing. He backed away till he felt that he had safely distanced himself from the edge. Once he had managed to catch his breath, he began to murmur to himself. As he did so, he crossed his hands over the eye slits of his golden mask and waited. Pressure built up beneath where his palms rested snugly against the openings for his eyes. His hands began to shake as he applied his strength to contain the inner force that was pressing against them. Finally, the time was right.

"Seek!" he commanded, as dark blue ooze burst through his eye slits, like projectile vomit. It was a torrent of the deepest indigo, splattering over the floor, collecting into pools, sliding together until it formed one large gelatinous mass.

"Find!" Pishtaco again commanded.

The blue ooze responded obediently. It moved slug-like over the cut stone facing of the cavern and slithered downward, hugging to the sides of the great abyss until it came to the opening leading to the lowest of the chambers. Creeping inside, it moved around the vacated cell of Ozcollo. Pishtaco could see in his mind's eye all that his magical seepage encountered. Atoc did not lie. Ozcollo was gone, so was Alliyma, who had been in the next tomb up. But Ussun was where he was supposed to be, as was Ozcollo, and Huallpa. Of course, Atoc had already made his presence well known but Pishtaco's ooze checked on him anyway, just to rule out his trickery. Atoc's tied-up bag of bones still rested against the cell wall just the way Pishtaco had left it so many centuries ago. His head, like the others, still poked out of the richly woven sack that he had been reverentially placed in by the Chachapoya. Pishtaco could tell that over the years rats had gnawed on it. This pleased him very much.

"Like what you see, Pishtaco? Enjoy the sight while you can."

"Enough of your sarcasm, Atoc. That pretty head of yours will soon be a home for river crabs. I shall not bother to speak with you any longer. Instead, I'll reign over you!"

With that pronouncement, Pishtaco shouted, "Sach'am-ama!" and clapped his hands.

The ooze now vaporized into the purest shade of indigo. It sought out the bodies of Atoc, Ozcollo, Huallpa and Ussun and then blanketed their corpses with its dense vapored hue.

The eyeless sockets of the dead magicians began to glow with a bright red light — deeper in red than any dye made from the mash of cochineal bugs. The red light engaged the blue, attempting to burn through the foggy shroud that Pishtaco had cast over them. These opposite ends of the color spectrum now did battle, advanced, gave ground, mixed and swirled, eventually fusing to form a new color. A spinning dark magenta rushed up and out of the tombs, filling the upper-most section of the great cavern with a purple light that spun faster and faster as it rose into Pishtaco's burial chamber.

"Sach'amama!" Pishtaco once more shouted

As he did so, two heads with large ears formed within the column of twisting light. As the light softened and faded from view, a bit of the long necks that those two heads were attached to emerged. Covered in forest greenery, it stretched out through the doorway of Pishtaco's mausoleum all the way down the steps of his pyramid. There it ended in a tail that coiled and uncoiled in an agitated anticipation.

Immediately Pishtaco fell to his knees and lowered his gaze. "Welcome Sach'amama, mother of the forests. I, the lowly Pishtaco, guardian of Inti's treasure, once again beseech you. Your exaltedness, Paititi is again under assault and the great treasure of the Sapa Inca, Inti's gold, may be stripped from this last city that still reveres the only true gods. Help me, Sach'amama, for all that has been and for all that may someday come to pass."

At first the two-headed serpent didn't answer Pishtaco's plea. Instead, her tongues flicked at the air, tasting it for the flavors that were to be offered in the upcoming sacrifices.

"Pishtaco!" the right head engaged him, peering down at him scornfully, "This air is rank, old, musty and decayed. There is little life in it, if any. How are you honoring us? Do you have several villages full of people trussed up in the great square of Paititi? Odd that we cannot savor their essence. When we are awakened from our slumber our appetites are keen and we can catch the aroma of the smallest morsel on the gentlest of breezes. Has our drowsiness affected us? If we stand here with our tongues out in the air long enough will we suddenly be aware of the great delights that you have collected for us?"

Unsure as to what to say, Pishtaco began to stammer. "Oh, magnificent mother of the jungle," he said placing his forehead flush against the stone flooring of his tomb, "this menace that of late we have spoken of has taxed me so much that I regret that there are few human offerings worthy of your belly. All but these have been used in the defense of Paititi."

"Pishtaco, have our eyes grown so old as well? We see nothing to be sacrificed."

Stumbling to his feet, Pishtaco scrambled over to where the old woman was cowering among the dead maidens. He reached down and caught her under her arms and yanked her onto her feet. Once she was up and teetering on her feet, he pointed to the old men who were trying to hide themselves behind a newly formed wall of stacked chicha pots.

"Behold, Sach'amama, I have living souls for you. This old woman has seen her days but she once was married to a tribal elder and bore him six sons and seven daughters. And those men over there were once renowned for their hunting skills. The one crouching behind the yellow pot killed a jaguar with a single arrow. Tell me, oh great one, how should I prepare these fine tidbits for you? Slice their throats and let them bleed out so you may lap up their blood? Set them on fire, so that you may smell the sweet fragrance of their burning meat before devouring them? Or simply throw them from the cliffs of Paititi and let their wailing be a treat for your most sensitive and discerning ears?"

The pupil slits in Sach'amama's right head narrowed as those in her left head widened and just before her right side could speak the left beat her to it.

"Ha-ha! Pishtaco. I have lived to see this," she said, as she enunciated each syllable with a throaty lisp. "You've preyed so long upon this land that you have driven off or killed off all of your game. Look at you. You are not in much better shape than those you propose to sacrifice. Oh, let them go, Pishtaco. There is but a sliver of their souls left in them and they will be with Supay soon enough. I am satisfied with the belly laugh that you and your fellow ancients have brought me. It is more satisfying than heartburn."

Her lack of interest in his victims had taken Pishtaco aback. Her remarks concerning his own physical condition had wounded his pride. Even though Sach'amama's more compassionate left head was addressing him, he knew it would be beyond suicidal to dispute this situation with her. So, he bowed to her submissively and was about to release the old woman when to his dismay Sach'amama's right head took charge of things.

"I see no reason for such charity. We were sleeping under the old kapok tree snoozing, beneath the forest's floor, for several centuries. Then, Pishtaco here awoke us from our deep slumber to this time, a time I would much rather have slept through. So, I am irritated, and I am hungry for my breakfast after so long a nap. Yes, Pishtaco, release those bloodless wretches of yours. But you are a different matter. For you, Pishtaco, are just fit enough to pay honor to us with your own death. I say we should beat Supay to it and roast your flesh. Come, come Pishtaco, it's not like you haven't been in a great snake's belly before."

Pishtaco placed his whole body prostrate upon the flooring of his tomb. He quaked in fear like he had when he was a child and was taken to Amarucancha the House of the Great Serpent. This was always the way with the two heads of Sach'amama; once you had an agreement with one, the other would overrule it.

He was now dealing with Sach'amama's right head. She was cold, logical and exacting. Pishtaco feared that they would first dine upon him, and afterward force his spirit down the great chasm to Ukhu Pacha, where it would be reheated as a leftover for Supay. Pishtaco now regretted taunting Supay by placing his tomb above his kingdom. His little joke had backfired, serving only as a fast way of getting him to Hell. Not funny...well perhaps to Supay...Then, to Pishtaco's relief, the left head decided to intervene.

"Pishtaco, before my right half devours you, perhaps you could tell us a little bit more about how Paititi is under assault. I see no such signs of it."

"Oh yes, goddess of the Amazon…and of all life between the mighty Andes and the great delta by the eastern sea. I will! As you had foretold unto me, a most peculiar witch with the most unusual and strange powers would come here from the foul lands of the Norte Americanos. I have confronted many a sorcerer and sorceress in my long life but never one such as she. Her powers are growing. She is learning her craft as she approaches. And she is near, very near. I have watched her long in her travels. At first, she seemed confused and moved in circles, but her movements have straightened out. Now, she is coming straight up the Rio Marañón to Paititi. I tried to stop her. I sent Chinkirma Mama to deal with this witch and her odd assortment of almost-people. That worked when the Spanish first came…when you, oh magnificent Sach'amama and Chinkirma Mama saved our dear Inti's treasure from the grasping Spaniards. But this time, Chinkirma Mama failed, and she has died at the hands of this sorceress."

"Wait, Pishtaco!" Sach'amama's left head interrupted, "This norteamericano witch killed Chinkirma Mama?"

"More to the point," declared the right head, "how did Chinkirma Mama become persuaded to go find this witch in the first place? Did you manage to find sufficient sacrifices to squander on her? And explain to us why it is up to us to defend Inti's gold. Where are Mama Killa, Mama Sara, Kuychi, Pachamama, Catequil, Kon, Urcuchillay, Ekkeko, Paryaqaqa, and above all where is Inti? Is he so proud that he cannot protect his own treasure?"

"I cannot tell you why the gods have hidden themselves. It is bewildering to me. Inti could come down from the sky. His light alone would have boiled the Farquhar, turning her and the shadow people into nothing more than a mist rising above the Rio Marañón. But when she was moving in circles in the forest there was no time, all had stopped, only the witch moved. Years went by and all was still. Inti and Mama Killa were fixed in the sky! They couldn't get free of her grasp! I fear to speak this, but perhaps she has frightened them?"

"I remember something crawling on my back," insisted the left head to the right. I wanted to scratch at it but found I could not."

"Yes," the right said, "I remember this as well, but Inti and Mama Killa afraid, Pishtaco? Of this...this...you called her a Farquhar? I have never heard of a Farquhar. Is she some demon of Supay?"

"I know not my, great lady. Once, through my spells, I found her in another land, Norteamérica. This was before she came here. When I saw her, she was on a throne wearing a strange cap attended to by some servant with a Spanish name...Hernandez, I believe."

"A Spaniard!" the right head snapped.

"Yes, Sach'amama, another Spaniard. They must still be in pursuit of the gold. They are a greedy people and will never forget about it. But I, Pishtaco, am ever vigilant. As I said, I tracked this witch to this Spaniard and was watching him teach her how to control her power, when he blundered. He called her something like... Penny. The Farquhar considered this to be impertinence on his part and lectured him. She was more than a Penny; she was a Penelope Gertrude Augusta Farquhar."

"A Penelope Gertrude Augusta Farquhar," the left head exclaimed, "such a mouthful of words must have great magic associated with it."

"Yes, she has. More than I have seen in the living men and her magic is growing stronger every day. You see why I fear, Sach'amama? Inti's treasure sustains our people. It is what keeps all of us from Ukhu Pacha. It isn't just Pishtaco who is held above the world of the dead, it is the whole of the Inca people...and forgive me...their gods. For once the gold is gone and distributed amongst the outsiders, the memory of all of us will fade. Yes, they will keep us alive for a time in their writings but soon, like our quipus, our talking knots; no one will be able to read the writing. It is happening now and in less time since our empire was vanquished, their books will be like our quipus, and the memories that keep us from falling into Ukhu Pacha will fail."

The eyes of the twin serpents widened. Pishtaco was now no longer in jeopardy of being eaten by one of the heads.

"This is why Chinkirma Mama faced the Farquhar and with no need for sacrifices?"

Pishtaco was about to assure the left head that this was the case when the right head blurted in, "You are so naïve. Chinkirma Mama always had a thing for our Pishtaco, here. And Pishtaco knew how to milk it. Chinkirma Mama gladly went to her death, her fishy heart pounding with romance for her man here...if that's what you can call this walking corpse."

"What's wrong with romance?" the left head insisted.

"Nothing, from Pishtaco's viewpoint. She did his dirty work, and he didn't even have to bloody his sacrificial blade. I suspect that Pishtaco was attempting to get the job done on the cheap."

"I shall kill these villagers right now, Sach'amama!" Pishtaco said, as he pulled out a golden knife from beneath his tunic.

The right head of Sach'amama laughed at him derisively. "Put that away, Pishtaco. There isn't enough blood in any of them to even dribble a spot upon this floor. Send them home."

She looked into the eyes of her other head and there seemed to be an unspoken agreement passing between them.

The left head spoke. "Well, Pishtaco, if you wanted to have something eaten you shouldn't have sent a lovesick electric eel. We will go and greet this sorceress who has panicked you and show you how it is properly done. We will not do it as a favor to you, but because this witch took the liberty of wandering upon our back. That being said, Pishtaco, listen well, we are not the fools. You do not guard the gold for Inti, for the Inca people or for the memory of the gods. You keep it for the magic that you can draw from its ancient fashioning. Unlike the rest of our world, it is still fresh, as untarnished as the day it was crafted with fire and spells. It still speaks of our greatness. It is what keeps our memory alive."

Then, a strange series of guttural sounds came from both the heads as they bobbed back and forth. Pishtaco knew what this was. He knew this was how snakes told jokes to one another. Though Pishtaco couldn't understand what the joke was about, he felt it only prudent to join in with a timid chuckle.

As he quietly snickered, a dark magenta cloud formed, first about the heads and then throughout the body of Sach'amama. The opposite ends of the color spectrum within the cloud began to pull apart, tugging and yanking until they were at last free of one another. These two columns of color, red and blue, began to twist, turning faster and faster until they formed into what might be described as a pair of spinning tops. The whirlwinds churned up the ancient dust within Pishtaco's tomb before bouncing down the steps of his great temple side by side, and quickly disappeared beneath Paititi's jungle undergrowth.

As they vanished from Pishtaco's sepulcher, all of the old and infirm sacrificial victims hobbled up onto their feet. Many were looking down, but a few had the courage to look straight into Pishtaco's eyes expectantly.

"Okay, I heard her," Pishtaco said, with a degree of aggravation. He swept his hand towards the doorway. "Get out of here. Go!"

His victims did not need for him to tell them twice. They scampered past Pishtaco and scurried down his pyramid steps much faster than they had come up.

CHAPTER FOURTEEN

Inti's Gate

Four ears flapped like giant bat wings within the stiff current of the Río Marañón. Immense ears made it easy for Sach'amama to hear paddles dipping into and out of the river. She could also hear river water racing around a pair of canoes, tracing their outline. Though the occupants didn't know it, Sach'amama was gathering information through the river touching the boats like a blind man feeling faces. From the changes in pitch and timbre within the water's flow, Sach'amama could tell that there were two boats heading her way, that they would be nearby in less than hour and that one boat contained one person and the other boat contained…no one.

Sach'amama lifted her heads up out of the water and now listened to the air. She could hear five distinct voices echoing off canyon walls a few miles away. The witch and her shadows would soon be near. Sach'amama contented herself with the knowledge that once this chore was over, and she had devoured all five of them, she would be free to glide off into the jungle. She had just spied an interesting patch of thickly growing ferns. She thought that that might be the right spot to sink down into the forest floor and rest for a century or two. Then, if some more adventuring Spaniards came upriver looking for Paititi's gold, well, it would hardly be any effort to reach over and gobble them up from there… and again go back to sleep.

———— 《》 ————

As the dugouts curved around a great bend in the river, Penelope and her companions were confronted with a stark contrast between two distinct environments. To their east was the hot steaming jungle of the Amazon and to the west were the high promontories that marked the start of the four thousand, five-hundred-mile-long Andean Mountain range. For some distance, they had passed barren hills and stark cliff faces on the western side of the river. Strangely, as they wound their way further along this great bend, they were confronted with a mountain peak that was not barren like others. It was covered in the same swampland vegetation that they had been seeing along the entire length of the eastern side of the Río Marañón.

Dense steam rose up from the river, engulfing the boats in a thick misty shroud. The paddlers could just discern a new island that lay ahead of them smack dab in the center of the river. It too was covered in jungle, but the vegetation appeared to Penelope as being slightly different, more exaggerated; thick long-stemmed plants dominated, with large craning blossoms that drooped down like oversized banana flowers. There was nothing like them on either shore of the Río Marañón.

As Penelope's small flotilla moved deeper into this twist of the river, Sir Ernest became very excited. He brought his paddle inboard and raised himself up to a standing position. His dugout rocked violently with this unsettling motion, causing his new bride to glower at him as though the tropical heat had just evaporated his senses.

"Sit down, dear, or you'll capsize us!" she said, in a tone full of wifely authority.

"No. No. Look dear," Shackleton said, adopting the apologetic tone of a husband, "Paititi!"

"Where? I don't see it." Ada remarked, looking confused and beginning to believe her diagnosis concerning the tropical heat.

"Just to the right of the island, you will see several large rocks. Watch as the haze moves about them. It's an old river landing. Let your eyes move up from there, about twenty feet or so, and you'll see what must be the bottom of a gate. Look carefully, the whole thing comes into view intermittently as the fog ebbs and flows about it."

"Yes! I see it." Now she, too, rose to her feet as their canoe began to turn and drift backwards. "Billy," she hollered across the river to the other canoe, "Paititi, it is there!" she pointed. "Can you see it?"

Billy Bowlegs looked intently at the haze about the shore, then nodded. Adding with a shout, "I see it all right. It's Inti's Gate."

"Right over there, Penelope," Belle exclaimed, "Can you see it?

"What? Where?" Penelope questioned. "I see nothing but jungle."

"Do what Sir Ernest suggested," Belle Starr insisted. "Follow up from those rocks and look through the gaps in the mist. It will come together for you."

Penelope stared hard but saw nothing. She shook her head, "We have to get closer. It must be my eyes." Billy and Belle began to paddle hard to get her closer to the spot so she might get a better look, as Ada and Ernest came up following close astern.

The island now lay amidships with the rock quay close on their right. And even though most of the fog had burned off, Penelope could still not see the gate that they were all so excited about.

Billy held out his paddle, pointing to the exact spot where the gate stood, "There. Right there. You see it now, right?"

"No, I'm afraid I do not. Can you develop myopia in a dream? I must be losing my eyesight."

"Pishtaco," Billy said with growl. "It is not your eyes, Penelope. He's in your brain manipulating and distorting what is out here. You are going to have to fight him. Drive him out! Or you will be no better than blind when you confront him!"

"You're right but I need to see him to get at him. This won't do. He has to be up there somewhere looking down at us casting his spells at me. Get us to that island over there. I'll climb up the high ground and just might be able to see where he is hiding up there."

Both boats soon fetched up upon the shore of the island and were quickly tied off on some dense roots that bordered the length of the island like a wall of wicker. Billy and Sir Ernest drew out their machetes and hacked a path through the dense undergrowth until they had cleared a route to the top of the small hill that Penelope had pointed out. There the combined crews assembled to gaze upward to the top-most crag of the great cliff of Paititi.

"Anyone see anything?" Penelope exclaimed.

Billy shook his head as everyone else peered up at the distant rock formations.

"He's hiding up there somewhere. But I can't see that far to tell where. We're too far away to see a movement or a shift in the shadows. That wizard is hunkered down somewhere. The mighty lord of Paititi has the balls of a hen. A hen with no huevos!" Billy yelled upward. "I say you just blast at the cliff face and hope you don't create a lot of parrots for all of your trouble."

Penelope took his advice and raised her hands upward to a likely spot for Pishtaco to be lurking, then she let it rip. The skulls of her fingernails glowed with a brilliance that they had never shown before. Even her gaucho boots glowed with the magic coming from her ten skull-painted toenails. Her fingernails were so blinding she couldn't bear to look at them. This time the fire that was expelled from her fingertips was much more concentrated, like laser beams or a death ray from a classic 1950s Sci-Fi movie.

Boom! A bit of the high steep face of the cliff vaporized into a cloud of dust.

"Can you see the gate now?" Ada inquired.

"No, nothing but greenery."

"Then keep trying till you do."

Boom! Boom! Boom! Penelope's fingernails began firing off successive shots. Shelling the cliff with her magic, puffs of smoke were erupting everywhere around its peak. Every couple of salvos or so she'd look down to see if the gate had yet appeared, then readjust her aim and begin to fire again.

Of course, Pishtaco was up there, surrounded by hundreds of headless chickens that he had been forced to sacrifice to help him blind Penelope to the sight of the gate. He had managed to avoid the barrage by ducking whenever he felt a surge in the magical properties of the atmosphere. Though he had been cowering behind a rock, he couldn't resist gazing down upon these overconfident upstarts and grabbing bits and pieces of their conversations as they echoed up from the base of the cliff. This was great fun, especially since he knew what was going to happen next.

"It's no use," Penelope sighed. "I think my fingers are shot. They are getting very tired."

"Let them rest awhile," Ada said, encouragingly. "We'll make camp here for the night. No point in us trying to get up there today anyway. It's just too late in the day. You can take another crack at him when you think you are again ready for it."

"I'm not sure I will ever be. My fingers really hurt," Penelope said as she held both hands out in front of her, as if she was examining her cuticles after returning from Carmen's Get Nailed, Spa and Beauty Salon.

Boom! Her left ring finger unexpectedly went off like a Roman candle. A bolt of flame arched up into the air and then crashed down onto the cliff face. It caught Pishtaco by surprise. He had no idea it was coming. The first blast caught him right between the eyes of his golden mask, which sent a whirling ball of fire into his brainpan. There it whizzed about circling his skull's inner circumference where bone meets brain. He was poleaxed. With a deafening screech that could be heard well below on the island, he felt his legs and arms shoot outward. His body crashed backwards upon the rocks as all of his ancient brain cells discharged at once. Half a millennium of memory came cascading through his head. He lay upon the stone twitching as the fireball continued its orbit inside of his head.

"I see it!" Penelope screeched. "It's there!" Now it was her turn to point.

Yes! Yes! That's it!" Billy shouted encouragingly.

A huge stone gate loomed before her about a third of the way up the mountain. It was made of giant stone boulders cut to lock into one another without any need for mortar.

In the center was a huge wooden door that appeared to have been firmly closed for centuries. Moss grew over and across the seam between the wooden gate and the stone that surrounded it. Beyond the mere size of the structure, what set it apart from any structure she had ever seen, was the massive lintel, and in the center of this lintel was the image of the sun god, Inti, cut deeply into the stone.

——— «◇» ———

The fireball inside Pishtaco's head lost its force. It faltered and fell deep into his brain, where it hissed and spat and finally died out. Pishtaco slowly regained control of his consciousness. He crawled up upon one of the rocks that he had previously peered over and again gazed down upon his adversary. Then, beneath his plumed, golden mask, his lips curled upward into a smile. His head contained half a millennium of memories, and only one was now of any importance. He would latch onto that memory for the time being, just in case Sach'amama failed.

He now turned his attention back down upon the Rio Marañón. For, he knew what was going to happen next.

——— «◇» ———

A high-pitched whine mysteriously began to reverberate throughout the little island. The little bones within Penelope's ears began to vibrate sympathetically with this peculiar sound. She felt like her body was going numb. And, even if Ada and Ernest, Belle and Billy might or might not have had tiny bones tucked away deep inside their phantom ears, the effect was the same. In fact, it was more so. Penelope was able to fight the sound, push through it, as though she was resisting a stiff wind. However, the others were paralyzed by the buzzing as far as Penelope could tell. It made her wonder if the noise had found the place in her brain where they all lurked and had managed to numb it, like an injection of Novocain into the gum surrounding an abscessed tooth.

After a struggle, Penelope managed to will herself out from the envelope of noise to regain her mobility. She moved towards the source of the sound, at the far end of the island, upriver from where they had landed.

At the very tip of the island there seemed to be two little peninsulas, long and narrow, like causeways, but leading nowhere. The sound was coming from there…,or just below there. Large bubbles were making froth upon the surface of the Rio Marañón exactly where the slivers of land ended. As each bubble surfaced, it burst open, releasing more of the mesmerizing sound that was coming up from the bottom of the river.

As Penelope placed her boot at the beginning of the peninsula to her left, everything swiftly changed. Without warning, the two slivers of land rose up out of the water. She stepped back in horror. The sight was more terrifying than that of Chinkirma Mama pulsating with electrical death in the night. Here before her were twin necks with twin serpent heads towering high above her. Huge fangs dripping, with gallons of river mud, opened wide above her head. As four large, deadly eyes peered down at her, four giant ears fanned the air about them.

A guttural laugh arose from the twin serpent's belly, coursing up their throats. Penelope could feel the sound moving under her feet towards their open mouths and guessed that she was standing somewhere upon their chest. The only sound was the crude laughter; her traveling companions were all silent, still frozen, like they had been in Xuphuri's camp, as if they had been turned to stone.

"Well, she's a game one, isn't she?" The right serpent head said, inclining her head to the left.

"Apparently so. I see why she makes Pishtaco so nervous. Never had anyone resist our song before. Quite something, that. And look, she glows. How about that?"

"Who or what are you?" Penelope demanded, stamping her foot upon an upper rib.

"My, she is annoying," the left head said to the right. She then craned her neck downward so that her head was level with Penelope's. "You know I rarely talk to my food. But since you've gotten this far and managed to evade Pishtaco's very best magic, perhaps I'll place you above a light snack and give you the respect one might have for haute cuisine. We are Sach'amama."

"And what is that?" Penelope imperiously demanded.

"Oh, the arrogance of food these days," the left head said to the right.

The right nodded in sympathy, but then turned her attention back to Penelope. "We are Sach'amama, the mother of this great forest you see about you. It is all our children — the trees, the birds, the insects, the animals, all of it — stretching from these massive mountains, down the great rivers to the sea. Now, just say that you are impressed, and we will get on with the digestion of you."

"No! You are not going to eat her!" An arrow streaked upward and impaled the right nostril of the right head of Sach'amama.

"Ouch! How did you get free?"

"You're not the only one who has some magic, you dumb-ass, two-headed snake!" Billy Bowlegs said, shaking his bow. He then turned to Penelope, "Run! You rescued me; now I'm going to rescue you!"

But Penelope didn't run. "Thank you, Billy, but I am not going to run. I've magic of my own and who knows, I might just turn them into parrots."

The right head then said, "Oh how romantic. I love romance. Apparently, they like to rescue one another from the jaws of death. Perhaps it heightens their passion. How I hate to break up a set but let's start with this bit of fluff, we then can eat the rest as appetizers and have the one with the red sombrero as our entrée."

With that, she reached down and grabbed the squirming Billy Bowlegs up into her jaws.

"Oh please, please don't eat him," Penelope implored.

"Hahaha," the left head laughed as the head right tightened down on her grip. "Tell you what, we might eat him and we just might not. But let me propose a little problem. You'll have to guess what both of us intend on doing with him to get him back. We might want to let him go. We might not. And be warned, it's hard to get both of us to agree on anything. But let's say we do agree on this occasion, what will it be? Don't answer quickly. Think about it. And, to make this even more interesting for you, let me add that if you guess wrong, we will, eat him and you, and those other friends of yours who are all on our back. And let me assure you that you'll never be able to turn us into parrots before we do that."

"But how do I know that if I guess right, you'll keep your word?" Penelope insisted.

"Well, I am a goddess, that should count for something..." Sach'amama's right head hissed as her long tongue darted out from under the clasped body of Billy Bowlegs. "Sorry," said the left head, "I meant to say we are a goddess." She then looked down at Penelope and explained with a bit of embarrassment, "Having two minds and just one body can be a bit confusing."

"Oh, I know," said Penelope. "Try it with six or even seven."

The left head seemed puzzled by this remark but chose to let it pass. "Where was I? Oh yes, of course we do lie on occasion, but not too often. If we were lying to you that would make all of this too easy and a bit silly and so boring. We can't always have our way... no excitement in that. Chance has to come into play to liven things up. So, what will it be? Come, come, you have to choose."

Penelope began to breathe deeply and hurriedly, as she looked into the eyes of the left head and then the right. She couldn't make up her mind what to say and was losing her patience. She wanted to use logic. She knew that it was there. She remembered this problem from somewhere. Where? Then it occurred to her.

"It's a paradox. The crocodile paradox!" she blurted out.

The right head tossed Billy into the air and the left dutifully caught him. "No crocodiles here, we ate them all for lunch while we waited for you."

The left head tossed Billy back into the jaws of the right so she could speak, "Ha! You are on to something. What do you know of paradoxes?"

"You've presented me with one — the crocodile's paradox. I had this in my junior year's logic course. The problem involves a fallacy of logic. It goes that there was a father whose son was caught by a crocodile. The father begged the crocodile to return his child, just like I'm begging you to do the same. The crocodile offers a bargain, it pledges to return the child if the father can guess if he will eat the boy or not. If the father guesses the crocodile will give back his son, he may or may not have guessed right. So, if he guessed wrong, his son will be eaten. But, if he guesses that the crocodile will eat his son, the crocodile is in a bind. If he intended on eating the boy, he must give him back. But, if he didn't intend on eating the boy what does the crocodile do since the father had guessed wrong?"

At first, the right head of Sach'amama shook with bewilderment. Then, she tried to speak while clutching Billy between her teeth. But her words came out as confused and unintelligible mumblings.

The left head then offered to explain, "She's very good with poetry, you know. And, her vocabulary is much more extensive than mine, but when it comes to math and logic, she's on the same level with those crocodiles of yours. But to be truthful, I had forgotten that one. I would have never suggested it if I had. Must be getting old…well I am, as old as the world. Everything is getting rundown these days. Do you know Achilles and the Tortoise?"

"Oh yes, my favorite. From Zeno of Elea, fifth century B.C. Achilles is racing a tortoise. Achilles gives the tortoise a head start, but Achilles is much faster, so he must win. Since there are an infinite number of points he must cross to even catch up to the tortoise, he can never win. All the while, the tortoise is steadily advancing to the finish. Therefore, since we cannot get between point A and B due to an inconceivable number of finite points in-between, motion is illusory and everything associated, including our existence, must be."

"Yes! Yes!" nodded the left head enthusiastically, as the right rolled her eyes skyward. "All illusory, quite correct! Well, I am quite impressed Ms. Penelope Gertrude Augusta Farquhar, is it?

"Miss"

"Oh yes, Miss. Sorry."

"Well, job well done. You know, I'm now disinclined that we should eat the little fellow here."

This statement caused Sach'amama's right head to launch into a vehement mumbling protest, due to the fact that Billy Bowlegs body was acting like a sock that had been stuffed into her mouth — only his spoonbill feather could be seen, vibrating between her lips.

"No. No. Let me handle this. There's more here than you think...or even I had thought."

The right head rolled her eyes, but she did as she was asked and did calm down a bit. The left craned her neck downward so that she was eyeball-to- eyeball with Miss Farquhar. It seemed to Penelope, as the hot foul reptilian breath passed over her, that Sach'amama was examining every crevice of her through the pupil of her eye.

"Oh yes...thought so," the left said as she raised her neck back up. She then turned to her right head. "Drop him."

The right head offered a few muffled objections, but the left was emphatic, "Drop him!"

The right complied, and Billy fell to the ground, unharmed except he was drenched in the serpent's slobber. Before the right could launch into another complaint, Sach'amama's left head added, "However you might eat her instead."

The right head of Sach'amama was pointing in the direction of Belle Starr, who was still held trapped by Sach'amama's spell.

Eagerly, the right head's maw descended upon her, and Belle disappeared into Sach'amama's belly in one long gulp.

"Belle! Belle! You ate Belle, you horrible big-eared snake!"

Sach'amama laughed, "I would have hoped that you could have thought of a better insult, but you must be getting tired from your journey — odd that the people in your party keep getting gobbled up. You'd best go deal with Pishtaco. He only eats small children. But to be honest with you, Belle wasn't very filling. Not really worth the effort."

As Penelope stood looking in horror at the beast, Sach'amama's right head turned to her other head and asked, "What now? Do we eat all of the rest except for Billy and Penelope, since you obviously have a soft spot for these two?"

"No, but we would be doing her a favor," she said nodding towards Penelope. "We should go. This battle is between Miss Farquhar and Pishtaco. We really should never have interceded on behalf of that old magician in the first place."

As she said this, the twin heads and their gigantic snake's body slithered out of the Rio Marañón, forcing the now fully awake Countess Lovelace, Billy Bowlegs and Sir Ernest Shackleton, to follow Penelope's lead and scramble for the canoes. They had just managed to slide them off of her back, and into the river as Sach'amama slithered into a great hole that she had constructed ages ago on the forested side of the Rio Marañón. The tip of her tail was the only thing showing by the time the party had crossed over to the ancient stone quay that jutted out before the great gate of Paititi. As the boats were secured to the dock, Penelope took a long look back at that last bit of Sach'amama and saw it disappear beneath the ground, and as Sach'amama sunk under the Amazon forest, so too did the remains of Belle Starr, the famous bandit queen.

CHAPTER FIFTEEN

Paititi

As Sach'amama left the river, a tidal wave of water tumbled off of her back. It radiated out from where the goddess had been, forming into waves that now vigorously slammed into either shore of the Rio Marañón. An oily slick had been left behind. It gently rocked in the middle of the river.

Belle Starr was gone. Penelope thought about this and the other deaths that had occurred on this journey. As she did so, the blood vessels near the surface of Penelope's skin widened, and blood rushed into her face as she reddened with rage. The adrenal glands within her body began to pump vigorously as her liver dumped massive amounts of glucose into her system. It was fight or flight time! And Penelope Gertrude Augusta Farquhar had made up her mind as to which it was going to be.

She spun round to where Billy, Sir Ernest and the Countess Lovelace were standing. They had assembled beneath the Great Gate of Paititi and were now observing the transformation in their dream host's physical appearance with great astonishment. The change was quite dramatic, much more so than donning the new clothing she had recently acquired. She hadn't sprouted fangs or horns. Her face wasn't that of a snake or a dragon. No, it was the same face...but it expressed an entirely different attitude. Its muscles were set hard and angular, and there was no sense of joy or pity or tenderness, for that matter, in her eyes. She was angry, very angry. It was apparent that she was no longer

involved in this quest just because Xuhpuri had told her that
it was the only way out of her dream.

She looked into their eyes probingly, and then shouted,
"Pishtaco dies! He dies today!"

"PISHTACO DIES! HE DIES TODAY! PISHTACO DIES!
HE DIES TODAY! PISHTACO DIES! HE DIES TODAY!"

The words echoed upward off the ancient cliff face of
Paititi towards the craning ears of Pishtaco, who had been
peering down upon the party, amazed that they had escaped
the power of Sach'amama, when he heard Penelope Farquhar
pronounce his death. He thought that she just might be able
to pull it off — the witch had repeatedly survived his magic,
killed Chinkirma Mama and beguiled Sach'amama. And
now, she was declaring that she would end his four hundred
and nineteen years of evil rapacity, dissimulation and gross
cupidity upon this very day. This unnerved him. So, Pishtaco
abandoned his observation post among the rocks high above
the great Gate of Paititi and fled towards the inner part of his
city. He had an idea, a desperate idea, but it just might buy
him a little time.

Penelope's surviving mental aberrations looked upon
her in wide-eyed astonishment. Then, seeing her come
marching toward them, they quickly moved to either side of
the immense wooden door that barred the main road leading
up to Paititi.

"Hey? What? If anyone is going to get rid of you guys it's
going to be me — not a fat eel, nor a two-headed snake or
some old — not quite dead —wizard covered in gold!"

"Well, I guess that's reassuring," Billy rejoined. "We'll do
our best to keep on your good side."

Penelope just snorted as she trudged past him. Stopping
in front of the gate, she looked it up and down and then
asked, "How long ago do you think it was when this thing
was last opened?"

"Hundreds of years?" Ava speculated. "No idea, really.
But I don't think the Chachapoya use it much these days."

"Humph, well maybe the four of us can give a go at
pushing it open before I try to move it with my fingernails. I
want to keep all the juice that's in them for pretty boy up top."

The four formed a parallel line in front of the gate. Penelope then held out her arms with her palms facing forward. The other three did the same. "Okay, on three we rush it. One - Two - Three!"

Four sets of hands rammed into the surface of the gate. It shattered. Large chunks of wood and a shower of splinters came raining down. A cloud of sawdust caused Penelope to wheeze and cough violently. As the air cleared, Sir Ernest dusted himself off and reached for a chunk of gate from the large pile of debris that had accumulated around them.

"Dry rot," he ventured after examining it. "Too much fungus in these parts — not clean and pristine like the Antarctic. Billy, why couldn't you have taken us to the South Pole? I don't care much for this heat."

"Because I didn't want to us to starve and have to eat sled dogs, like you did."

"They didn't taste that bad you know. Much better than penguin. However, when I ordered that the ship's cat, Mrs. Choppy, be prepared for dinner, there was nearly a mutiny."

"You ate your dogs and a cat?" Ada said with alarm.

"Yes, dear, we were marooned and starving."

"I'm not comfortable with that. You should have mentioned this before the wedding," she said with a half-smile.

"Oh...of course...sorry my love. But anyhow, you are right, this gate hasn't been used for centuries."

"Don't try and ingratiate yourself with me now. I think your crew would have been right if they have clapped you in irons."

"But my love..."

"I do weddings," Penelope interrupted, "not divorces. And right now I'm on my way to a funeral — Pishtaco's. Are you coming?"

Her remark put an abrupt end to any further banter concerning Sir Ernest's Antarctic culinary habits. Everyone sheepishly fell in line to begin the steep ascent up the old road that the Chachapoya had cut into the rock face. Ironically, they were following along the same route that Siwar Q'enti had traveled to awaken Pishtaco, but with quite the opposite intention. Soon they were passing through the outlying villages of Paititi, long abandoned, with terraced gardens whose shapes could barely be discerned through the dense covering of vegetation. Spreading canopies of trees had replaced the roofs of the ancient houses.

Only the structures that had been sculpted into the rock face seemed to be free of the omnipresent plant life. Most of them were high above the road; no doubt with a commanding view of the Rio Marañón. They were in a series, one after another, row upon row, and gave the appearance of a giant honeycomb made of stone. Penelope guessed that they were rough-cut tombs that had once held the Warriors of The Clouds' dead. Below those lifeless nests, built against the basalt, bounding the left side of the road, were two-tone whitewashed houses, that had been painted in shades of rose just below the windows. They looked sort of like roadside inns for weary travelers making the mountain trek up to Paititi.

Here, Penelope stopped to turn and look behind. Billy Bowlegs was bringing up the rear. She shouted to him "Hey slowpoke, Mr. I-Have-All-The-Answers-Guy, what do you think those were for? I wouldn't have imagined that the Chachapoya had invented motels."

Billy walked over to one of the houses along the road and peeked in through an open window.

"These people, like the Inca, found it very hard to let go of their dead. They treated them as though they were alive. But apparently nobody is at home now."

Penelope frowned, "What a creepy lifestyle these Chachapoya had", then added, "I certainly can think of better places to live when I'm dead. Just place my mummified remains among my tea roses, which if all goes well, I'll be seeing them by tomorrow morning."

In all there were six of these accommodations that once held the most notable Chachapoya corpses. Each was placed just a small distance from the next. Billy Bowlegs had taken it upon himself to go first. He walked up to each doorway or window and peered in, making a big tongue-in-cheek announcement to Penelope that there were no evil spirits inside. His antics continued till he walked up to the last house in the line. As Billy was readying himself to thrust his head through yet another window, a head appeared in the window.

"Shit!" Billy exclaimed, as he stumbled backwards.

"Don't shoot Miss Farquhar! I've heard that is an expression of your people. I do hope I've gotten it right," Pishtaco said as he thrust his hands out the window as though he was surrendering. "Forgive me for not taking the time to have a little chat with you earlier, but your motivation was unclear to me. Now I think I have everything buttoned down in my mind. Perhaps we should have a little parlay before you attempt to destroy me? Please note that I did stress the verb attempt. Not trying to be arrogant, but the matter of my destruction remains to be tested."

Penelope had her hands and nails at the ready. "Pishtaco, why shouldn't I blast you right now down to Ukhu Pacha? I've been told that Supay is very eager to get his hands on you."

"Yes. Yes. That is no doubt the case. He is not one of my fans. However, I am a tad unclear as to what that has to do with you. Supay and this entire world you have managed to plop yourself into is a very long way away from the Lorenzo de Zavala School of Science in Austin. Again, another Spanish name... But no matter, the fact is that I think you've been duped, Miss Farquhar, misguided by your present company. You and I have been divided by their treachery. I confess that it took me too long to reason out what was taking place. If I had discovered this earlier, I would have made a civilized attempt to contact you. This is to my regret. If you could see beneath my mask, you would now be noting a kindly, and I would add, benign smile. For, I do bear you no malice, Miss Farquhar. You see, we have both been betrayed."

"Pishtaco, I'm really getting the urge to incinerate you like I incinerated Chinkirma Mama. I really don't want to hear whatever nastiness you are cooking up."

"Oh yes, poor Chinkirma Mama. Not very ecofriendly of you to kill such an exotic wetland creature. I imagine that the biology department at your university would give you a low mark for that one. And, of course, you could incinerate me as well," Pishtaco said, stammering through the mouth hole in his mask. "If I were you, I might very well entertain that notion. I am not a wizard to be trifled with. Yes, I certainly have gotten older, and my powers are weaker, the cause of which I would like to share with you... But I'm getting ahead of myself. If you destroy me, you've been promised by... what's his name...oh of course, Xuhpuri... odd that I've never heard of this Xuhpuri until recently. Now the forest is alive with talk of him. But I digress; I've been told that Xuhpuri says that when you kill me your dream will be over. Being out of this dream is something you seem to really want?"

"Yes. But as I've mentioned, I've developed a real hankering to destroy you as well."

"Blast him while you can, Penelope!" Billy Bowlegs shouted. "He's just beguiling you. Weakening you with words!"

"Kill him!" Ada barked, as Sir Ernest picked up a large stone and made a run at Pishtaco, as if he could smash the sorcerer's brains out.

Pishtaco simply twiddled one of his fingers in the air and the three of them suddenly slumped over, their heads dangling above the tops of their feet.

"That has happened to them far too often!" Penelope exclaimed. "I'm sick and tired of everyone around here messing with my voices! You guys either turn them off or stick them into your mouths!"

"Calm down, Miss Farquhar. I will restore them in a moment! And I appreciate your anger. It is understandable — I have put you through a lot of bother. So, has Xuhpuri, for that matter. But in my case, it was misguided. You must hear me out. We have much to discuss."

"Okay, Pishtaco, move out of that tomb and sit down upon your hands in the middle of this road. If you even think of moving a finger towards me or Billy, Ada or Ernest, I will turn you into ash. I'll let you have your final words, then it will be time for you to go see Supay."

Pishtaco did as he was told. His lean frame bending down at the knee joints until he fell backwards upon upturned hands.

"Is this what you had in mind, Miss Farquhar?"

She grunted her assent as she trained her glowing nails upon the eye slits of his mask.

"Most kind of you, Miss Farquhar. May I continue?"

"Go ahead but don't take too long. I'm getting anxious to wake up in my bed."

"Of course, you are. It has all been quite an ordeal for you. But have you considered that if perchance I kill you, you might just wake with a yelp in that four-poster bed of yours on Guadalupe Street? Yes, I know where you live. You see, Miss Farquhar, I have been checking up on you. Done a lot of homework."

"Yeah? Well, I have never had any privacy before, so why would I expect any now? Get on with it."

"How awful. But as I was saying, Miss Farquhar, there you are bolt upright, forehead beading with sweat, pulse racing and then comes the calm — the relief of knowing that it was all just a very bad dream...or was it? You will, of course, question that. At times, we all do. During the day, we construct a logical world, but late at night we pull it apart into absurdity. Yet, which is the real one? You must have considered the question?"

Penelope just frowned at him.

"Well, I did, lying in my tomb as people moved away from Paititi and the memory of me faded. There I was, weakening, stretched out on a stone slab, only perceiving the passage of time through a succession of putrid odors that came off of my rotting flesh. Miss Farquhar, I went from smelling like rotten eggs to spoilt cabbage and finally to an odor akin to garlic gone bad. And I assure you that these stretches between the various stages of my own putrescence gave me plenty of time to think upon such matters. Then, sometime after the gaseous bugs had all finished dining on me, and my scent stabilized to that of my old goatskin sandals, I realized that our heads are nothing more than slop buckets that catch the discarded thoughts of the gods. You see, there is no reality beyond these scraps and parings that the great god Viracocha orders to be thrown down to us ..."

"Did I just see your right wrist move? Do you think you can distract me so easily with all of your baloney? Beguile and then kill me? Pishtaco, I'm not going to allow you to do that. The real question here is why am I wasting so much time before getting around to killing you?"

"No, no... please! It was an involuntary reflex. That's all. I was merely about to suggest that no matter what happens, there is a possibility that you will find yourself again in your room in Austin. Whereas the rest of us may just vanish — will-o'-the- wisps of your overactive dream state."

"Yes, but I'm sure that Ada and Sir Ernest and Billy Bowlegs will be returning with me to my couch with the psychotherapist. They've been traveling with me for some time."

"Indeed, they have! Which brings me to the topic of our little chat. My dear Miss Farquhar, I regret to inform you that the Chachapoya have settled in your brain. And, in so remote of a place, I would have never have thought to seek them out... I mean the Bremond Block of downtown Austin, Texas," He chuckled adding," Penelope...May I call you Penelope?"

"No."

"Of course not, I do understand. Miss Farquhar, the Chachapoya have colonized your head like the Spanish colonized the lands of the Inca. I want you to think about all of those years, medicated, analyzed, trussed up in mechanical restraints at the East Hampton Psychiatric Center, and to realize it had nothing to do with you or your weak father's suicide or you stabbing that abusive mother of yours, or any psychiatric condition of your own."

"That's crazy talk...I mean I take full responsibility for my own mental imbalances... Hey, what's the scam? Your magic isn't working, so you are going to attempt to manipulate me with verbal trickery? And, if that doesn't work, do you intend on garroting me like you did your grandmother?"

"Oh, my dear grandmother, Ciqui Ollco. I see that you have been checking up on me as well. You know, I'm still fond of my grandmother. So many centuries have passed since I murdered her, but my love for her has not diminished with time. Of course, I had to have her garroted. What else was I going to do? I had learned all I could from her. It would have been foolish, in fact overly sentimental, to have allowed her to live. Couldn't have a second-rate sorceress meddling in my work. She started to think she had some control over me due to being my grandmother. But I assure you that I had it done lovingly — flowers strewn about her feet, musicians played a love ballad as the rope tightened."

Pishtaco began to laugh, a reedy laugh, which seemed to take a great deal of effort to force its way up through his decrepit windpipe. "Miss Farquhar, is it you who are trying to distract me? Make old Pishtaco angry? Get him all riled up so you can zap him and permanently shut him up? Apparently, I am touching upon a subject that you really don't want to know about? Do you enjoy having those voices in your head? It is understandable that you think that Pishtaco is dangling some bait in front of you before the trap comes down. But still, it is curious that you aren't more inquisitive. I mean, I have just told you that the Chachapoya colonized your head, and your reaction is to change the subject to me executing my grandmother. Perhaps you fear that I intend on taking them away from you? Well, let me assure you that I will. They're going back right to where they belong."

"All right, Pishtaco, spit it out. Let's see if you can do what Doctor Hernandez and a bunch of psychiatrists in East Hampton couldn't."

"Oh, but I now fear that by exposing the truth to you, it might make you lonely. You'll have to go out and make real friends."

Penelope's fingernails were heating up and glowing red.

"Ah...I see that I must come to my point," Pishtaco said, as he motioned to the whitewashed house that he had just come from. Would it surprise you if I told you that in this tomb was Billy Bowlegs and that the other five once belonged to Ada, the Countess Lovelace, Sir Ernest Shackleton, Belle Starr, Cecile Fatima and the one at the far end used to house the remains of René Descartes?"

"What?"

"Oh, I see that it does surprise you. Well of course it does. Why shouldn't it? Miss Farquhar, with some regret I must inform you of who they actually are. As you may know, while

I governed the Chachapoya, I enslaved them and attempted to obliterate their culture. This is how things are done if you want to destroy any vestiges of a people's rebellious nature, which the Chachapoya had so often demonstrated that they had. So, after the initial slaughter and intimidation, I went about annihilating everything they had ever taken pride in."

He looked up at Paititi's cliff face. "Those corpses in that beehive network of tombs the Chachapoya had carved out had to go. No ancestor worship or clan pride could be permitted. So, I tossed all non-essential mummies into the Rio Marañón. That was a lot of work but I actually found myself doing some of it myself — actually it was quite a bit of fun. Oh...I see that your nails are becoming very impatient. So, I should maybe get to the point."

Penelope gave a slow nod of agreement, adding dryly "Get on with it."

"Well, that far tomb, the first one you passed, belonged to Orotongo, a huge man known as the bear. He was the first great Chachapoya shaman. He was very powerful and much revered. His essence was deep in this culture, and I knew that it would be hard to erase his memory, that of other five from his people's consciousness. I realized that I might throw all six of these wizard's mummies into the Rio Marañón and watch them float away and their spirits would still come back here to help empower their people. What a thorny problem."

Pishtaco rhapsodized about his accomplishments. "It occurred to me that the best way to control this situation was to build a great temple to me. Of course, I had the Chachapoya build the other temples to the gods before mine. Our gods had to come first. They have eyes to see, ears to hear, noses that smell and skin that feels. They are not just illusory concepts. You cannot play them easily. They know what you are up to. So first came the twelve temples. The one to the far west of my grand municipal square for the gods I had dedicated to Mama Killa. Opposite to her to the far east, is the temple that I had built to my beloved Inti. On the north side of the square the temple of Pachamama, goddess of the Earth. The other eight temples I clustered on either side of where my two great boulevards crossed —

Kuychi, the rainbow god — Mama Sara, mother of maize — Kon, the god of rain —Catequil, god of lightning, to the south. Across the way, flanking the northern road, I had the temples to Paryaqaqa the god of water, Ekkeko, the god of wealth, Urcuchillay, lord of animals…and, of course, there is one there for Sach'amama, whom I believe you have met. I topped this whole magnificent project off with the grandest of all temples, the one to me, which was built on the far end of the southern boulevard. I had the Chachapoya place it directly over their most sacred spot, the well to Ukhu pacha.

Here is where your friends come in. My temple was constructed with seven layers, with my remains intended for the top of the well and each layer going down, successively, to house one of their shamans. Thus, I brilliantly incorporated their power into my own. As long as they were stuck under, me, the people revered the spot and consequently, forced to revere me. My strength grew and I quickly learned how to dominate the souls of Orotongo, Alliyma, Ussun, Ozcollo, Huallpa and Atoc. That is for a while I did. Then, as I have said, I grew weak. The memory of me was fading. But somehow these third-rate magicians learned to grow stronger. How did this happen, Miss Farquhar? How?"

"Beats me, Pishtaco. Something you ate? Bad cabbage cooked in rancid garlic with rotten eggs?"

"Ha! Ha! You have a delightful sense of humor, Miss Farquhar, sarcastic and biting, just like another acquaintance of mine, Atoc. You know, one of the six Chachapoya shamans that I removed from these tombs and transferred to my own. You see, recently this Atoc made a joke at my expense. He said that I have the balls of a hen — a hen with no huevos. Isn't that funny, Miss Farquhar?"

Penelope knew he was making a point but at first it didn't register. Then, she placed where she had heard it. Pishtaco read the drawing realization on her face.

"Yes, that's right, Billy Bowlegs said that. How odd that a Seminole Indian would be using a Peruvian expression? I guess culture these days spreads everywhere and across the world. Or could it be…?" Pishtaco then gave a little chuckle. "Yes, your Billy Bowlegs is my prisoner, Atoc. You see Miss

Farquhar I'm neither your enemy nor your tormentor. You have Orotongo, Alliyma, Ussun, Ozcollo, Huallpa and Atoc to blame for your condition. The voices in your head came from some Chachapoya mummies that I stripped down and placed in bags — the bags of old bones that I had placed below my crypt. I do apologize for the intrusion into your life. You must believe this, if I had known what they had been up to I would have instantly put a stop to it. Thanks to their manipulations of your head, you spent years in a mental institution, pumped with chemicals and placed in hospital restraints. They fed off of your thoughts and your life, because they had none of their own. Kept from Ukhu Pacha by me, and eventually forgotten by all but me, they must have reached out and found a mind that could receive them...that would be yours."

"I don't believe you. This is just some ploy to gain the upper hand and destroy us! It really is time for you to head to Ukhu Pacha, Pishtaco!"

"Oh, that might be easy, Miss Farquhar, I mean, if you can pull it off. I confess that I became considerably weaker after this little adventure of yours dispatched Orotongo, that would be René Descartes to you — Alliyma was your Cecile Fatima and Ozcollo, your wild west girl, Belle Starr, to Ukhu Pacha. But perhaps, their absence now makes you a little weaker too? Now we have these three to consider." Pishtaco pointed to Sir Ernest, Ada and Billy, their heads still dangling over their feet, swaying ever so slightly. "I know them as Atoc, the youngest and last to have died of this lot, and the other two, your star-crossed lovers, the Countess Lovelace and her adventurous swain, Sir Ernest Shackleton are actually Huallpa, full of joy and Ussun, the plum eater. Oddly, they were, here too, star-crossed lovers who died of fever — a plague of some sort had hit Paititi. It was so kind of you, Miss Farquhar, to help them out with their wedding. Well, here we are, at the end of their stories. What should you and I do with them now?"

Penelope just stared at the three with her mouth agape, not quite prepared to take in all of what Pishtaco had just said.

"You know, I thought that Siwar Q'enti awoke me because you had come, just like the Spanish, for my gold...I mean, Inti's gold," he quickly added, as he looked toward the sun. "But that was not the case. You are here to do their dirty work — kill me and get my shamans destroyed in a way that would oblige Supay to welcome them into Ukhu Pacha. It still puzzles me why Viracocha commanded his hummingbird to wake me. Perhaps it was to make me aware of this Chachapoya plot? What puzzles me more is how did six wizards manage to crawl into your head. Should we ask Atoc how he did it? I think so."

Taking advantage of Penelope's apparent state of total confusion, Pishtaco jumped to his feet and began to walk in a tight circle around the slumped body of Billy Bowlegs. He then snapped his fingers. Billy rose up to his full height, and in the process, took a swing at Pishtaco, who nimbly backed away from the blow, with obvious anticipation that it would come. Pishtaco made some sort of sign with his hands, which again froze Billy into place...except for his thoughts and his voice.

"This is how he normally is in his cell, Miss Farquhar, but with far less meat on his bones. Atoc, we are just curious, how did you pull this off? Come, come, speak or I might do something nasty to Huallpa."

"No, you won't!" Penelope was starting to come to her senses. Raising her hands to draw a bead on Pishtaco's mask, she added, "When did I say you could get back on your feet? Back on the ground and sit on your hands again!"

"Sorry...sorry. Just trying to be of some help," Pishtaco said, as he lowered himself once again onto the surface of the road. "And so far, I believe I'm succeeding where Doctor Hernandez has failed.

Pishtaco then cautiously placed his hands under his rump and continued. "You know I wouldn't really hurt dear Huallpa ...I mean Ada. We have been together too long, though it does perplex me as to why you care. Anyway, I'm sure Mr. Bowlegs, won't refuse to enlighten you. I mean, what choice does he have since the truth of this matter has now been revealed to you by me, Pishtaco. Apparently, I'm your only real friend. Go ahead, don't be shy, take my friendly advice and ask old Atoc a few questions."

"Atoc!... I mean Billy! Is this true? Why? Why would you do this? Cripple a little girl like that?" Penelope was in disbelief, more saddened than angry.

Billy was shamefaced. It took him several attempts to speak and finally he said, "I'd like to say that it wasn't me and I had nothing to do with it, but I did. If it is any conciliation, and I doubt that it is, I was the last to join in."

"Speak up Atoc! Speak up! Miss Farquhar needs a full and detailed explanation concerning this appalling manipulation of a young child's life. Totally reprehensible, I must say, Atoc. Go on, speak up."

Though Billy was galled by Pishtaco's jabs, he summoned his dignity. Looking Penelope squarely in the eyes, he began to explain. "You have to understand that we all had been dead for centuries. At first, it didn't matter that we were still in Kay Pacha. Our people revered our memories, and to a certain extent, we still were able to participate in the lives of our people, the Chachapoya. Our bones were cared for, people made offerings to us, our skeletons were dressed up for public festivals, paraded through the streets and honored by all. Everyone came to consult with us. So many questions from all types of people were brought before us. We were very often able to help. We discovered that just because we were dead didn't mean we couldn't speak, and we did — through their dreams. We would crawl in their sleeping heads and stage our little fantasy plays. Our intervention helped them. So, what if we were being kept far away from Ukhu Pacha, we didn't care. We were still important to the living, even made friends with them. Our thoughts stayed with them. When they died some of them were able to stay with us for a while, until the memories of them had been lost to the living."

"Yes. Yes. Atoc, get to the point. We have been detaining Miss Farquhar far too long."

Billy Bowlegs glowered at Pishtaco, then swallowed his pride again to continue, "He's the one, Pishtaco is the reason why we did it. His army slaughtered the Chachapoya. As he likes to brag, he cleaned out the tombs — threw all of those living souls down into the Rio Marañón. He then had us carted off to the temple he had built for himself, which later served as his tomb. His magic was so much greater than ours. We could not stop him as he enslaved our powers and joined them with his own. We were now aiding, not only in the terror and subjugation of our own people, but in endless cruelties of anyone who crossed his path. And, to our frustration, Pishtaco wouldn't fade! Memories of him lived. He refused to go down to Ukhu Pacha, like every other thing that had ever lived. Pishtaco made sure that his legend thrived, kept alive as it was retold by the campfires in the jungle."

"Once again Atoc, could you hurry this up? By the time you are done the memory of the entire world will have faded and gone down to Ukhu Pacha."

"Eventually, Pishtaco had weakened enough atop his stone slab that his powers were kept alive only by bush gossip. When that happened, we had the freedom to cast our thoughts about, plunge our minds into our old memories, or even create our own dreams. This was all we could do while Pishtaco slept. We were entwined with him. The memory of the six sorcerers lived on, coupled with the memory of Pishtaco. His tale had become our tale and so we were not permitted to make that journey down to Ukhu Pacha."

"It was Orotongo who discovered you. He was most brilliant of the Chachapoya. He alone, not the Inca, invented the quipu, strings and knots, which he used to preserve history, and to compute the movements of the sun, the moon and stars. He was our greatest mathematician. So, when Orotongo discovered a mind — a mind very far away — a mind that would let him in whenever he wanted to be there, not just when she was sleeping, he entered it and stayed there for some time. When he eventually returned back to his thoughts in Pishtaco's tomb, he whispered to the rest of us about this strange new world. He had discovered a lonely girl with a mind gifted in mathematics — a lonely girl crushed by a domineering mother. So then, over a decade, one by one, all of us made our way into that exceptional but fragile little girl's head. However, Orotongo felt it best that we not reveal who we were. He said that knowing of our reality would crush her more than what had already happened to her. So, Orotongo had each one of us wait until you, Penelope, happened upon someone you were interested in — someone who no longer was alive..."

"But of course," Pishtaco interrupted. "Miss Farquhar, have you read some accounts about the six people who have been playing with your brain?"

"Biographies, yes," Penelope murmured, feeling ashamed over how willingly she had let the voices in.

"So Atoc...I mean, Mr. Bowlegs," Pishtaco said chuckling, "You insinuated yourselves into her mind by pretending to be the characters she was reading about?"

"Yes, not to make any excuses, Penny. Sorry, I meant Penelope — but it was agony for me to stay in my cell and hear, year after year, Orotongo, Alliyma, Ussun, Ozcollo and Huallpa tell of you and your world. I could see no way I could justify going to it. It was like being a candiru fish, a tiny vampire fish that stealthily enters someone's body and sucks its blood...but in this case, your thoughts. But then it occurred to me that we could manipulate you into coming here. That maybe someone who was actually alive, might be able to destroy Pishtaco with our help, and send him down to the waiting Supay. Perhaps then we would be free. Orotongo agreed to set all of this into motion if I would join him and the others.

Atoc hurried to add, "When I suggested that we should make plain who we were and what we wanted to do, he grew irritated, insisting that revealing too much to you, other than a fantastic and crazy dream, might cause you even further mental harm than we had already caused. He felt it best to just expand upon the craziness that you had become accustomed to rather than adding some new form of madness. And so, I agreed in hopes that we could destroy Pishtaco and free you as well."

"Ha! Ha! What a spin, Atoc," Pishtaco, exclaimed. You've always been a clever one. But I must say you had me going for a while. It was a nice try. When you announced that Supay had taken Orotongo and Alliyma, it really did throw me into a panic. Did the six of you know that by me having your dream-shapes destroyed, you would be received in Ukhu Pacha by Supay?"

Atoc shook his head, "No, at least, I didn't. I don't believe any of us knew how involved Penelope would become in crafting the dreams that we had concocted for her. She has this controlling nature. Everything in her house is just so. When we entered her mind, she did the same with us. We had to conform to being those people she had read about — taking us over utterly, like you do when you make up one of your spells. But the difference is that you would let go of us. She wouldn't. Orotongo, Alliyma, Ozcollo, Ussun, Huallpa and Atoc became René Descartes, Cecile Fatima, Belle Starr, Sir Ernest Shackleton, the Countess Lovelace, and Billy Bowlegs. Our sense of being was overridden. We were trapped in the fantasy that we had created. Only when we were summoned back by you to help with your magic, did we become ourselves again. Although we were still trapped within Penelope's reality, we simultaneously resided within your tomb, where you imprisoned us. I don't know why, but whenever you called us back Penelope's dreaming would stop. It was like you hit the pause button. I really think that she is comfortable with us in her head. When you were finished draining us of our magic, her mind would again seize hold of us. It is amazing but true, Miss Farquhar has a very strong spirit, apparently more powerful than our own. Perhaps that's why she is such a great sorceress? Perhaps that is why Orotongo chose her to kill you?"

"Wait a minute! I might be crazy but I'm not that crazy. No one could be that crazy," said Penelope.

"Yes, you are," Pishtaco interrupted. "Stop raving and please shut up."

"What do you mean shut up? Who do you think you are? I'm going to blast you so far into Ukhu Pacha, it will take Supay and all his demons digging with shovels to find you."

"No more threats, please. We will get to all of that destroying Pishtaco nonsense in just a moment. So, Orotongo had thought that Penelope was capable of doing me in? Ha!

What a fool. Seriously? This deranged woman?" he said as he contemptuously pointed at Penelope.

"Deranged! Okay, Pishtaco, here we go. You are meat!" Penelope shouted.

"Calm yourself Miss Farquhar, and think, why am I talking to Atoc right now instead of your laughable Mr. Bowlegs?" Pishtaco said, now rising to his feet. "Because your power is faltering. It began to falter when I started to poke holes in this illusion. Your dream is failing. You are becoming part of my reality."

"Yeah? Right! Tell it to Supay!" Penelope screamed as her nails heated up from black to hot tamale red, to a lacquer finish sunburst orange, reaching peak power with a shade of supernova white with glitter. Then, she let it rip! The combined exhaust of five F1 engines in a Saturn V rocket ship was like the flickering flame on a match head compared to the blistering fiery fury that now came from Penelope Farquhar's fingertips. Pishtaco was sheathed in fiery plasma of ionized gas. Nothing of him could be seen. Then it all came to an abrupt halt. Her scorching inferno seemed to get stuck. It was no longer blinding. In fact, it wobbled around Pishtaco as if it were encased in a terrine of gelatin.

Though Penelope thought nothing could have survived that initial blast, Pishtaco exited from what was now a gooey mess of supernatural powers, flicking off the bits and pieces of Penelope's magic that still clung to him as she looked on in amazement.

Pishtaco shook his head sympathetically and then said with a sigh, "I am afraid that is the best that you can do now. But there is no need for you to reproach yourself. We are too evenly matched. So, I'll be taking my wizards and be going home." He turned towards Atoc, who seemed shaken by the recent events. Before Atoc could speak, Pishtaco flexed a finger, instantly reverting Atoc, Ada Lovelace and Ernest Shackleton back to what they really were, three bags of bones. Pishtaco then reached down, picked up the bags and threw them over his left shoulder.

"Leave them here, Pishtaco. You've got your gold. Let them free. Please!" Penelope pleaded.

"Please? My-my you are desperate for a family, aren't you? But no — they come with me. I fear there will always be somebody coming over the Andes or up the Rio Marañón looking for Inti's gold and these old wizards will someday come in handy. My advice to you, Miss Farquhar, is that you leave this place and get on with your life."

"How? If I knew how, I would."

Pishtaco turned to the high cliff that dominated Paititi. "My guess is that you should throw yourself off that mountain. It might just do the trick. You could find that you wake up out of this dream and are back home...or you might be smashed upon the cliff face. That's what happens when I toss people from it. But with you? Well, give it a try."

Pishtaco then turned away from Penelope and began walking up the road towards the inner city and his tomb — with the three bags containing Billy, Ada and Ernest still over his shoulder, swaying with each one of his footsteps.

CHAPTER SIXTEEN

Ghosts of the Chachapoya

As Pishtaco disappeared into the vines and overgrowth that hung over the ancient road leading up to the God's temples and his tomb, the silence became unbearable. They were all gone. Penelope's mind was once again her own — her thoughts were now hers alone. She was free! Oh, how she had wished for this moment! But now that it had come, the sudden stillness was frightening — even more so was the lack of companionship. Yes, they were often irritating and meddlesome, but they were her voices — her confidants — her colleagues. They had worked together as a team to understand this strange world, as well as the equally bizarre one that they had left behind when they boarded a plane. Above all else, they were her friends...her only friends. And she was not going to let Pishtaco carry off what was left of them, even though they were just sacks of the old bones of rather deceitful Chachapoya wizards. They were her rather deceitful Chachapoya wizards, whose souls had shared her mind since she was a young girl, and she wasn't going to let go of them without a fight.

So, she followed after Pishtaco, though this proved challenging since the rainforest vegetation didn't give way as she climbed higher along the ancient route. However, the air did. Penelope was forced to maneuver her way through the dense jungle growth that seemed to heal itself and grow more abundant as she slashed and hacked at it in an attempt to get a glimpse of Pishtaco on his way back to his tomb.

With each step, she managed to take, Pishtaco took many more. Her lungs hurt, her breathing was labored, and she felt the need to retch from lack of oxygen.

Penelope had to stop and take a rest. She needed to breathe in as much air as she could before she could take up the trail again. Sluggishly, she moved on. Even though her going was slow, at one point she did manage to catch sight of Pishtaco. Summoning all of her strength, she cried out after him. It was a feeble shout, but Penelope knew that Pishtaco had heard her. Though he didn't turn and face her, he did make an exaggerated movement with his hips, so that the three bags of bones hung over his shoulder rocked back and forth.

After several hours, Penelope finally arrived at the hidden plaza atop Paititi. At first, she thought the heavily forested mounds that surrounded her were nothing more than very large, odd-shaped hillocks. Then she remembered how Pishtaco had fairly gushed about his architectural achievements.

"The one to the far west of my grand municipal square for the gods I had dedicated to Mama Killa. Opposite to her to the far east, is the temple that I had built to my beloved Inti. On the north side of the square rises the temple of Pachamama, goddess of the Earth. The other eight temples I clustered on either side of where my two great boulevards crossed — Kuychi, the rainbow god — Mama Sara, mother of maize —Kon, god of rain —Catequil god of lightning, to the south. Across the way, flanking the northern road, I had the temples to Paryaqaqa, the god of water, Ekkeko, the god of wealth, Urcuchillay, lord of animals...and of course, there is one there for Sach'amama, whom I believe you have met. I topped this whole magnificent project off with the grandest of all temples, the one to me..."

This was Pishtaco's temple complex!

Penelope knew that since there were temples on either side of her that she must be on one of the two large boulevards that he had described. Though it seemed no more than an alpaca path, she guessed that if she followed it to its end it might take her to where Pishtaco had constructed a grand temple to himself.

It took a while, but after some serious plodding, Penelope eventually reached the first step of the last temple along the trail. It lay smack in the middle of what Pishtaco had described as the Southern Boulevard. She knew that she had found the right temple as soon as she reached the place. On the steps leading all the way up to the upper landing were a series of stone carvings that were partially covered by ferns and moss. What the vegetation hadn't shrouded left no doubt as to who resided here. It was the sort of ghoulish motif that would be well-suited for the lair of any witchdoctor, conjurer, necromancer, or boogeyman. There were the standard array of skulls and bones, human souls being eaten by the hideous fiends, and beasts devouring hearts. Of course, it was all meant to cow and terrify anyone unfortunate enough to come close to them. Perhaps there were simpler ways to announce that Pishtaco was interred here, but nothing could be quite so dramatic.

Penelope laid her right foot upon the first step, and as she did so she could sense the tens of thousands of other feet that had been placed upon this spot. Some had come in sandals of leather and twine, some had come shoeless, their feet dirty and heavily callused, and some had come with feet that were clean, unblemished, but all of them had come unwillingly. Depressions had formed in the stone over the centuries from where these reluctant feet had trod. Near the top of this staircase, foot-worn hollows in the stone turned into a long continuous channel where the owners of these feet gave way to fear, faltered, and were grabbed by attendants to be pulled up to where Pishtaco stood.

As Penelope neared the top, she could see into the darkened tomb that contained Pishtaco's living remains. He was there, somewhat preoccupied, because it took a while for him to notice her.

"Ah, Miss Farquhar, you've taken me by surprise. I would love to invite you in, but the place is a mess. I just was tiding up a bit — putting old bones back where they belong. But my, my, aren't you persistent. You should have realized by now that there's no way you are going to get them back. Now that they are all tucked away in their little rooms, they will stay there until I have need of them…and no going on any more adventures, I will see to that."

"Pishtaco, I don't know how to barter with you. In fact, I won't. So, if I have to pull down this sad temple of yours block-by-block, I will. Just release Huallpa, Ussun and Atoc. They don't have to come with me. They can be free of the both of us," Penelope said, as she tried to force her way into his sepulcher.

Pishtaco held his hands out and effectively blocked her, "Well, well," he cheerily exclaimed, "that does sound like a good deal…for them. Listen to me, Miss Farquhar, I have found that the longer I live the more I feel the need to. Life is addictive. You must see my point? So, there is no way I am going diminish my powers so you can go on having weird conversations in your head. Besides, there is always someone coming around the bend of that damned river looking for the treasure. I need all of the magic I can muster just to protect it. And I very much doubt that Viracocha would have sent Siwar Q'enti to revive me again if Inti's gold was meant to be in a private residence or put on public display in one of those gold museums. I've heard that they have some in Lima and Bogota. Besides, by rights, the gold should be mine…I mean Inti's, of course."

"Pishtaco, no one's seriously coming after your gold if all of this is just a dream that I'm having back on Guadalupe Street. Once I wake up, you and all of Paititi will go wherever dreams go to. You'll be quite safe there, I imagine. And I certainly won't be bothering you again."

"So, you say…hmmm…you know, Miss Farquhar, I am willing to chance it. As I said before, your quickest route back to Texas is off of that cliff," he pointed for the second time this day to his sacrificial promontory. "The ledge is right up there, conveniently located no more than 1,715 steps from this temple. Yes, I've counted them. I've been up there enough over the years. Beautiful view from up top, you can see the river and the Amazon basin stretching for miles. And I am confident that once you have jumped you won't be bothering me anymore. I have tossed so many from that cliff —Chachapoya, some Inca and people whose tribal names

I've long forgotten — none of them ever came back to annoy me." Pishtaco laughed at his joke, but his voice grew more ominous. "So please do us both a favor and get on with it."

"Not without Ada, Ernest and Billy!"

The flash from her fingers scattered sparks all around the entryway. Electricity pulsed up and down the opening to the tomb but could not penetrate inside. Her sparks spat and sizzled, glowed blue, but only had enough force to define the shape of what was blocking it, an invisible door protecting Pishtaco, who stood on its other side.

He laughed out loud again. This time it was a great deep laugh. "Oh please, Miss Farquhar, my old frame cannot take such amusement. My ribs will start sticking through this embalmed hide of mine, and that won't be a pretty sight."

"Come out of there and face me, you coward!"

"Oh my, yes I can be a coward when it is necessary. But as I've told you, we have become too evenly matched. No good could come from it for either one of us. We would both survive and much worse for wear. If I could, I would gladly send you down to Ukhu Pacha this very moment. But I cannot. As I keep urging, the cliff is right over there, and it is your only hope. Now, good day to you, Miss Farquhar. This conversation wearies me, and I need my rest."

With this, he turned his back on her, walked over to where his stone slab was suspended high above the cavern, climbed up upon it, and went to sleep.

Penelope stood speechless by the opening. It took some while for her to collect herself enough to move from the spot.

——— ‹› ———

Stunned, she wandered aimlessly down the southern boulevard to where it intersected with the north, east and west roads that all joined in the center of the great municipal square. They formed a great cross, which provided access to all of the temples that lay off it. Penelope didn't know quite what to do. The memories of her days, or perhaps centuries, within her dream kept presenting themselves. She had walked back and forth on this terrain for some time — passing the temples of Mama Killa, Inti, Pachamama, Kuychi, Mama Sara, Kon, Catequil, Paryaqaqa, Urcuchillay, Sach'amama and even Pishtaco's. She didn't know how many times she had gone by them. She'd been walking a long while, but it wasn't quite as long as when she had gone walking in the forest near the mining camp. But it was long enough for both the sun and the moon to make many appearances.

There was something odd about this route. It was gnawing at her. It started to bother her more than the thoughts of her own predicament and those of Ada, Ernest and Billy. There was something obvious here that was whispering in the inner workings of her head, but what that was wouldn't come forward and announce itself.

She had become familiar with all the back streets and byways of the upper level of the city of Paititi. However, there was one area she avoided with great fear, but she knew that she would inevitably walk there.

Finally, in a self-induced trance, Penelope began her ascent up the narrow rock-cut staircase that led to Pishtaco's favorite place of slaughter. At the summit of this cliff, the ancient, volcanized rock was covered in a thick patina of blood from all of Pishtaco's victims. The drop from here was staggering. Thousands of feet down, his victims would have ended their terrifying descent upon jagged rocks that had once been part of the promontory but now bordered the western bank of the Rio Marañón. With her final step forward, Penelope allowed her foot to dangle in the air. Like a boy who had climbed to the top of a roof peak to balance one leg on a ridge cap, she was daring fate. Perhaps Pishtaco was right? This just might be the way back to her bed on Guadalupe Street. Perhaps he was wrong, and this would be the end of her? Either way, it was becoming tempting. Whichever way it turned out — the silence of death or life back in Texas psychiatrist-free — would be a bit of an improvement. Curiously, normalcy was starting to lose its appeal for Penelope. The special world she had maintained within her had become very dear to her.

Perhaps there was really no Pishtaco and she had just been caught up in a very long, intensely delusional episode in her own personal ravings? In that case, she might wake up with her voices still secure within her crazed head. Then, everything would be as it was. Yet, somehow, she felt safe with that outcome.

Swaying over the precipice, gently buffeted by a breeze, Penelope decided to allow all thought of her survival to ebb and hoped that the cliff would make the decision for her. There was no point in walking anymore. And she had done all she could do here. It was time to go somewhere — anywhere.

Gazing out upon the great jungle basin below her, Penelope thought that this could be the last thing she would see in her life, and that was good. The scenery was breathtaking; the sun was again setting within this dream and casting heightened colors and shadows all over. Yet, despite the darkening skies, Penelope could still make out the rainforest, stretching out in the distance. Her eyes were taking in all of it, well beyond that which normal human eyesight would allow. Even the curvature of the Earth didn't hinder her. She could see the Atlantic and the great river delta, where the forest's rivers joined the sea. If this was to be her last view of the world, there could be nothing more glorious than for her to close her eyes upon this. And that was what she intended to do — close her eyes, go limp — and fall. She took several deep breaths; the way Doctor Hernandez had taught her to begin her meditation. This made her feel fairly relaxed. She moved her weight a smidgen forward. Then something below caught her eye.

Penelope was able to pull herself back just in time, before she would have had no choice but to spatter herself on the rocks below.

Whatever they were, they were coming out from beneath the jungle canopy and congregating in large groups at the eastern shore of the Rio Marañón. She guessed that these things were aglow with magic — perhaps it was with the same kind of magic that had been glowing in her? Penelope couldn't make out much detail, they were too far off, but it struck her that they might be kindred spirits. She could see even more of them glimmering under the trees far off into the Amazon, and they were all heading her way.

She watched attentively as the last blob of light made its way out of the forest and onto the edge of the riverbank.

There, unimpeded by water depth or rapids, the whole mass of them moved across the Rio Marañón and onto the landing, and then rushed through Inti's Gate. Penelope lost sight of them there but knew that they were on the very road that she had taken to reach the hidden plaza because the whole northern side of the mountain was awash in light. Their coming was like a second dawn. Soon the leading edge of the lights was in the plaza.

All of the temples were now becoming visible from the glow. Penelope could now make out the temples of Mama Killa, Inti, Pachamama, Kuychi, Mama Sara, Kon, Catequil, Paryaqaqa, Urcuchillay and Sach'amama. They had been stripped of their vegetation and bathed in a golden light. They must have looked as fresh as the day their capstones were laid. Even Pishtaco's great sepulcher was rid of its jungle covering. All of the temples had been deforested... all except for one temple, and it had but one tree.

It was the old kapok tree, the one that Cecile had called a spirit tree, or ancestor tree. It was the very tree that she had shaken her rattle at in Xuhpuri's camp, the tree that had been covered in handprints from the people who had lived here — the one that Cecile claimed that people went to it after they had died. There it was again! Either it had been there all along, hidden from view by all of the vegetation, or the glowy things had brought it with them. But there it was, smack dab atop Pachamama temple, and now it was being surrounded by what Penelope had come to realize were thousands of glow-in-the-dark people.

———— «» ————

Pishtaco had seen the lights as well; the brilliance nearly blinded him as he lay resting upon his stone slab above Ukhu Pacha and quickly drew him to the opening of his burial chamber. He gazed out, down the great boulevard to where the light had collected about Pachamama's temple. He knew what he was looking at and it was a sight that did not agree with him. For there, gathered around the old kapok tree, were the spirits of all of his victims, will-o'-the -wisps of horror that had been flitting among the jungle's shadows for centuries — keeping his memory alive.

CHAPTER SEVENTEEN

Inti's Gold

It was no big deal postponing her death; Penelope knew that she could always hike up the staircase to the cliff later on. It was somewhat reassuring to her to know, that if she was forced to roam the streets of Paititi long enough, she would inevitably find herself back here. Death would take care of itself in due time. For right now, neither waking up in her bed on Guadalupe Street or dying on the rocks below Paititi was particularly appealing. So, why not take advantage of this dream, especially since it was beckoning to her with more to offer?

Penelope sprinted down from Pishtaco's cliff but found that she couldn't keep up her pace. Penelope was forced on several occasions to stop and catch her breath. The fact that her lungs labored so hard disturbed her. It made her think that throwing herself down onto the rocks by the Rio Marañón might have been far more painful, dream or not, then she originally imagined.

As she got closer to Pachamama's temple, it became apparent that these bioluminescent folks were locals, possibly Xuhpuri's lot, but with some other individuals mixed in. They were gussied up in fancy garb. Penelope knew that they were high-ranking men and women. There could be little doubt that they were no longer alive. Most of them bore disfiguring scars and wounds, but their flesh, though it glowed gold, was devoid of any other color and quite translucent. She could see clear through them. It didn't take an advanced degree in mathematics from the Zavala School of Science to know that they were some sort of ghosts and more than likely all had a bone to pick with old Pishtaco. Fortunately, for Penelope, they didn't seem to be irritated with her; in fact, just the opposite.

At first Penelope had hesitated, coming to a stop when she had gone close enough to see what she was dealing with. As she approached, she saw broad smiles breaking out upon every face. Thousands of faces, thousands and thousands of careworn, unhappy faces erupted with great joy as they took a knee before her. Among them there were children, footless children riding on the backs of adults, who insisted that they be lowered so that they too could show respect. Penelope wasn't quite sure what she was walking into, but the sight of these forlorn spirits overcame any pretense of stoicism that she might have had. Her emotions were now set free — she ran from child to child kissing and embracing them —crying as she clutched their insubstantial flesh.

Grief, theirs, hers and the whole planet's overtook her. She sobbed — sobbed and sobbed until an elderly woman, who wore more otherworldly finery than the rest, came up to comfort her.

Grasping Penelope by the hand, she looked into her eyes sternly, and then pointed to her own throat, where a deep cut had been made from a garrote.

She led her through the gathered crowd, which parted as they came. This grand lady then led Penelope up the steps of Pachamama's temple to the very top where she bid her to sit. She made a sweeping motion that took in all of the temples within the great square of Paititi. Penelope obediently lowered herself onto the uppermost stone of the temple. As she did, the entire crowd of apparitions sat down as well.

As Penelope gazed out, she could see that Pachamama's shrine and the entire street below were covered with squatting specters, each glowing like a lantern, radiant with a particular soul.

All were silent, nothing moved. All eyes, living and dead, were fixed upon the grand boulevard that led down to where Pishtaco's shrine stood, off at the far end of the temple complex.

For some time, they stared in that direction. None of them would have been surprised to learn that Pishtaco was staring back. That is, when he had a free second to glance out from the doorway of his tomb and take it all in.

Pishtaco knew that he didn't have much time. He knew she would figure it out. He would have to keep all of them out. So, he was pulling out all of the stops, every bit of magic that he knew would be needed. Muttering imprecations with his spells that not even he had heard before, Pishtaco wove a great invisible barrier about the entrance to his bedchamber.

Penelope could see the sparks and wild colors coming from his lair and guessed that he was busying himself. But why? She wasn't exactly sure. There was something she was missing. Everyone else seemed to know what that was but her. She tried to refocus. Here was the great square of Paititi before her. She was sitting atop Pachamama's temple. She was staring down the boulevard that ran from north to south to where Pishtaco's temple was. Along the sight of her vision were many other temples, all bordering the grand boulevard that led east to west. Inti's temple was to the east. Mama Killa's temple was at the very end on the western side. These two grand boulevards formed a great cross with four temples occupying the ends of the cross with eight other temples positioned along the four arms of this cross. There was Kuychi, the rainbow god's temple, Mama Sara, mother of maize temple, Kon, the god of rain's temple, Catequil, god of lightning's temple, Paryaqaqa, the god of water's temple, Ekkeko, the god of wealth's temple, Urcuchillay, lord of animals' temple and Sach'amama the twin serpent's temple.

There was something here... something mathematical about this layout. But Penelope just wasn't quite sure what. Oh, how she wished René hadn't died in the plane crash. If only Orotongo the Chachapoya who pretended to be Descarte was here, so he could coach her a bit like he had done when she was in school.

Then it hit her, of course Descartes! She was staring out at his Cartesian coordinate system! The north south boulevard was a giant y-axis and the east west was a giant x-axis!

"Minus one minus two!" she shouted as she remembered the floating trunk in the river that opened up with Descartes' mechanical daughter bouncing up and handing her a card with only -1 -2 written on it. All of the ghosts now turned and grinned at her as she announced, "The other six temples represent positive and negative coordinate positions along the x-axis and the y-axis. Which means that -1-1 would be the temple of Paryaqaqa, the god of water, on Inti's side of the x boulevard. And -2 y would be below it on Pachamama's north boulevard. So, that tells me that -1 -2 would intersect right where the temple of Ekkeko, the god of wealth stands... Inti's gold!"

Penelope threw both of her hands into the air and hopped about in a tight circle as she proclaimed to the spirits, "Pishtaco, we've got him!"

She charged down the steps, summoning everyone to follow. The ghostly horde fell in line right behind her. Soon they were at the foot of Ekkeko's temple. They climbed to the top, then back down again — around and around they went — searching for something to indicate where the treasure might be hidden. All levels of the structure were examined. The ghosts seemed to pay particular attention to the carvings in the stones, but when Penelope questioned them, they just shook their heads. There were just no clues. But then, as Penelope headed back up to the top of Ekkeko's temple, hoping she had overlooked something, she noticed that many of the ghosts were starting to congregate on the east side of the shrine. It was where the foundation dipped into the ground, as though the structure had once been impacted by some tremor or that the footing was so soft that it had simply sunk into the earth. From where Penelope stood, it was like watching a colony of ants discovering a sugar cube. More and more ghosts came running to this spot. Soon they were all situated about this imperfection in the architecture.

The crowd dutifully gave way as Penelope asked if they would let her get closer. At the very fore of this gathering were the footless children that Pishtaco had buried around the perimeter of his temple. Though memory of Pishtaco had dwindled so that the people in the forest had almost forgotten about him, occasional glimpses of these children fleeing through the jungle upon the backs of other spirits had helped keep his memory alive. That was an unexpected consequence of their flight. But now they had returned, and they burned with a desire for revenge — their tiny hands clawed at the ferns and mosses that concealed a lintel stone. As they dug deeper, throwing out mounds of dirt around them, a doorway was exposed. Whatever had once barred this opening, wood? beaten copper? magic? had failed over time.

It took little time for a large opening to be excavated through the doorway. The children backed away as Penelope, accompanied by the old woman, who was now being escorted by a tall man with a round shield and an axe, moved forward. The three of them took turns peering in, then crawled together into the chamber. The glow emanating from Penelope, the old woman and the tall man, who was obviously once a great warrior, lit up the room. It bounced and shimmered and ricocheted off thousands of golden artifacts. There were piles of gold nose plugs, rings, ear pendants, golden arms, masks devised to look like various gods, golden bats, golden flying fish, golden jaguars, golden ducks, goblets of gold studded with sea blue and forest green chrysocolla, golden arm bands and leg bands, as well as sacrificial axes. There were heaps upon heaps of golden sunbursts displaying the face of the divine Inti, as well as golden statuary crafted to mimic his heavenly appearance. The biggest ear pendants were at the bottom of the pile with the smallest on top. So, it was with all of the plunder that Pishtaco had seized after he had ambushed and murdered General Rumiñawi. It all had been sorted, meticulously graded and categorized and then placed into an appropriate mound of treasure based upon its subject matter, function and size. Here in the great vault, beneath the temple for the god of wealth, it was obvious that Pishtaco had lovingly cared for every piece of the Sapa Inca's missing ransom. He no doubt knew where each object was located, what its history was and what price other men would have paid for such a thing. It was a museum of gold, but unlike the Museo Oro del Peru or the El Museo del Oro in Bogota, this museum's Inca treasure had no visitors, only an ever-vigilant curator.

Penelope was dumbstruck; she was having a hard time taking in the vastness of the place and for a moment had forgotten why she was even there. Then the old woman and the tall warrior turned to face Penelope. At first, contemplative, then quizzical, then their expressions resolved into a moment of realization, as their ghostly eyes turned and met each other. Penelope could see that something had been decided and that she had been left out of the decision process.

The warrior gathered up as much gold as he could carry, so did the old lady. As they did this, other spirits came into the vault and began to pick up treasure. Soon the space was crowded with the specters of the Chachapoya. Fathers and mothers began handing up rings and amulets to the footless children they bore upon their shoulders. All of Pishtaco's treasure was quickly turned over to the hands of Pishtaco's victims.

"Exactly," Penelope said, with a tad of hesitance, "We must take this to Pishtaco and force him ..." She couldn't finish what she had planned to say to them because they had all turned in unison and streamed out the doorway of the treasury.

Penelope was left standing inside the emptied vault without even a nose plug to take with her. She ran out into the great quad and saw that her companions were all heading to Pishtaco's temple. She raced on after them but only caught up with them once they had come to a stop.

Pishtaco's temple was now ringed in the glow from tens of thousands of people whom he had once murdered. Each defiantly held a bit of the treasure above their heads. Inti's gold, radiant with the light from their spirits, transforming what would have been the dead of night into the brightest day.

However, he was not cowed. He hurled curses and spells down upon them. And when that proved to have little effect, he concentrated his powers on fortifying his doorway. For this he used his best incantations, ones that even he was afraid to speak.

Penelope's dream had suddenly been taken over. She was in the back of the crowd and now had to push and elbow her way to the front to again take charge of it. As she broke through the outermost perimeter of souls, she could see Pishtaco laboring to protect the entrance to his tomb and to the great cavern that led to Ukhu Pacha. Multi-colored lights showered and exploded as Pishtaco imbedded his magic deep within the stonework. If Penelope was going to act, it would have to be now.

"Pishtaco!" she yelled up from the lowest step of the pyramid. "Pishtaco, as you can see, I have your gold! I have Inti's gold, all of it! I've left nothing behind in Ekkeko's temple but an old spider. The gold is mine. So, you'd better look at me and start to parlay or we'll walk off with it."

"Parlay?" The word caught his attention, as she had hoped it would. "Parlay? Are you proposing some sort of compromise? I did not know that was in your nature. Do go on, but what is there to compromise on? The gold is Inti's, the gold is mine, but do tell me how we are going to COMPROMISE on this."

"If you could have taken the gold back you would have done it by now. Even if we cannot get at you through your doorway, there is nothing stopping us from ferrying it across the river and scattering it all about the Amazon. That's quite a big jungle."

"Why, yes, it is, Miss Farquhar. It would be a bit tedious tracking it all down, but I have time. And I assure you, no matter how long it takes, it will find its way back to Ekkeko's temple. Actually, that might be doing me a bit of a service. If I am out and about in the rainforest looking for the lost Inca gold, slaughtering anyone who might get in my way... well, that would certainly keep my memory fresh in people's minds. But still, it is not the way I want to spend my senior years. So, we are back to this compromise you seem to have in mind. I imagine you don't want to spend the centuries chasing after me while I chase after the treasure, so do speak."

"Simple, you release Ada and Ernest and Billy, and we drop the gold and leave."

"You are still missing your family? Oh, how sad. Why would I release Huallpa, Ussun and Atoc to you when we have already discussed how evenly matched we are? Sounds like a great deal...for you!"

"Release them and I swear that I will throw myself off of that cliff of yours."

"Right…of course you will. And of course, I believe you. No, sorry, if you want terms, here they are: First, you will put the gold back where you found it. And secondly, you will have these luminous corpse friends of yours slink back to wherever they have come from. Only then will I release Atoc. Truthfully, he has been dreadful company over the centuries, and I would not mind being rid of him. Even with Atoc no longer enslaved by my powers, I think I can match you with just the magic coming from Huallpa and Ussun… locked away in their cells. Besides, let us be truthful, it is Atoc whom you really want back in your head."

That stung, but it was true. Penelope knew that she desperately wanted Billy Bowlegs tucked away in her thoughts…just Billy.

Pishtaco watched her face carefully. Then he laughed and exclaimed, "Well, Billy will be exchanging one prison for another, but I see that we have a deal."

The tall warrior moved out from the throng of spirits. This sight forced Pishtaco to cut short what he was about to say. It was apparent that this ghost had briefly unnerved Pishtaco, but he regained his composure.

"So, you have more than just dead Chachapoya with you, Miss Farquhar. General Rumiñawi, you've finally gotten your gold back, have you?"

Pishtaco gave a derisive laugh, "Look at all of you, you half-starved wraiths. The only reason you can face me here today is because of me. Your stay in Kay Pacha has been prolonged because of me. You have piggybacked upon my memory. What a contemptible lot of anemic ghosts — ghosts who have had to flee into the jungle out of fear of me, where a fleeting glance from a terrified hunter sustains your pathetic memory. Yet, when he stumbles back to his village does he speak of you? No, he announces that he has seen yet another victim of great Pishtaco. You are horrors held on earth to give me life."

Pishtaco began to laugh a deep and hearty laugh filled with confidence. "They speak of Pishtaco, don't they,

General Rumiñawi, when they spy you in the shadows? Poor General Rumiñawi, look at you; you are no more than an afterthought. The memory of you is weak — so weak that you cannot even muster energy to speak with me."

General Rumiñawi lurched forward, as though he was ready to charge up the temple steps and rip Pishtaco's throat out, but then he checked himself.

"Yes. Yes. That was wise of you. If I have turned all of you into what you are today, imagine what I could do to you if I really had to think hard on it. What a pathetic lot you all are, tying your hopes upon the appearance of an insane girl. What fools. I keep the best wizards in all of Kay Pacha in cells beneath my feet, and their spirits are forced to obey me. Imagine what I can do to you. And their memories are so strong that they can even speak...well...one even speaks too much..."

The old lady now forced her way through the other assembled spirits, taking up a position next to the general. Throwing her hands out, she gestured wildly toward Pishtaco as her face contorted with the blackest of emotions.

Pishtaco took in a deep breath, staggered back a bit, and then recovered his balance. This registered upon the face of the old woman who seemed pleased.

"Why it is my grandmother, Ciqui Ollco, the dear woman who sheltered me from the death sentence proclaimed by the Sapa Inca — the dear woman whom I had to have garroted because she wanted to control those powers which she had given to me.

"So, like General Rumiñawi, you never reached Hanan Pacha and are but a muted silhouette, a pantomime player here to strut about, no doubt in search of some scrap of your former glory. Truly, I would have wished you better."

Ciqui Ollco was enraged by this retort. Her face contorted menacingly as she ran up to a ghost who was bearing a golden sunburst that depicted Inti and wrenched it from his hands. Holding the god of lights symbol high over her head, she motioned with it for everyone to follow her. She rushed onto the first step of Pishtaco's stepped pyramid and froze — nobody was following her.

"State of the universe, grandmother dearest, everyone is just concerned about saving their own skin...or whatever that glowing material is about you. But who am I to talk? As you know, I am all about saving my own skin...as decomposed as it may be. Well, now that you all have received this nice little lesson on what you can and cannot do, please place all that gold down in a nice big pile before you return back to the jungle to once again pursue your dank and lonely spectral existences."

A few ghosts did, reluctantly, pile their gold trophies upon the lowest step of Pishtaco's temple, and quickly backed away in fear. Pishtaco took a great deal of pleasure observing this and shouted down his thanks to them from the doorway to his tomb.

Then a third spirit came forward from out of the crowd.

"Oh no, yet another? Who is it going to be this time? The Sapa Inca? Oh, perhaps Pizarro has been nurturing a grudge against me? Oh, whomever it is, come forward and let's get this over with. This is all just too much of a distraction."

The third specter moved with small steps, head down and shoulders hunched. It reached the first step and went onto the second.

"You are a brave one. Okay, why are you here? Did I slit your throat and cast you from the heights of Paititi? Perhaps I did that to your children...or were you around when I was into fire and made all of those burning sacrifices?"

"No, you did not do any of those things to me. I was killed on your death bed and my corpse was then laid by your feet."

This ghost unnerved Pishtaco. There was something extremely unsettling about it. For one, it spoke.

"I don't recall ordering any sorcerer to be garroted upon my death. I had them all killed well before that. So how is it that you can speak? Even my grandmother doesn't have enough magic left in her to muster the slightest of grunts, so tell me why you can speak yet the others cannot?"

"I can speak," she said as she slowly raised her head, "because I am the only one here that hasn't spent themselves on hating you. I can speak because I am the only person whom you ever felt remotely fond of."

Her head rose so that his eyes met hers.

"Imasumaq!" Pishtaco gasped.

"I can speak because I once loved you."

Luminescent tears slid down the cheeks of the woman who had once been Pishtaco's concubine, the woman whose parents had named How Beautiful.

Pishtaco stammered searching for words, "But...but... Imasumaq...I did not order you to be...killed. They...they... they just assumed that you had to be killed. Custom, that is all..." As Pishtaco stood looking down upon her and the assembled crowd, his golden mask grew dull. The magical forces that he had arrayed in front of him weakened, becoming blurry and incoherent. Pishtaco appeared more like a drowned man lying on the bottom of the Rio Marañón rather than an exalted wizard atop his funerary temple.

The transformation, the wavering of power, was not lost on anyone assembled there, least of all Ciqui Ollco. She held up the golden sunburst of Inti again and charged, passing the first step, passing the second step and Imasumaq — then on to the third and fourth. Then the throng of spirits at the base joined her. All the magic guarding the doorway shattered as they rushed through the entry and over the prostrate and now trampled Pishtaco.

Ciqui Ollco jumped into the great cavern leading to Ukhu Pacha. General Rumiñawi then threw himself over the stonewall leading to the underground realm of Supay. The multitude of spirits became like water spinning in a great drain as they cast themselves into the cavern, each holding a bit of Inti's gold. Soon the gold was gone. It had returned to where it came — to Supay in the other world.

Imasumaq was slow coming up the steps. When she entered the tomb, all of the other ghosts had gone. She sat upon the stone wall and gazed upon her corpse, still nestled among the other women who had been sacrificed upon Pishtaco's death. Then, she stared pityingly at Pishtaco, who was just managing to lift himself up on his elbows.

He saw her, looking so serene and so peaceful, and then managed to raise one arm to motion her to move away.

"Pishtaco, my dear, yes, your powers did come from Inti's gold and your grandmother, Ciqui Ollco, and the captive sorcerers, Orotongo, Alliyma, Ussun, Ozcollo, Huallpa and Atoc, and also from the tens of thousands of Chachapoya that you have murdered. But mostly it comes from you being more scared of dying than the rest of us." Imasumaq then let herself go, falling over backwards down into Ukhu Pacha.

Apparently being trampled by a mob of angry ghosts had proved to be no more injurious to Pishtaco than a pillow fight at a sleepover. Pishtaco felt a great need to point this out to the ghosts, but they had all gone off to Ukhu Pacha. He had to confess to himself that he did feel some remorse over the demise of Imasumaq, but Pishtaco believed that women enjoyed martyring themselves — even more than he enjoyed martyring them.

Just a second's worth of sentimentality had made him vulnerable. No more than a spasm but it had cost him Inti's gold. He wasn't sure how Inti would feel about that. Inti hadn't been around much these days. Perhaps he wouldn't mind that the gold was now in the keeping of Supay? Perhaps the god was indifferent but certainly Pishtaco wasn't. This could prove to be a fatal blow to him. There was too much magic wrapped in it. Every piece was caked with his and other sorcerers' invisible spells. Pishtaco was astonished that after all of the centuries that had gone by, he could still feel the slightest twinge of romanticism. How sloppy. Now he would have to survive with just his golden mask and three bags of old bones.

Then he recalled those gold museums in Bogota and Lima. Of course, it would take him a while to figure out how to break into them — certainly not dressed as he was now — but there were all minor complications compared to what he had been through during the past four centuries.

"Why don't we settle this here and now?"

Pishtaco looked to the entry to his tomb and standing there was Miss Penelope Farquhar.

Pishtaco shook his head and rose to his feet while brushing off the dust that had accumulated from hundreds of years of his poor housekeeping. One of those minor complications had just presented itself and truly it was time to deal with it.

"Miss Farquhar, I assumed that you were traveling with your friends and that you were now being entertained by

Supay down in Ukhu Pacha. Please, do not let me impede you on your journey. Do jump, I promise not to interfere."

"Let me rephrase that so an ancient creep like yourself can understand me. It's time to say bye bye, Pishtaco. You are right, Supay is going to be entertaining them with you billed as the main feature."

"You forget that it is now just you against me...me and Ussun, Huallpa and Atoc."

"No, not with Ussun and Huallpa!"

Both Pishtaco and Penelope turned to look at the stone wall that bordered the circumference of the great cave that led to Ukhu Pacha. Standing on top of it with their heads just touching the underside of the slab that served as Pishtaco's funerary bed, were a man and a woman dressed in the regalia of high Chachapoya sorcerers.

"Wait! What do you think you are doing? I forbid this!" Pishtaco screamed.

As he did so, Penelope stretched out her fingers and hit Pishtaco full in the chest with a blast from her skull and crossbones painted nails.

Pishtaco staggered back towards the wall. As he did so, Ussun and Huallpa joined hands and for a few fleeting seconds once again appeared to Penelope as Sir Ernest and the Countess Lovelace.

"It is time for us to truly die, Penelope," said Ada, as Sir Ernest nodded.

"No wait!" Penelope shouted, for once in agreement with Pishtaco. But then Ada and Ernest turned and jumped.

Enraged, Penelope felt the glow from her fingertips intensify, and she gave out another blast but it was countered by a shot from Pishtaco's hands.

The two rays of power collided and struggled with each other as Pishtaco and Penelope each moved forward and then had to give ground. Then, four hundred years of determination began to prevail. The strength of Pishtaco's power was growing more and more as Penelope's faded.

Then, two hands from behind Pishtaco's grabbed his mask and ripped it off. It was Billy Bowlegs standing on the wall...

"No! Billy! No!"

But Billy ignored her. Still holding Pishtaco's mask, Billy Bowlegs blew Penelope a kiss, then tossed himself down into the bowels of Ukhu Pacha.

"B-I-L-L-Y!" Penelope shrieked as she watched him disappear into the great hole. In a rage she pivoted, extending her fingers to give Pishtaco another blistering with the heat from her hands, but that was no good. Nothing was there. What powers she had had seemed to have disappeared with Billy. But Pishtaco was in the same situation. He was staggering by the rim, a tottering rotten length of flesh that looked more like roadkill than a man.

This must have been the first time his face had been exposed to the air since he had been laid to rest atop the stone slab that had held him for centuries above the sacred entryway to Ukhu Pacha. He was decaying rapidly. His lips had gone, fully exposing gums that held but a few teeth. His cheekbones popped through his leathery skin as one eyeball dropped from its socket, as did what was left of his nose, where Siwar Q'enti had previously touched it.

Penelope now saw her chance. She rushed at him and grabbed him by his throat to push him backwards towards the cavern. As she did so, the last bit of flesh on his face fell to the floor. There was no skull underneath. Instead, another head emerged, like an insect breaking through its protective covering at the end of a hard winter. A new face appeared. It was younger and healthier.

"MISS Farquhar, you mustn't attempt to apply reason to these hallucinations of yours. Regrettably, there is no cure for your condition. Please, stick with your regimen of medication, and practice your meditation. Our goal is to confine these episodic delusions — Inhibit them, if we can." The face of Doctor Hernandez's brightened and he laughed. "Well, that's what I would have said before I had run all of those tests on you. There's good news for you, MISS Farquhar. You don't suffer from schizophrenia after all."

"What?" Penelope was baffled, forgetting for a brief second who she was dealing with. "What are you trying to say?"

"What I am trying to say is that you are suffering from what we have labeled dissociative identity disorder. Sort of detailed daydreaming. A mental disorder to be sure, but very treatable, with a few years of counseling. I would venture that it is quite possible that you will be able to rid yourself of all of those imaginary friends of yours. No doubt your illness was brought about by severe childhood trauma, that is frequently the case, and not due to your genes or a biochemical imbalance.

Odd thing about dissociative identity disorder, it can be misdiagnosed as schizophrenia. In fact, and this is the kicker, MISS Farquhar, the whacky symptoms associated with the disease are rarely present before psychiatric therapy. It's worrying but some psychiatrists are apparently leading their patient into such extreme mental states."

Stunned, Penelope relaxed her grip. Then, Pishtaco began hooting with laughter. It was the first time she had seen his mouth contort with laughter. He looked as if he was going to bite her. But he didn't. Instead, his hands reached up, clasped the tops of his ears, and then tugged at Doctor Hernandez's face till it came off. Pishtaco then flipped it over his shoulder so that it fell down into the opening of the cavern, as a new face appeared.

It was her mother's!

"How do you think old Felix Gruber got his medical wing for bipolar and schizophrenic disorders? That cost me a pretty penny but well worth the cost.

In blind rage, Penelope's threw every ounce of strength she had into tightening her grip about, what appeared to be, her mother's throat.

"Oh, go ahead, choke me. You've tried to murder me before. But you chose a knife then. I'll tell you again what I told you when you stabbed me, perhaps this time you'll understand? But I doubt it. You were always such a daddy's girl. You only listened to daddy. No time for your mother but always time to go off with daddy. And my, how he did dote upon you. Would you like to see it? Can you remember?"

The whole body of Pishtaco began to transform. What had been a tobacco-colored cadaver with the pale head of an old woman with blue-rinsed hair gradually changed. It grew fat and bald and had no clothing. There was her daddy and there was nothing to cover his nakedness except for a lavender plush bunny, which he gripped by the ears over his genitals.

This was the deepest cut that Pishtaco could inflict. Penelope again screamed, but this time she pushed him backward with every ounce of magic and strength that she had.

Over the stone wall, the two of them tumbled into the great emptiness.

The time seemed to slow for Penelope, but Pishtaco moved on ahead of her at an accelerated pace. Soon she was all alone in the void. It was a little like skydiving, seemingly standing still as she hurled downward. She could see herself ahead and behind — her arms and legs spread out catching the non-existent air. It was as though she was between two mirrors. There appeared to be an unending series of Penelope Farquhars. Images of her receded in multiple copies — all wearing red capes, smallish red sombreros, black jackets and black skirts, all growing smaller and smaller in countless iterations both above and below.

They were all the same except for minor differences in size and opposing positions. And they were all disappearing into a single point of perspective. Each was a valid copy of Penelope Gertrude Augusta Farquhar. Perhaps it was mere happenstance or fate that selected which Penelope Gertrude Augusta Farquhar would now be crashing into the floor of Ukhu Pacha.

She slammed into the blackened soil of Ukhu Pacha with a great thud. The sound of which reverberated throughout Supay's realm. The pain from the impact was beyond description; all of Penelope's ribs snapped; her knees shattered, and so did her back.

Groaning, and with some effort, she just managed to lift her head from where the force of her collision had imbedded it deep into the musty earth. Opening her eyes, Penelope's attention immediately became fixed upon someone whose pain was worse than her own.

Pishtaco's screams were piteous and incessant. There would be no opportunity for him to charm, con or beguile his tormentors with his nimble tongue; the pain that was being inflicted upon him had flung aside any thoughts that he might have had in his head. His mouth was no longer any good for talking and only served as a megaphone for his torment.

A large red, manlike creature with two long twisting horns sprouting from his head was directing similar, but smaller versions of himself, on how to properly apply fire to Pishtaco's body. An assemblage of flute players now gathered around him, and improvised a melody to go with Pishtaco's screams.

The horned being must have sensed that Penelope was now conscious, for he turned about to face her, then after eyeing her over, walked towards her.

Though she was in horrible pain, Penelope, unlike Pishtaco, was still able to think clearly. It was obvious who was approaching. It was Supay. She didn't know if she should panic or be grateful. She had brought Inti's treasure and Pishtaco to him...

The opening above her suddenly began to disgorge every imaginable kind of creature. White-bellied spider monkeys, rufescent screech-owls, giant land snails, golden-headed quetzals, tapirs, red creepers, glasswing butterflies, giant armadillos, jaguars, malachite butterflies, gold mantled howlers, hyacinth macaws, tree sloths, crimson-rumped toucanets, and pink tarantulas began raining down upon her.

When they stopped, peacock bass, red-bellied piranha, grey and pink dolphin and a vast colony of bulldog bats, orange-winged, orange-cheeked and yellow-crowned, rose-faced and blue headed parrots, scarlet-shouldered parrotlets, military macaws, red-green macaws, blue and yellow macaws, scarlet macaws, chestnut-fronted macaws, cobalt-winged parakeets, white-eyed-parakeets, golden plumed parakeets and maroon-tailed parakeets came plummeting through Paititi's deep portal to Ukhu Pacha.

The creatures of the Amazon formed a towering mountain of life upon Penelope's back. Once they had darted, crawled, hopped, plopped, slid, or flew off, the gods that had ruled over them came down. Down came Mama Sara, Kuychi, Catequil. Kon, god of rain, landed between Penelope's shoulder blades. Then, Urcuchillay, the lord of animals, fell upon her head. So, it went, one after another, all of the gods colliding into Penelope as though she was some sort of pillow that had been strategically placed to cushion their fall. Sach'amama then made her appearance with a loud thump and took her time slithering off. Finally, Mama Killa came down, as Inti crashed behind her.

Supay had stopped moving towards Penelope when all of creation began to rain down upon her. Now that Viracocha's creations had moved off into vastness of Ukhu Pacha, Supay again began to approach her.

Penelope shivered with fear as he bent down. He saw this, so he gently stroked her hair. As he did so, his crimson face with horns like an Oryx began to dissolve away. A crown of feathers replaced his horns and his skin turned brown and wrinkled. Now, the only thing red about him was the color of his hair. It was Xuhpuri.

"You did all that was asked of you, our goddess of the Earth, and much more. You have brought Pishtaco and Inti's gold down to Ukhu Pacha, and you have called everything else in as well. This is good. The cycle now renews, and the madness has left. Viracocha is pleased."

Xuhpuri kissed her on her forehead and then slowly moved away. "Time to heal Pachamama. Time to die. Time for all of us to die."

———— 《》 ————

Like a helicopter coming in for a landing, Siwar Q'enti moved deeper and deeper into the great cavern that led to Ukhu Pacha. Finally, he came out the end. At first, he buzzed over to Xuhpuri, who smiled at Siwar Q'enti as the divine hummingbird hovered by one of his ears. Then Siwar Q'enti moved off from him, dropping down to be level with Penelope's face. He moved up close to her and then pressed his long tongue gently to the side of her upper lip.

This is when Miss Penelope Gertrude Augusta Farquhar died.

CHAPTER EIGHTEEN

The Spider Leaves

The golden orb weaver began working out from the central hub of its web by first pulling the strands of the inner-most circles into its mouth. This was a delicate maneuver and had to be done carefully. Choosing a wrong strand might cause the entire web architecture to collapse. One by one, in the reverse order of how they had been laid, the sticky threads were consumed. Once the last of the spirals had been removed, it was on to the anchor threads — which had been adhered to two of the posts of the four-poster bed. Nothing was wasted. All was digested quickly. The silk contained protein — protein that had to be stockpiled in the spider's silk glands — protein that was needed for the spinning of the next night's web.

The bridge thread between the two posts was eaten. There was nothing else to do but leave.

Leaping off of the bed and onto the bedroom floor, the golden orb weaver scurried under the door, down the steps and finally negotiated its way outside and into one of the many gardens.

———— «» ————

The sensation was like riding alone on an elevator up to the penthouse of a skyscraper. There was no conversation. There was no feeling of awkwardness, as when the elevator is full. No one was observing her, commenting, or offering advice. It was a tiny space, but a space free of people.

This elevator ride seemed to go on forever as it ascended upward — then it came to a stop and the doors opened.

Sunlight poured through the bedroom dormer windows and penetrated through the sheet that had been pulled over her head. There was no escaping the fact that it was morning, and it beckoned to Penelope to step out of her elevator.

As Penelope tentatively pulled the lace-fringed sheet off her head and peered about, it was apparent that she was indeed in her room. There was her curios cabinet filled with Miocene fossils — megalodon shark's teeth and skate rasps. There were her rare seashells, her prehistoric flint projectiles, too. There were her framed beetle and butterfly collections, as well as small piles of polished agates, minerals and flashy semiprecious gemstones. She was the only person she had ever heard of who would have such things in a bedroom. So, it must be her bedroom.

It was a new day and a beautiful one at that. The prisms dangling from the rim of her rose shade reading lamp were catching the sunlight and casting rainbows about her lavender walls. It was a beautiful day! The dream had ended, and her voices may have gone. So far, so good, Doctor Hernandez would be so pleased!

Penelope was so happy she could hardly contain herself as she sat up in her bed and poured herself a bit of water from her Royal Albert water pitcher. As she took a sip from her apple-green hand-blown water glass, she noticed something was terribly out of place. Someone had been in her room. There was an ashtray on her bed stand with a spent cigarette in it. She had told Francesca, the woman who cleaned her house, that she was a nonsmoker, and that she wouldn't appreciate it if Francesca smoked in the house. What was even more curious was that Francesca apparently smoked cigarettes in an ebony cigarette holder, for there was one in the cut-glass ashtray that contained the cigarette. This was very strange because Francesca never struck Penelope as a smoker, nor as a smoker who smoked with such pretense as to own an ebony cigarette holder. Of course, Penelope was going to have to bring this to her attention. Still, the cigarette holder looked rather fancy and appealing. She thought that she just might take up the habit herself.

But how could she waste her day being absorbed with such trivialities? The day was new! Pishtaco was but a nightmare and so far, her head was free of Cecile, Ernest, Ada, René, Belle and Billy...could she but hope?

Penelope hardly could contain herself. She leapt out of her bed. She felt like skipping about her room, like when she was a little girl, but contained her enthusiasm long enough to run over to one of the dormers, throw back the curtain, raise up the sash of the window and let the fresh morning air come flooding into her room. This struck her as odd; the air on Guadalupe Street was stale, city air. But the thought quickly left her as she espied her lovely gardens radiating their magnificent colors in the bright...Mediterranean!!!... sunlight. The tea roses, the red columbines, the deep blue salvia, the snapdragons, the white foxgloves, and the borders of lavender Mexican petunias and fiery red coleus were exactly where she had planted them...but where had Guadalupe Street gotten to? It was gone! Her property now ended at the edge of a cliff. There was no Guadalupe Street. And beyond where it should have been, was a vivid blue harbor full of sailboats and other pleasure craft...and there also was a mountain just to the right of her with pastel-colored villas stacked on top of one another going up its side...

"Senorina! Senorina! You must get dressed! You must get dressed quickly!" Penelope turned from her bedroom window and gazed at her bedroom door as it opened.

"Senorina, please," came the familiar voice, "he's here! He's here. Oh, it's so exciting!"

It was Francesca, but she had abandoned her customary yoga pants and tee shirt for something very different, for something quite formal— a black dress that buttoned up the front and was edged with white piping around the collar, pockets and sleeves.

"Francesca...I'm glad you are here. I don't feel well. Something is terribly, terribly wrong. You must call Doctor Hernandez. Doctor Hernandez, he will prescribe something. Perhaps hospitalize me?"

"Who is Doctor Hernandez? You no longer use Doctor Di Moze?"

"Who?"

"Di Moze. You use Di Moze all the time. He's a good doctor. You don't like the sleeping pills he gave you? You weren't getting any rest and the filming was just so nonstop."

"What filming?"

"Signorina, come here. Let me see if you are running a temperature."

Francesca grabbed hold of Penelope with both hands and pulled her towards her. She then placed one hand upon Penelope's forehead.

"As I suspected. You are not running a temperature. It is those jitters again. Who could blame you? You have been under a lot of strain. But I thought that after last night's cast party, you would begin to relax. No matter, it's a new day. And you have nothing on your calendar. Well...except for Mr. Grant."

"Francesca, you aren't making any sense...nothing has made any sense since I left Doctor Hernandez's office."

"You mean Doctor Di Moze. But don't worry; Francesca will get you all ready. And to think he is wearing a white tux. I bet he had it on at last night's party. Perhaps he has been wandering the streets of Capri since you came home. Oh, I put the box of roses he brought for you on the table in the foyer. He is standing there next to them. Mr. Cary Grant, who would have ever thought I would have talked to him in person? He said that he hopes to take you out for brunch at the Ristorante Cerio. Of course, you are going to accept, it is good for your career," she laughed, "and it is good for Francesca to get an occasional look at him."

Forcing a dazed Penelope into a white satin robe, Francesca pushed her mistress till she was in front of her ivory inlaid dressing mirror, then combed out and brushed her hair.

"There, perfection! But you need to smile, Signorina." Francesca then took her index fingers to Penelope's cheeks and pressed on them. "Come on Signorina, for Francesca, smile."

Penelope was having a hard time expressing anything but absolute shock. Penelope Farquhar was not the person she was looking at in the mirror, nor was it some Andean mother goddess of earth and time. Gone was the short tenacious-looking, blue-eyed blonde. A tall woman, with deep brown bedroom eyes and ample cleavage had replaced her. She had become one of those drop-dead gorgeous types, with a bronze tan that people would die for and a small beauty mark... on the side of her upper lip...

"There, Signorina, you look beautiful, and it was no work on my part. Come. Come. He's waiting downstairs."

Francesca prodded the reluctant Penelope out the door of her bedroom and onto the balcony that overlooked the ornate vestibule just below. She stood next to Penelope, propping her up, as they both gazed down upon the Hollywood heartthrob.

An older and very handsome man had been watching the two of them as they entered onto the balcony; being an actor he knew that timing was so important. His cue had come. Throwing his hands up in an extravagant way, he announced, "My dear Penny I spent my night wandering down the Via Matermania until I found a wooded area that looked out over the Tyrrhenian Sea. There I proclaimed your beauty to the stars, the wind and the waves below me until the sun rose up overhead. Then I made my way here. Please, allow me the privilege of treating you to brunch at Cerio. I've been there and Cerio has the best prosciutto panini in all of the Bay of Naples. And perhaps, if you will allow me, this evening we shall go dancing! You will accompany me, won't you, Penny?"

For a few seconds, she thought about her new situation. But then, Penelope's response came quick.

"That's Signorina Penelope Agostina Geltrude Fargnoli!"

She wasn't really cross with him. How could she be? Grant looked so handsome standing there in his white tuxedo with a trendy red scarf wrapped about his head. You know, the ones with the fashionable spoonbill and egret feathers that stick out the top?

Author's Note

The Q'eros Prophesy

The Q'eros are an Incan tribe of roughly 600 people who fled from the conquistadors to the mountain tops of the Andes. They have preserved an ancient Incan prophesy that states that five hundred years after the conquest of the Incas will come a new age, one that will supplant the age of greed and destruction that had followed in the wake of the conquistadors. The prophesy is called the Great Change. It proclaims that madness will end, and harmony will be restored when the condor of the south and the eagle of the north fly together. Pachamama is greatly revered by the Q'eros people. The Q'eros were first brought to world attention in 1955 during an ethnological expedition headed by Dr. Oscar Nuñez del Prado of the National University of Saint Anthony the Abbot in Cuzco.

The Inca emperor, Atahualpa, was ordered garroted by the Conquistador Francisco Pizarro in 1537.The Inca Empire collapsed with his execution.

Glossary

Amarucancha House of the Great Serpent, was a palace in Cuzco that contained a courtyard full of snakes and a giant snake within.

Atahualpa was the last independent Inca emperor.

Chachapoya were a nation of peoples from the northern Andes who were known as The Warriors of the Clouds. Shortly before the arrival of the Spanish conquistadors, the Inca conquered them. The Chachapoya had a massive mountaintop citadel in Kuelap, which can still be seen today. They also had a tradition of mummifying their dead and placing them in shelters or niches on cliff faces.

Chinkirma Mama the love-sick electric eel is purely my own invention, though partly inspired by a painting of Pablo Amaringo's concerning a story his grandfather told him about rubber tappers who were attacked by giant leeches while camped along a river. See "Ayahuasca Visions — The Religious Iconography of a Peruvian Shaman" paintings and commentary by the shaman Pablo Amaringo, with analysis from the Columbian anthropologist Luis Eduardo Luna. Published by North Atlantic Books. Chinkirma is Quechua for electric eel.

Ciqui Ollco. For the purposes of this story, Ciqui Ollco is Pishtaco's grandmother. As a real-life historical figure, she was the mistress of Topa Inca Yupanqui. Upon his death, Ciqui Ollco attempted to place her child upon the throne but was stopped by the Sapa Inca's sister/wife Mama Ocllo Coya who prevented this by declaring Ciqui Ollco to be a witch. Ciqui Ollco was most likely executed, and her son banished from court.

Corpse Vine, also known as Ayahuasca, is a vine that is brewed into a psychedelic broth and used by shamans in the Peruvian jungles for spirit healing and dream quests. I would refer you to the above mentioned "Ayahuasca Visions — The Religious Iconography of a Peruvian Shaman".

Cota Coco was a lost Inca city discovered in 2002. For the purposes of this story, it is the secret city of the soothsayers, where black magic is practiced.

Cuzco was the capital of the Inca Empire.

René Descartes' Automaton, Francine. Descartes did have a mechanical girl with him when he boarded a ship bound for the court of Queen Christina of Sweden. His machine was thrown overboard after superstitious sailors searched his quarters and discovered the apparatus concealed within a box.

Footless Children In 2016, thirteen Inca sacrificial graves were discovered about temple ruins in Chotuna-Chornancap, Peru. The remains dated back to the 14th and 15th centuries. Six of the thirteen sacrificial victims were children, of these, two had had their feet amputated. The sacrificing of children was not an uncommon event in the Inca culture, in 2018, at the Las Llamas site, the sacrificial remains of 140 children and 200 llamas.

Hanan Pacha was the upper, heavenly, realm within the Inca religious belief system.

Doctor Hernandez is Penelope's research psychiatrist.

Huayna Capac was known as The Young and Mighty One. He became the ruler of the Inca people after his father, Topa Inca Yupanqui. Some attribute the construction of the place known as the Amarucancha, House of the Great Serpent, to him.

Inti was the sun god of the Inca people and the son of Viracocha. The Inca royal family believed that they were his direct descendants. He was worshiped in the form of a golden disk, and it was believed that gold fell to earth from the sky in the form of Inti's tears.

Kay Pacha was the middle, earthly, realm within the Inca religious belief system.

Lucid Dreaming is a technique that has been occasionally employed by psychiatrists in matters concerning psychosis. The method utilizes a subconscious prompt to alert the dreamer that he is dreaming, and then, through exploiting this knowledge the dreamer is able to manipulate his dream.

Mama Killa was the Inca goddess of the moon. She was the daughter of Viracocha, and the sister and wife of the sun god, Inti.

Mama Ocllo Coya was the Sapa Inca Túpac's sister/wife.

Monitored Meditation to Control Schizophrenia is an experimental procedure where a patient is trained to mentally manipulate an object on a screen while in a meditative state. It is hoped that such cognitive training will produce morphological changes to areas of the brain vulnerable to schizophrenia, so that patients will be able to ignore inner voices — a little like weightlifting for the mind.

Paititi is the Peruvian equivalent of El Dorado, a lost city of gold that was hidden in the jungle and served as a refuge for Inca people fleeing the Spanish conquistadors. Vatican archives contain a document written around 1600 by a Spanish missionary, Andres Lopez, in which he described Paititi as being filled with silver, gold and jewels. Adventurers and archeologists have long been searching for its location.

Pachamama is the equivalent of mother earth. She is the fertility goddess who sustains life and in some legends is the daughter of the creator god, Viracocha. All begins with her, all ends with her. She is the great cycle of renewal.

Palla, the word means noble lady or princess in Quechuan, the language of the Incas. In this story, it is the name of a huge green anaconda that is kept at the Amarucancha, House of the Great Serpent. Such a snake supposedly did exist.

Pishtaco was a legendary Andean bogeyman who preyed upon the indigenous people. A Spanish priest, Christobal de Molina, first mentions him in 1574. He was described as a slitter of throats, who drank blood, ate human fat and had a particular fondness for abducting children. For the purposes of this story, he is the illegitimate son of Topa Inca Yupanqui, the emperor of all the Incas.

Pishtaco's Cave to Ukhu Pacha touches upon the myth that the first Incan royal family emerged on earth through a cave in a mountain, Paqariq Tampu, in Cuzco. The area was subsequently built up with many Inca shrines and buildings. The Incas also felt that underground streams and caves led to Ukhu Pacha. For further reading, see the "Narrative of the Incas" by the 16th century Spanish interpreter, Juan De Betanzos. De Betanzos wrote down the ancient legends as told to him by his wife, the Inca princess, Dona Angelina Yupanqui, who was the late Atahualpa's (the last Inca Emperor) principal wife. The book is readily available in print.

Pyramids, large triangular structures made of stone or adobe brick that were used for the burial of nobility or for religious services associated with various gods. In the Supe Valley of Peru lies the oldest city in the Western Hemisphere, Caral-Chupacigarro. It is believed to have been constructed between 2,500 and 2,000 B.C. by the Norte Chico civilization. This site was discovered in 1948 by Professor Paul Kosok, chairman of the Department of History and Government at Long Island University, but it wasn't until 1974 that detailed mapping of the city was made. So far, it has been determined that the site consists of six large pyramids with thirty-three lesser temple complexes. These structures, like in the story about Pishtaco, align with the movement of celestial bodies and were associated with various gods. The Caral-Chupacigarro pyramids pre-date those of the Egyptians by about 100 years.

Francisco Pizarro was the Spanish conquistador who conquered the Incas in 1537. He held the Inca emperor, Atahualpa captive and demanded ransom for his life. Nine months later, after receiving a vast amount of treasure, Pizarro had Atahualpa tried and executed.

Qasa means frost in the Quechuan language. The fictional character by that name represents a real person who was a high minister in the Incan Empire. One of his responsibilities was providing and maintaining snakes for the Amarucancha, a palace also known as the House of the Great Serpent.

Quipu are Inca knotted strings used in an array of strings to manage accounts and other forms of data.

Rumiñahui, General was an Incan general who was sent out to collect some of the ransom that was demanded by Francisco Pizarro for the release of the Sapa Inca, Atahualpa. When Pizarro had reneged on his promise to release Atahualpa, and instead had him garroted, Rumiñahui took the 750 tons of gold that he was conveying and hid it in the mountains where the Spanish would never find it. He was defeated by the Spanish conquistadors at the Battle of Mount Chimborazo, eventually he was captured and tortured to death, but he did not give up the whereabouts of the hidden treasure.

Sach'amama is a big eared, twin-headed serpent with hypnotic eyes. She is the goddess of the Amazon Forest. Her name means mother tree. She sleeps within the forest floor and is very cranky when disturbed.

Second Death. The Inca felt that a person was not truly dead till they had become forgotten (social death occurring sometime after biological death). In a similar vein, dead members of the aristocracy would retain their property rights, and servants tended to their mummies, which kept their memories alive.

Siwar Q'enti is the royal hummingbird that can travel between the three realms, Hanan Pacha, Kay Pacha and Ukhu Pacha. It is considered to be a spiritual guide and the only living creature to have seen Viracocha's face (the supreme creator god.)

Supay is the god of death and ruler of the underworld (Ukhu Pacha.) He is associated with miners and is still worshiped by them in the Andes.

Topa Inca Yupanqui was the emperor of all the Incas and for the purposes of this story, the father of Pishtaco.

Ukhu Pacha is the Inca land of the dead where Supay, god of underworld dwells. Supay judges souls, which results in either punishment by demons or reward and renewal with new lives in Kay Pacha (the earthly realm) or in Hanan Pacha (the heavenly realm). Ukhu Pacha can be accessed through caves of deep springs. During the early days of Spanish mining operations, the indigenous miners required rituals be performed to soothe the disturbance of Ukhu Pacha. The realm is also associated with the earth mother goddess, Pachamama, in relationship to harvest and rebirth.

Viracocha predates the other gods. He became the overarching creator within whose domain all gods and people exist.

Xuhpuri is another invention of mine. However, the shaman's name means macaw in Chayahuita. Chayahuita is an endangered language spoken by many tribal people in the area of the Amazon basin where the story takes place.

If you enjoyed this read...

Please leave a review.

It takes less than five minutes, and it really does make a difference.

Reviews should answer at least three basic questions.
(But won't give the story away.):

- Did you like the book? *("Loved the book! Can't wait for the Next!")*
- What was your favorite part? *(Characters, plot, location, scenes.)*
- Would you recommend the book?

Your review will help other readers discover this book. Consider leaving your review on Amazon, Barnes and Noble, Apple iBooks, KOBO, Goodreads, BookBub, Facebook, Instagram and/or your own website.

Brian Hades, publisher

To leave a review on Amazon

~ Even if the book was not purchased on Amazon ~

1. Go to amazon.com. Sign into your Amazon account. If you do not have an Amazon account, you need to create one and activate it by making a purchase. Amazon will check to see that your account is active before allowing you to leave a review. Amazon has some restrictions, such as not leaving a bias review. For more information on Amazon's policies please read Amazon's Community Guidelines for book reviews:

   https://www.amazon.com/gp/help/customer/display.html?nodeId=GLHXEX85MENUE4XF

2. Search for and find Pishtaco by Mark Patton, then click on the book's details page.

3. Scroll down to find the Write a Customer R Write a customer review eview button. Click it.

4. Select your star rating. A rating of 5 is best, 1 is worst.

5. If you have a photo or video to share, add it to the upload box.

6. Add a headline.

7. Write your review.

8. Press the SUBMIT button

To leave a review on Barnes and Noble
~ Even if the book was not purchased on BN.com ~

1. Go to barnesandnoble.com and sign up for an account.
2. Search for and find Pishtaco by Mark Patton, then click on the book's details page.
3. Scroll down to the review section and click on the Write a Review button.
4. Select your star rating. A rating of 5 is best, 1 is worst.
5. Add a review title.
6. Write your review.
7. Add a photo if you wish.
8. Select if you would recommend this book to a friend.
9. Select appropriate TAGs.
10. Indicate if your review contains spoilers.
11. Select the type of reader that best describes you (optional).
12. Enter your location (optional).
13. Enter your email address.
14. Checkmark that you agree to the terms and conditions.
15. Press the POST REVIEW button.

About the Author

At nineteen Mark Patton was a helmsman for the Woods Hole Oceanographic Institution. By his mid-twenties he was flying out of Otis Air Force Base for the National Marine Fisheries Service. After graduating from Northeastern University, he became a roughneck for Delta Drilling. He left Texas to become a police officer and later a head of Natural Resources on Cape Cod. Retired, he is now pursuing his longtime passion for writing.

Need something new to read?

If you liked Pishtaco, you should also
consider these other EDGE titles...

The Haunting of Westminster Abbey

by Mark Patton

Romance Amidst Chaos...

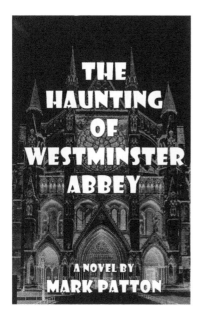

Wallace Butterfield, British architect, knew that he has been a failure at nearly everything, including relationships. But what he didn't know — couldn't know — was that he was special. He would have been amazed to know how exceptional he really was.

Wallace's only hope is an invitation from Reverend Poda-Pirudi, chairman of the Westminster Abbey Foundation, London, England, to bid on the design for a new tower for the Abbey.

Unfortunately a coven of absinthe-drinking Witches have taken an interest in the architect special quality and have decided that they will do anything (kidnapping, torture, or even burning at the stake) to get what they want from him.

What do the Witches want? Will they succeed in burning Wallace at the stake? Who is Reverend Poda-Pirudi and what can he do to try to save Wallace?

Super-Earth Mother

The AI that Engineered a Brave New World

by Guy Immega

Get ready to explore a new world with Super-Earth Mother

Super-Earth Mother is a thrilling Hard Science Fiction novel that reveals questions about humanities' future; exploring genetic coding, developing artificial intelligence, and building space vehicles that travel beyond the stars.

What will it be like to settle into some 'home-like' planet's environment? How will we survive the journey there? What will happen after we land?

Super-Earth Mother answers these questions and more.

It is the story of an Artificial Intelligence machine named Mother-9 who uses synthetic biology to grow generations of human beings best suited to survive on the earth-like planet Velencia, where the first Human colony of genetically engineered babies will learn to survive and thrive.

Super-Earth Mother is a thrilling quest and the ultimate in sci-fi adventures.

Shadow Stitcher

An Everland Mystery

by Misha Handman

Selected as one of the year's most compelling debut novels for Kobo's Emerging Writer Prize, Shadow Stitcher is guaranteed to delight.

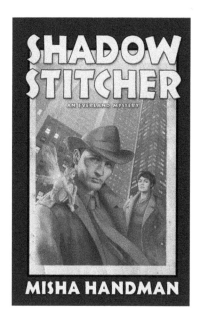

This fast paced Noir mystery has a great cast of easily identifiable characters, a plot both easy to follow and intriguing, and an ending that will leave you satisfied.

A former pirate faces mobsters and magic in 1950s Neverland.

Basil Stark isn't the man he once was. A reformed pirate and private detective, he walks the line between criminal and hero, living in the corners of what was once the island of Neverland, its magic slowly fading into the new world of the 1950s. But when a routine missing-persons case turns into a murder investigation, Basil finds himself pulled into a tale of organized crime, murder, unstitched shadows and dangerous espionage. With only a handful of fellow outcasts and a stubborn determination to bring a killer to justice, will he survive the many people who want him dead?

For more EDGE titles and information about upcoming speculative fiction please visit us at:

www.edgewebsite.com

Milton Keynes UK
Ingram Content Group UK Ltd.
UKHW011927140823
426877UK00002B/26